ALSO BY CATHERINE BUSH

Minus Time

The Rules of Engagement

The Rules of Engagement

Catherine Bush

Farrar, Straus and Giroux

New York

Farrar, Straus and Giroux
19 Union Square West, New York 10003

Printed in the United States of America
First published in 2000 by Harper*Flamingo*, Canada
First published in the United States by Farrar, Straus and Giroux
First edition, 2000

Library of Congress Cataloging-in-Publication Data
Bush, Catherine, 1961–
    The rules of engagement / Catherine Bush.— 1st ed.
      p. cm.
    ISBN 0-374-25280-7 (alk. paper)
    1. Canadians—England—Fiction.   2. Man-woman relationships—
Fiction.   3. London (England)—Fiction.   4. Women scholars—Fiction.
5. Toronto (Ont.)—Fiction.   6. Dueling—Fiction.   I. Title.

PR9199.3.B797 R85 2000
813′.54—dc21   00-035442

Grateful acknowledgment is made for permission to reprint excerpts from the following:

Paul Muldoon's *Madoc: A Mystery*. Reprinted by permission of Farrar, Straus and Giroux.

"Small Town Boy," by Steve Bronski, Larry Steinachek, and Jimmy Somerville, © 1991 Bronski Music Ltd. (PRS) & EMI Virgin Inc. All Rights o/b/o Bronski Music Ltd. administered by WB Music Corp. (ASCAP). All Rights Reserved. Used by permission. Warner Bros. Publications Inc., Miami, FL. 33014.

For those without whom

and for my sisters

The night I wrote your name in biro on my wrist
we would wake before dawn; back to back: duelists.

—Paul Muldoon
"Asra," from *Madoc: A Mystery*

I

LUX WAS COMING. Already she was somewhere in the wide expanse of London. My awareness of her presence unsettled me vaguely. Sometimes, before she flew in to visit, I dreamed strange dreams. Like a breeze, she stirred up things.

Midafternoon, I rode the Northern Line home to meet her and stared at the people scrunched on the surrounding banks of seats. Across the aisle, a man in aviator shades sat sketching in a notebook—I wondered if wearing dark glasses in the underground made the world easier to draw. Another man, sweating profusely, clutched a tabloid paper without reading it. Beside him, a woman in a golden sari clamped two polythene bags of groceries between her feet. Out of curiosity, I tried to imagine how each would look transformed by anger. How would the soft, relaxed line of the first man's lips contort, or the sad-eyed desolation of the second man's face, or the woman's dreamy distraction? I studied the first man's hands, dark fingers grasping a pencil, the thick wales of ruddy skin over the other man's knuckles. The woman's fingers were laced and folded over the pleats of cloth in her lap. I wondered what violence each was capable of and what was the worst act of violence they had committed in their lives so far. Had any of them ever punched someone, or drawn blood? If so, how did they explain their actions to themselves?

And, as often when traveling through London by bus or train or underground, I tried out my own version of the ark question—the ethics dilemma that high-school teachers and university philosophy professors liked to confront us with. You are in a lifeboat with a group of people but there is not enough food or water for everyone. Will you split what little there is or toss some survivors overboard? Who will stay and who will go? If I were stranded in a boat with these people—or if a bomb exploded on the train *right now*—who would prove to be the most resourceful, the least likely to panic? What risks would any one of them be prepared to take?

Lux had called me two days before at work. I was in the back room of the Centre for Contemporary War Studies when Moira Ikagoro, who runs the office, answering the phone and monitoring arrivals, put the call through.

"Arcadia?" Lux said.

My heart gave a little start. Part pleasure, part— "Hello, you." I touched my free hand to one of my hair combs. "Where are you?" Because, with my sister Lux, you never knew.

"In Toronto."

"Not in London."

"Not yet."

"But you'll be here tomorrow."

"Almost bingo," Lux said delightedly. "Day after tomorrow."

"Is this business, or—"

"Well, we're shooting something, and then we're flying on to Johannesburg to do some more shooting. You know, mostly music, and how things have changed for musicians since—kind of a post-election thing. But of course I want to see you."

Lux made a habit of sudden annunciation. Sometimes I'd pick up the phone and she would be ringing me from Ankara or Moscow to tell me that she'd be stopping off in London the next day; or she'd be just about to board her plane at Pearson airport in Toronto; or she was in the air, in a 767, four hours away.

"Do you need somewhere to stay?"

"No, we're staying at that same place near Piccadilly as last time. A bit grungy, but it's fine."

"So do you want to make plans now or just ring me when you get in?"

"I'll call you when I get in," she said. "I'll *ring*."

That night, I dreamed in green: a flurry of leaves, a green body on the ground, a girl in a green dress climbing a mountain of steps toward a plane. I woke up sweating.

Arcadia. Lux. What sort of people would give their daughters names like these?

My father, Benedict Hearne, was the one principally responsible. A nuclear engineer, he believed that naming children was not something you undertook lightly—that names should mean something, herald something, have a certain resonance. My mother has told me how, before I was born, he would come bursting through the door of their tiny Ottawa apartment, snow in his dark hair and nestled in the tweed of his winter coat, and shout out possible names. Bliss. Adam, if it was a boy. Atom. Or Molecule. My mother had argued against my name, on the grounds that I was bound to be teased, but my father had argued back that children will be teased no matter what their names are, no matter how common or peculiar, the ingenuity of childhood will always think up something, and I tend to agree with him.

His passion convinced her—the light in his face, the fervor stretched tight beneath his skin. He would lean beside her at the kitchen counter, or kneel by her rocking chair, pressing his cheek to the sleeve of her butter-yellow cardigan, dreaming a landscape for her. At thirty, he was a year younger than I am now. He'd rub her fingers and ankles, swollen in the late stages of pregnancy, and pull loose the barrette holding back the nearly black, growing-out bob of her hair. A blue fluorescent strip light burned above their heads. A north wind hissed in the pine tree outside the window. I don't believe he imagined idyllic fields and rolling hills dotted with sheep, no quaint pastoral landscape, but giant trees and brilliant light and bare knees of granite poking up through the earth. *If it's a girl*, he whispered to my mother, Anne, *we'll call her Arcadia.*

I started up from my desk as the front gate clanged shut and Lux strode through the front garden. She galloped down the outside steps that led to my basement flat (the garden flat, for in the rear there is a tiny plot of grass surrounded by flower beds). In one hand she swung a newspaper-wrapped bouquet, her black leather knapsack jouncing from her shoulders.

When I opened the door, she flung herself into my arms. "I'm knackered," she said, grinning at the English word. "It's good to see you."

"You, too," I said, and it was—to feel, as we kissed, the pressure of her arms, inhale her secondhand-smoke-and-cinnamon-chewing-gum aroma. There was an odd relief in this. She handed me the bouquet—sky-blue delphiniums. "Mmm.

Thanks. Everything all right? You're early." Which Lux almost never was.

She nodded. "We were actually shooting in Camden—not very far away at all—I didn't realize before. This band called Fishwater. It's a pun on this Brazilian dish. *Feijoada?* Someone told me. The lead singer's Brazilian and about seven feet tall—he's been on the cover of some of the music magazines lately, but I don't suppose you've seen him."

She hosted a world music show called *Mundo*, produced in Toronto but aired on various music TV channels around the globe. Sometimes, late at night, I would curl up in my study and watch her. Lux Hearne in Havana, tracking down Cuban punk bands; Lux Hearne in Nairobi swinging to the rhythms of Swahili funk.

Just as strange was the instant's disjunction I felt now between Lux in person and on-screen. Live, she was smaller, slighter, as is true of most people who appear on TV, though her features remained forceful—dark eyebrows, wide mouth—and there was no change in the husky, buoyant timbre of her voice.

She dropped her knapsack to the floor. "How's the book?" she asked.

"Fine," I said. "Coming along."

I knew Lux's interest was largely polite. She did not care, on the whole, to talk about the work I did, not my job at the Centre, not my study of military intervention as a defining feature of late-twentieth-century war. Even now, both she and my mother hoped (it seemed to me) that war studies was something I would outgrow or pass through. Nor did they want to delve too deeply into why I did it, for this would mean invoking a past that none of us really wanted to discuss. At least my father did not instantly shy away from the subject of my work, which I interpreted as a sign, if tacit, of some sort of respect.

I shut down the computer, watching the screen go blank with an audible ping.

When I turned, Lux had picked up her knapsack. Her white T-shirt hung loosely beneath the hollow of her throat. Her dark hair fell about her face in a mop of choppy curls. In the shell-like ridge of her right ear gleamed a row of tiny silver rings and in the skin just above her left nostril a fleck of ruby glittered.

"That's new," I said. Since I'd last seen her, eight months before.

"Like it?"

"Yeah, I like it. I do. Are you thirsty? Fancy something to drink?"

"Sure."

"Sparkling water, orange juice—or shall I open a bottle of wine?"

The May weather was warm and muggy; there had been days in a row of droughtlike heat. "Wine later," Lux said. Behind me, the heels of her red cowboy boots clumped down the hall. "But just some water for now." When I glanced back, I caught her peering, as she passed, into my bedroom.

"Mmm," she said. "Everything's so summery here. It was raining in Toronto."

In the kitchen, I laid the delphiniums on the counter and hoisted the electric fan onto the table. From the fridge I took a bottle of water, and poured some into a glass for Lux.

In earlier days, when Lux was still a deejay, she would stay with me when she came to London, sleeping on a foldout cot in the study. The first few times she came, I'd even gone out to Heathrow to meet her and together we'd ridden the underground back into town.

"How're Mum and Dad?"

I'd last seen my parents a little over a year before, in Amsterdam. My father had flown to Brussels for a conference on nuclear-waste disposal, my mother with him. I'd suggested meeting up in Amsterdam and had taken the hydrofoil across the Channel. This was how we saw each other now, in neutral territory. Singly, and once together, they'd come through London, though I preferred elsewhere. In Amsterdam we'd stayed at the same small hotel, eaten an Indonesian *ristafel*, gone to the Rijksmuseum. We spoke about their house in Toronto. We did not speak—had barely spoken over the years—about why I'd left the city. We talked about my father's work, but not necessarily, or not as often, about the implications of his line of work.

Each time I saw them there were a few more flecks of silver in their dark hair, but they were still slim and handsome people who evoked the glances of strangers as they walked, my father's arm slung round the collar of my mother's sky-blue coat, her hand raised to touch his.

"They're okay," Lux said. "I have a letter for you. And some photos. Dad's cut back a lot. He's doing some safety-related consulting, but not a whole lot—he was in the States recently and in Ottawa for some commission on underground storage of spent fuel rods. And Mum, she's all right. She's taking canoeing lessons."

"Canoeing lessons?"

She gulped from her glass. "At a club. On the lake. Sometimes she takes the dog out. She goes, you know, around Ashbridge's Bay? Or sometimes up the Don River, or along Cherry Beach and around the island."

I tried to imagine my mother in a canoe—a canoe!—nosing past scrub willows, the jetsam of urban beaches, around the derelict harbor lands. What was she looking for?

"I mean, she's fine," Lux said, and gave me a look, as if to add, who are you—you who aren't there—to judge her?

Judge either of them.

I pulled out a chair and sat down across from Lux. A breeze

blew in the open window from the garden and drifted against my skin. Nudging the heel straps free with my toes, I let my sandals drop to the floor. As Lux pushed up the sleeves of her T-shirt, the golden late-afternoon sun caught the round curve of her shoulders, lighting the little red heart tattooed just below her right one. "How's Haydee?" I asked.

Haydee, Lux's girlfriend, danced with a contemporary company and traveled as much as Lux did. I'd gone to see her perform when they'd last come through London, and, because Lux had asked me to, had gone backstage to meet her. Onstage Haydee flung herself through the air like a Molotov cocktail, fearless, topped with a head of raggedy, bleached-blonde hair. In person she was muscular but tiny, narrow eyed and feral. I thought she seemed nervous around me or silently judgmental.

Lux set down her water glass and rubbed her golden arms. "Haydee's great," she said.

Lux pulled her address book out of her knapsack and asked if she could make a phone call.

"Of course," I said, and listened as, red boots clacking, she made her way back down the hall toward my study.

Often, when Lux comes to visit—whether she stays with me or not—she gives out my number, and for weeks afterward there will be calls from people asking for Lux Hearne. Nasal London voices, voices with all manner of accents. Friends and what I assume to be various music-industry acquaintances. She seems to possess the lucky ability of making herself at home wherever she is.

At the kitchen sink, I rinsed the stems of the delphiniums, sliced off the ends with a knife, set the long stalks in a glass vase. Lux's voice drifted down the hall. From the fridge, I took out a bottle of New Zealand chardonnay, uncorked it, and, setting two glasses on the counter, filled them. Wineglass in hand, I unlocked the back door.

Heat from the sun-drenched flagstones rose through my bare feet. Some lie at crooked and tipsy angles, the cement foundation beneath them cracking, but at the flattest spot sits a weather-beaten wicker chair. I stepped out onto the grass beyond, testing the ground beneath for parchedness.

My idyll, I thought. My tiny paradise. I'd dreamed, when I first came to London, of living in a flat with a garden.

We spread a white sheet on my patch of grass and ate on that: cold chicken with rosemary, French bean vinaigrette. In the flower beds, yellow nasturtiums bloomed and the first rosebuds puckered like lips. A stray cat eyed us from the shrubbery until Lux threw it a scrap of chicken.

After we'd eaten we lay side by side on the sheet, staring up at the purpling sky, our legs in the shadow of the dwarf apple tree, our feet nearly touching the brick wall at the bottom of the garden. Lux's presence rippled just beyond my skin, and I was aware of the tug of genetic proximity, the intimacy of sharing the knobbly shape of our toes and the placement of a mole on our necks and the curve of our fingernails, a tug that, though not sexual, was erotic.

The scent of honeysuckle wafted over us.

"Cay," Lux said. Above the dimming rooftops and multihued windows, the sky had turned to plum. "I think you should come back."

I did not immediately say anything in response. It had been ten years—ten years almost exactly. There was nothing, really, that needed to be said. When I'd left, I'd sworn to myself that I would never go back.

"I'm not asking as anyone's go-between," Lux went on. "No

one told me to ask you—although of course they want you to. It's just me asking—saying, I think you should come back."

"I don't really see the need." I laid one arm across my forehead. "You come here and last year I saw them in Amsterdam. And Dad had a stopover at Gatwick the year before that."

"It's not the same."

"I'm busy," I said. "We all are. But I make the time."

"There's no reason to think you'd run into them." She wasn't talking about our parents this time. "Cay, it isn't a good enough reason anymore. Maybe in the beginning, but not now. I live there and I've never run into them. Ten years ago is history."

"It *is* history," I said, "but that doesn't mean I want to go back, or need to."

"Come home," Lux said.

"Lux, not right at the moment."

Another sigh gusted out of her. "Cay—" A phone rang through someone's open window, a sharp *brring, brring*, and at the sound Lux sat up hurriedly. "Is that yours?"

"No," I said, turning on my side toward her.

"I left your number," she said. "There's someone I'm trying to get hold of."

I WOKE IN THE DARK to the echo of Lux's voice wafting through the flat. *Come back. Why don't you come back?* I struggled to right myself in the landscape of the familiar: the white walls of my windowless bedroom, so small that the double bed engulfs it, the sea of white bedsheets. Rising, I pulled my old silk robe from the hook inside the closet door and slipped it around my shoulders. The turquoise numbers on the digital clock read 5:06.

In my study, at the front of the flat, I lit the gas fire, though it was far from cold. I flung myself onto the love seat, wrapped myself in the velvet throw that lay across the back. Love seat, ha. Yet there was comfort in this room, my white cocoon. I'd built a haven within these four walls. There was safety in the flicker of flame against the pale green ceramic tiles that line the fireplace; in the looped patterns of the worn Persian carpet (a jumble-sale find) on the floor. In the outline of the desk, the slim gray case of the computer, the black back of the desk chair. In the maps that cover the walls—maps dotted with pins and pencil lines to demarcate the world's restlessly new and shifting borders. Even in the titles lining the bookshelves, titles like *Slaughterhouse* and *How to Make War* and *The Origins of War*.

After breakfast, after two cups of strong black coffee, I shoved my sunglasses over my grainy eyes, stuffed some papers into my carry bag, and locked the door of my flat behind me. On the North London railway line to Highbury and Islington, a man in a blue linen jacket sat across from me. I imagined myself kissing him—more curiosity than lust, for I'll do this with all sorts of people. Ray Farr, my director, in the middle of a meeting. An old woman on a street corner. Would her lips be velvety or dry? How would his surprise transform him?

In Highbury, I crossed the street toward the green shimmer of Highbury Fields, passed the Boer War statue (reminders of war lie everywhere), and made my way along the row of terrace houses that line the park.

Downstairs, beside our door, there is only a discrete typewritten sign, one of three, beside the intercom. THE CENTRE FOR CONTEMPORARY WAR STUDIES, it reads. Upstairs, we occupy two rooms above a ground-floor barrister's office. We're a research organization, small and privately funded. We produce papers and video reports, collect documentation, do a certain amount of educational work, respond to media requests. U.N. personnel, aid workers, nongovernmental and governmental strategists, students, journalists all make use of our resources.

When I entered the office, at the top of a flight of creaky wooden stairs, Moira, solid and capable in a flowered dress, rose from her chair. The rest of us, including Ray, share the three desks in the second room, where in summer the two tall windows, sashes broken, are propped open with milk bottles and an electric fan whirs, while in winter we huddle around a small electric heater set in the middle of the floor. All this is deceptive, really—the broken window sashes, the heater— because the real office doesn't exist in any one place. I come in a couple of times a week for meetings and to sift through correspondence, and work at home the rest of the time. These rooms are our shell, the carapace that hides the telecommunication lines and fiber-optic cable and complex binary codes that store our information and connect us to each other, to colleagues, and to conflicts around the globe. We cross borders with ease this way, even though the computers are chained to bolts in the floor and the red eye of an alarm system blinks high on one wall.

I study war. I'm a researcher, a theorist, an associate director at the Centre. I have a degree in War Studies, and I like the baldness of that. Not Defense Studies or Conflict Studies or Peace and Conflict Studies. No one declares war anymore, some eminent analysts say. The concept of war is outmoded. But I don't see the point in talking around what we are really talking about when we are really talking about war.

A few people, men especially, still appear shocked when they find out what I do—not so much because I'm a woman, I assume, but because of the way I look. Because I like to wear long, clingy skirts and dark red lipstick and in boots with heels I stand as tall as they do. If I let loose my hair, it would fall halfway down my back.

If we were war correspondents we wouldn't have this problem, says my friend Lola Race, a military historian specializing in World War II aerial bombing techniques. Lola likes to wear bright stockings—fuchsia, lemon, lime—beneath tight black miniskirts. *To hell with looking butch.*

There are men, Lola says, *who actually dare to ask me if I shave my legs and underarms because they can't believe I do.*

Glamor, in female war correspondents, isn't seen as incongruous. They're permitted to be fascinated by war while trailing the allure of those who thrive in dangerous situations. They're women who race through sniper fire gathering stories about human suffering, who manage to win the confidence of hot-blooded, sex-starved young men brandishing AK-47s, who dash on lipstick by candlelight in a room in the partly bombed-out Sarajevo Holiday Inn.

But I'm no war correspondent.

Other people simply ask me why I do what I do.

There are things I want to know, I tell them. *Things I believe it's important to attempt to explain. I'd rather think about these things than not.*

AT THE END OF THE AFTERNOON, I left the office and cut south and west through Islington until I reached the canal. This stretch, as I turned toward home, is usually quiet. I had only anglers, bent over their rods, snacking on crisps, for company. A rat scuttled across the towpath and dove into a maze of nettles. Closer to Camden, under a copse of poplars, squatters had rigged up tents of plastic sheeting. Smoke puffed skyward.

Walking by the canal is like entering border country. The city as you know it disappears. Wildness asserts itself. People vanish—around corners, never to be seen again. Or they materialize as suddenly—a crowd of schoolchildren yammering under the rainbow-striped arch of a sewer pipe. Perhaps, when I stop to think of it (and I did not often stop to think about it), the canals remind me a little of the ravines in the city where I grew up.

I'd thought Lux might ring, at least to say goodbye, but when I reached home, there was no message from her. All I knew was that she was flying out to Johannesburg the next night.

In the morning, I again woke early to the interior ringing of

Lux's voice. *Come back, come back.* At five, in my nightgown, I went out and weeded the garden. I had no wish to go back. I did not want disruption. Better to keep the past in the past, to protect yourself through knowledge: that's what I've told myself. Later, after a shower and more strong black coffee, I packed up my laptop computer and escaped south, under the river, to Kennington.

Beyond the Fruitcake Patisserie and the Burst Your Thirst off-licence, past the spiked metal grill atop the police station's walled parking lot, spread the grounds of the War Museum. Bright lawns blazed beneath a glittery noontime sun—still green on the surface, although if you stepped onto the grass, the ground beneath was hard as tack. Children from a nursery raced about shrieking, in and out of the speckled light under the broad old beech trees. All that pastoral beauty. Sheep would not have looked out of place.

On benches in the deepest shade, old men in flat-topped caps rustled through newspapers. Nannies ambled behind pushchairs packed with sleeping babies, one—I noticed with a start—shielded by a tiny Toronto Blue Jays baseball cap.

Between the tall wrought-iron entrance gates and the steps of the museum itself a haze of rose blossoms spill forth in salmon and coral and lemony yellow and eggshell cream. Above the roses loom the huge twin barrels of a World War II naval gun, aimed north in the direction of the river, at the heart of the city.

As I passed along the length of gunmetal, the fragrance of roses drifted up, nectar sweet.

"Here's your ticket, love," said the man in the ticket booth when I flashed him my researcher's ID. Just as, when I'd entered the Camden tube station that morning, shifting through bodies, the bedraggled man hawking magazines had called out, "Buy a copy of the Big Issue, me love." I'd given him a handful of change. It amuses me to live in a city where one is called *love* so easily. I shrug it off. It doesn't offend me.

In the upstairs research rooms of the War Museum I was unlikely to be disturbed. Soundproof glass doors deaden the sounds of the museum itself: the cries of schoolchildren, the ricochet of mortar fire and explosion of bombs from the audio-visual displays. In contrast, the research rooms are cool and still and airy. In winter, sunlight shines through the tall, arched windows. By midsummer, the light comes filtered through the leaves of the beech trees, turning the walls a pale absinthe. The effect is calming, quite peaceful, actually.

I set up my computer on one of the wooden tables. In front of me, I laid out pages of statistics about increasing civilian casualties in military conflicts—for this is one of the crucial ways in which the nature and rules of war have changed throughout this century.

In classic considerations of war, two armies converge upon a battlefield, though naturally raping and pillaging and laying land to waste have gone on throughout history. But in 1917, Sir Hugh Trenchard, in charge of Allied strategic bombing during the First World War, first argued that using the air force to target cities and civilians could be a legitimate tactic for waging war.

By 1950, 50 percent of war-related casualties were civilian. These days, the ratio of civilian deaths to military is five to one. Over 80 percent, in other words. Nearing ninety, some say. Over fifty million dead in conflicts since the end of the Second World War. And rising. Even refugees in safe havens are targets these days. (Think of Srebrenica.) In the Balkans, the creation of refugees has become a specific strategy of war.

Across the room, a wispy-haired researcher stepped up to a tall metal cabinet and slid open one of the wide, flat map drawers. The hands of the old-fashioned clock above the door crept toward noon. Standing, I burrowed in my bag for my wallet and slipped it into my palm.

When I rang home for messages, from a call box in the basement, Lux's voice burst from the answerphone into my ear. "Cay, it's me. I'll try you at the office. Please call me as soon as you get this message, okay? It's really, really important." She left her number at the hotel. The next message was again from Lux. "Cay, are you there? Please pick up if you're there. Okay, it's eleven and I'm going out for a couple of hours, but if you get this, call me and tell me if there's a number where I can reach you. Or just come by the hotel, say, about three o'clock."

I rang the hotel and the receptionist put me through. On the first ring, Lux picked up the phone.

"It's Arcadia."

"Oh, Cay, I'm so glad it's you." Her voice rose, lightly frantic. "Where are you?"

"The War Museum."

She ignored that. "Can you meet me?" This was seduction. She assumed I would. She phrased it as a question but it was not a question. Whatever plans I had, whatever arrangements I had previously made, it was her conviction that I would cancel them in order to meet her. I owed it to her. Because I'd left. Because I lived here and she lived there. Something like that.

"All right," I said.

"Not at the hotel, but in Islington. Still at three. Is that okay? At the Café Olé on Upper Street. It's like about halfway up."

I was familiar with the Café Olé on Upper Street, since it was
not all that far from the Centre for Contemporary War Studies.
For all I knew, Lux had picked it simply because she liked the
name. She sent me postcards sometimes—from the Lime Lick
Café in Bangkok where they served Scram Bowl eggs. From the
Get In Inn in Istanbul. Once she'd written to me from the
Cosmic Side View Hotel somewhere in Kenya. She'd drawn a
picture. *I'm staring out the window looking for the cosmic side view.*
All I can see is mud walls and dust and a speck of sky. Maybe that
IS the cosmic side view.

I found her at a side table. She grinned and waved. "Thanks
for coming." And stood as I approached. "I'll buy you coffee or
whatever you want."

"Oh, please, Lux, sit, that's hardly—" The agitation she'd
evinced over the phone was not immediately in evidence.

I ordered a cappuccino from the skinny waitress and Lux a
café au lait. Orange sponge-painted walls surrounded us.
"Guess what," I said. "I heard a story today about the first escalator installed on the London underground and how they hired
a man with a wooden leg to ride up and down it to demonstrate
that it was safe."

Lux nodded. The tiny ruby in her nostril winked. She had
been too young to remember the time we'd first ridden an escalator together, though I did.

When I was two, just after Lux was born, we moved from
Ottawa, north up the Ottawa River to a small town upstream
from the nuclear-research facility where my father had begun to
work. White bungalows, filled with the families of nuclear
scientists, lined its crescents—a tiny, perfect suburb dropped
down in the middle of the woods. On the flagpole outside the
spreading low-rise of our school waved the red maple leaf of the
Canadian flag and a green flag emblazoned with the grin of
Elmer the Safety Elephant. On the road into town, there was a

security booth and a long, mechanized arm that, when lowered, blocked all traffic, but by the time we moved there, people were stopped and questioned far less often than they had once been.

I was five and Lux was three on the day that our mother took us to Ottawa, two hundred miles away, to visit the Eaton's department store. Lux had never seen an escalator before and if I had, I didn't remember it. We stood in terror at the bottom of the moving staircase and had to be coaxed onto the first step, but then, as we began to scroll upward, hands pressed to the metal sides, something lifted in us. By the time we reached the next floor, all we wanted to do for the rest of the afternoon was ride the escalators like some amusement-park ride.

Other things Lux did remember: our shared bedroom in the white bungalow, the gate in the plastic-coated chicken-wire fence that marked the line between tame lawn and wild trees. The TV game, which I invented and Lux took to like a drug (so that later I would feel oddly responsible for what she became). Because we were barely allowed to watch television, we made up our own TV show, *The Lux and Cadie Show*: we starred in it. We rescued imaginary hockey-star husbands from witches and marauders and an evil hockey-star brother who once tried to send the husbands in a barrel over Niagara Falls. We became secret agents. We interviewed each other. In the woods, in a circle of dappled sunlight, Lux would swivel her tiny hips with joy and clutch an invisible microphone. *And now*, she'd say. *Coming right up*.

When we came home from school, our mother poured us glasses of real orange juice instead of Tang, made from orange flavor crystals. No sweets, she'd say to us (no candies, we knew she meant), except on weekends. Once I saw her toss a Barbie, which Lux had been given for her birthday, into the garbage. (When I told Lux, Lux didn't seem to care.) She gave us old dresses—cotton minis covered in jazzy flowers, a sleeveless number in green velvet—to dress up in. She didn't let us watch any television she considered too American or too violent. She'd come to Canada from New Zealand, believing in a progressive future. She had a degree in English and art history. One afternoon, she dropped to her knees on the tiled kitchen floor in front of us, and said in a strange, fierce voice, *There are things I want to protect you from.* As if through will and diligence she could create a haven for us.

In the evening, she seated us to either side of her on the brown sofa and read to us from the *Blue Book of Fairy Tales.* Later, when we were teenagers, after we'd moved to Toronto, Lux started up a band called Babes from the Woods. She sang and played guitar, told me she'd always wanted to be in a band with that name. What I thought, looking back, was that we had grown up like children in a fairy tale, in a clearing in the middle of a forest, where things, at least at the beginning of the story, seemed safe.

"I need to ask you a favor," Lux said, leaning across the café table toward me.

"Mmm?" I said. "What sort of favor?"

She ran her spoon through the steamed milk of her café au lait. "To deliver something for me."

"What sort of something?"

"A package. For a woman named Basra Alale. A refugee. She's Somali." She kept her voice low.

"Here in London."

Lux nodded. Her curved lips were lightly chapped. Her whole demeanor breathed the belief that I would listen and agree with her. The irresistibility of her voice was rooted in this—not in a perceived need to win me over. She conducted interviews in the same way (I'd seen her), with an appearance of guilelessness, though it wasn't guilelessness, exactly. As if she could not imagine why anyone would not want to respond to her questions and reveal themselves to her.

"Lux," I said. I kept my voice as muted as hers was. "Please. Can we back up? Can you tell me how you come to be delivering a package to a Somali refugee? Or is there some musical connection I'm not yet aware of?"

She looked up. "There's this human-rights organization called Rights Now. Maybe you've heard of them. They're mostly based in New York, but they also have an office in Toronto. They were founded by David Raphael? The singer? You've heard of him, haven't you? They do a lot of work with people who are musicians or somehow involved in the music industry, but you don't have to be. They asked me if I'd do some stuff for them."

"Stuff, Lux?"

"Running errands. Delivering things. If I'm, like, traveling somewhere and they need someone to deliver something. Like money. Or cameras. Palmcorders." She gestured with one hand to show how tiny the palmcorders were. "So people can take them into places, dangerous places, and shoot things where you couldn't take a camera crew, then smuggle the tapes back out."

I asked her how long she had been doing this. I was surprised, for she had never breathed a word of it, and Lux had never struck me as particularly political. I hoped she didn't think of it as some extension of being on TV: playing secret agent.

"The last couple of years? On a couple of trips." She shrugged. "It's not that big a deal."

"Isn't it dangerous?" For surely there were risks.

"No," she said. "Not really. I just pass things on. To other people. It's not that suspicious. I mean, what's odd about me traveling with a palmcorder? I've never been stopped."

"What's happened with Basra Alale, then?"

"I can't get hold of her. I was given a number and I left messages, but she hasn't called me back. I called the Toronto office to see if they had any more information—she knows we were supposed to be trying to reach her. So I thought, you know, because you're here, because you live here . . ."

Wherever Basra Alale was, it was not likely to be in Central London. Possibly not on the underground, possibly miles away by bus. And first I had to find her.

"She's like about my age," Lux went on, "maybe a year or so younger. Before the war, when she was a university student in Mogadishu, she sang with this group—they were all students, I think, but she was the only girl, and I think she wrote the songs—about the trouble with clans. Some of their songs, anyway. At least one. How they should be abolished or made less powerful or whatever. She was arrested and beaten up, and then when Mogadishu fell, she fled to Kenya and ended up in a refugee camp. That's where Rights Now got involved with her—they knew about her from before. I think she has some family in London. It's taken a while—but that's why they brought her here."

"Have you met her?"

"No."

"I meant before this. I didn't know if—"

"All I've got is a Xeroxed photo of her. She only got here a couple of months ago."

"Why me?" I asked. I crossed one leg over the other. For there were other people, friends in London, whom Lux might have asked: a deejay named Daisy; a music producer turned trip-hop star named Tommy Singh, born in Mississauga, Ontario, whom Lux had met while they were radio-and-television-arts students in Toronto and who was still one of her best pals. "Why didn't you ask Tommy?"

She looked indignant, as if I had pulsed some tender nerve.

"Because you're my sister. Maybe I trust you more than Tommy. Why shouldn't I ask you, Cay?"

"There's no—"

"Are you saying you don't want to do it? You can't just sit around in your room all day writing about war, you know."

"Lux." I touched my fingers to one of the combs wedged in my hair, to cool bone. Her eyes had gone very round, as if she was frightened that she'd gone too far.

Perhaps she did not need me to help her, but wanted me to run this errand. Make me the go-between for once.

Perhaps she was not even supposed to be doing this.

I SAID YES, OF COURSE.

There were five thousand U.S. dollars in the package, Lux whispered, as she passed a brown envelope across the table. The amount surprised me. Just a little. To help Basra, Lux said, and to pay back the people who'd helped get her here. It did feel a little like playing secret agent.

That night, when I rang the number that Lux had given me, a woman answered and said in a soft, accented voice, but not as if anything were out of the ordinary, that Basra should be in later. I left my own number.

All the next day, I worked at home. I cut back my modem use so that the line would not ring busy for long stretches as I trolled the on-line reportage and firsthand testimonials from the world's wars (and non-wars). Lola rang, Ray rang, but no one else. I sat at my desk and thought, The work I do is perfectly valid. I'm a theorist. I hardly need to race about the globe. Besides, I value safety. And here in London I've found a sort of safety.

I thought about Somalia at the time of the U.S.- and U.N.-led intervention, by which point the country had ceased to function as a state—this was the argument—civil government having collapsed, riven by tribal fighting. Which made a mandate for intervention less like a call for invasion, a violation of state sovereignty—though, of course, the most crucial rationale for action was that thousands upon thousands of people were starving.

Five years ago there were still those who believed a military force could go in on the ground, restore stability in months, make a quick exit. That elite troops trained for hardcore combat could switch hats like magicians or tap dancers and function as peacekeepers.

I wondered exactly when Basra Alale had left.

At eight in the evening, I switched off the computer, shook out my hands, and stumbled blearily toward the kitchen, where I unlocked the back door and stood at the edge of the garden, breathing deeply.

The phone rang. The phone rang again, and I dashed back through the flat toward it. There was silence on the line, a gap, and then a sluicing of air or static or water. "Cay," Lux's voice said. "Have you managed to get hold of her?"

"Not yet."

Perhaps I sounded too nonchalant, though I did not mean to, and this was what riled her. It had been less than twenty-four hours since I'd said goodbye to Lux at the Angel tube station, after all.

"Cay—"

I shouldn't have done it, I know, but I hung up on her.

There's a sensuality to returning to a place where you live by yourself. Its smell newly asserts itself—its nest of smells, a concoction fruity with dust and decaying paper and coffee and sweet human musk and the hint of something metallic.

There's a sensuality to living on one's own. The lusciousness of solitude is a pleasure I subscribe to. The thrum of privacy beckons as soon as you step through the door. Rooms themselves become a kind of body, an extension of your own body or someone else's body. Yet there's no one to nag you when bits of food are stuck between your teeth. No one to notice if you stuff newspapers instead of food into the freezer, since it costs less to freeze something than nothing, or get up at 2 a.m. to water the garden; no one to stop you from eating a pear and letting pear juice dribble along your arm and down your chin.

The next evening, I went out for dinner at the pub across the street. Returning, trailing the scent of cod and chips, I locked the door behind me and ran my fingertips tenderly along the glossy walls.

When the phone rang, the noise was startling. I was sitting in the kitchen, hugging a cup of coffee. All was quiet in a way that seemed spectacular for such a huge city. No one was practicing the saxophone. No one blared Bronski Beat from some upper window in a fit of nostalgia: *run away, turn away*. Outside, gnats danced in the thick, dark air. I was not lonely.

When the phone rang again, I stepped to the counter and picked up the receiver.

"Hello," I said, clearing my throat. "Sorry. Hello?"

"Yes," a voice said, female, crisp and faintly halting. "I wish to speak to Arcadia Hearne." Ar*cah*dia, the voice said.

"This is Arcadia."

"Ah," the voice said. "Please. My name is Basra Alale."

She said she hoped she was not ringing too late. No, no, I said, not at all. Was she all right? She said she was. When could we meet, I asked her.

"Tomorrow night," she said, as if there were no choice in the matter, and perhaps for her there wasn't much choice. "Near King's Cross Station."

"Right," I said. "That'll be easy. Lovely."

Without warning, she pressed a palm to the receiver, or so it sounded, and I heard her muffled voice joined by another, male. Then she returned. "There is a café, please. Good Grub Café. On Omega Place. At eight o'clock."

I gave her my work number just in case, and told her I'd find it.

Good Grub, I thought. Like a joke, or a name that Lux might have had a hand in. As for Omega Place, I had to look it up in my battered *London A to Z*—a tiny cul-de-sac, just above the intersection of the Caledonian and Pentonville Roads, which I must have walked by numerous times in the past without ever noticing it, but there—invisible, visible—all at once it was.

I worked late at the Centre, then hailed a cab, which dropped me off on a gritty curb opposite a brick wall. High on its side hung a plaque bearing the faded words OMEGA PLACE.

Alpha, a voice whispered, *Omega*. The world wobbled a little. A boy, a blond boy, danced bare chested in a clearing, in the green light that filtered down through a ring of trees.

Suddenly, from the pocket of his jeans, he pulled out a knife. Small, blue handled. He flexed the blade. Flattening one hand against his chest, as if to frame a patch of skin, he began to carve into the flesh. Two diagonal lines that met at a point, a line that crossed between them. White lines turned red, the letter *A* coming clear as blood welled up.

"Evan, stop," I cried. Fear laced me—not just shock, but giddiness, like a new pulse.

He didn't look up, not then, not until he'd drawn a circle in the skin around the letter. Then he threw his arms open wide, blood trickling over his ribs, head tilted high, face gripped in a rictus of pain or ecstasy. "A and O," he said. "For you, Arcadia. Alpha and Omega, from the beginning to the end—because I'll love you forever."

I slung my bag across my chest, hand tight on it. Yet all this was familiar: the sweep of the Caledonian Road, the bottle of red wine smashed across the pavement; the darkened windows of the Pirate Book Shop; a woman in a doorway wrapped in newspapers, peeling an orange in a reek of citrus and urine; a man in a blue windbreaker hurling a string of vituperation at a woman in a miniskirt and white thigh-high boots, who threw up her hands, turned on her heel, and stalked away. Most familiar of all were the flashing lights, a block away, of the Family Amusement Palace Leisure Hall.

In the months after I first came to London, I haunted video arcades, and none more than the Family Amusement Palace. There were never any families, of course, and palace was hardly the word for it, although there had been some attempt made to fix the place up in the years since then. Lightbulbs blinked in a frazzle of enticement from the marquee outside. Plate-glass windows now filled one wall.

Inside there were always men—young skinny men, men with pockmarked faces, men in bilious nylon tracksuits, men whose pockets swelled and jingled with change. In the days when I hung out at video arcades, I, too, made sure there was change in my pockets, but I did not play the games that much. When I did, I did so halfheartedly, as a pretext for spying on the men. I watched their eyes and mouths, watched their fists slam and jiggle. The din was stupendous. It poured over me like a tidal wave, although I could soon distinguish the particular sounds of whistling bullets and high-pitched screams. Sometimes the men shouted out catcalls; often they ignored me, left me free to watch as they leaned toward their screens, stunned and consumed by the lure of games with names like Conqueror or Nadir or Fatal Combat.

Net curtains covered the windows of the Good Grub Café. Although the sign on the door read CLOSED, a yellow light shone within, like the glow of a cottage in the middle of a forest.

When I knocked, I could see, through the scrim of opaque lace that covered the door, a figure approaching; then the lock turned, and the door opened a crack. "Yes?" a man said, a white apron cinched at his waist.

"I'm Arcadia Hearne, I'm—" Oddly nervous.

"Yes," he said. "Please. Come in." From beyond the man's shoulder came a flutter of movement. A young woman rose from a table where she'd been sitting beside another man in a tweed jacket. The walls of the restaurant were covered improbably in red velvet. Little white fairy lights twisted around a glass refrigerator case filled with cans of fizzy drinks. Plastic flowers rose from tiny vases on the plastic-covered tables.

The young woman stepped forward, light on her feet, an expression of hungry expectancy seizing her face. "Greetings," she said, and held out both hands. I glimpsed a trace of the girl in the badly Xeroxed photograph that Lux had shown me.

"Basra?"

"Oh." She raised her fingertips to cover her mouth and, eyebrows rising, let loose a tiny laugh. "Yes. I am so sorry. Please. I am Basra." The palms of her hands, when she clasped mine, were dry and cool. She kissed me on both cheeks. Her head was bare, hair pulled back tightly in a grip at the base of her neck. She was tall and slim—lanky, willowy. The starchy newness of her clothes—bright white T-shirt, V-shaped denim skirt, white ankle-high trainers—might, on someone else, have looked awkward, a sign of being out-of-place, but only made Basra seem neatly self-possessed.

"I am so happy you have come," she said in her precise, surprising English. *Basra* as in the Iraqi city, I wondered. Bombed Basra, ancient Basra—once a cradle of civilization, once, so it was rumored, home to the Garden of Eden. I wondered if Basra Alale was, technically speaking, a refugee. The neighborhoods around my friend Tim's surgery in Hammersmith (down the street from a pub called the Adam and Eve) were filled with Bosnian refugees-who-were-not-refugees. They were all missing things, as Tim put it—an arm, a leg, an ability to sleep through the night, a city. And they were missing refugee status as well, for even this had gained a permanence that put it out of the reach of many people. They had instead what's called *exceptional leave to remain.*

"Yes. This is Wahid," Basra said. One arm traced a long arc toward the man in the apron, who ducked in a small bow. "And this is Amir Barmour."

The man in the tweed jacket stood, holding out one hand. "How do you do?" A smile rose along his lips. Not Somali, although Wahid seemed to be. Amir Barmour wore a blue cotton shirt beneath his jacket, bright against his sepia skin, and his voice sounded quite *English* English, as if he had, for all I knew, been born mere miles away in the vastness of London.

"Please, you must sit down," Basra said, as if she were simply a hostess inviting me to join a party. She stood beside the table, on which two empty Coke bottles wobbled. "And you must have a drink."

"It's all right, really."

"Oh, but you must."

The man named Amir pulled out a chair for me, then withdrew to a few tables away. I eyed the menu on a board above the bar—sausages and chips, eggs and chips, eggs and beans and chips. Cheap English food. "A cup of tea then, that would be lovely."

Up close, once she had seated herself, Basra's long face seemed solemn, her eyes very round and heavy lidded. A tiny scar nicked the skin beneath one eyebrow. "Lux—my sister— was sorry not to be able to meet you."

"I, too, am sorry," she said gravely.

Wahid cleared away the Coke bottles and served me tea in a little tin pot, a china cup and saucer, a shortbread biscuit. Once he had retreated, I lifted my bag into my lap, unbuckled it, and, pulling out the manila envelope that Lux had given me, handed it to Basra. She laid the envelope on the table. Lifting the hem of her T-shirt, she unzipped a cloth money belt tied around her waist, folded the envelope into it, and zipped up the money belt with such purposefulness and alacrity that a moment later, hands clasped on the table in front of her, it was as if she'd done nothing at all.

Do I believe in pure altruism, true selflessness? I don't know. I was curious about Basra. I wanted to ask her questions. Where had she learned her English? In the refugee camp, at university? I wanted to know what her relationship was to the man named Amir, who sat, one arm folded over the other, with an expression of alert impassivity on his face, as if he were attentive to everything that transpired but did not want to seem too involved. Lover? Escort? Some sort of guardian?

"When did you leave Mogadishu?" I asked her.

"Three years ago."

"Have you been in Kenya all that time?" She nodded. "How did you get there—by sea or overland?"

"I walked through the desert," she said.

Another woman (in a pearl-gray suit, as we ate roast quail in an upscale Notting Hill restaurant) had told me how she had fled Mogadishu just after the dictatorship had fallen. She had found places for herself and her mother on a small boat crammed with other refugees, a boat bound for Mombassa, Kenya. The trip should have taken twenty-four hours. They were at sea for ten days with no food and almost no water. One woman had died, Halima told me, as she lifted a quail wing in her hands and delicately stripped the meat from the bone.

Halima was a high-level aid worker. In the days to come, she was flying back to a refugee camp in southern Sudan. (Where victims of that civil war were also starving.)

I thought, too, of a story my friend Patrick O'Daire, an Irish journalist, had told me. About the road to Basra. Route 80. The highway from Kuwait City along which, at the end of the Gulf War, the Iraqi army had fled.

He had traveled, at the end of the Gulf War, with a British squadron to Kuwait City and, with stubborn persistence, managed to snare a driver and vehicle to take him out along the road to Basra. In the midst of its flat expanse, he asked his driver to stop, and climbed out. The road, apart from the chugging of his own vehicle, was silent. The tarmac beneath his feet was pitted with holes, which he knew to be a telltale remnant of cluster bombs.

It was easier to walk than drive, because the road was nearly blocked with vehicles, jammed along the road and at the side of the road: saloon cars and milk-delivery vans and Japanese-made sedans, among others, all turned in one direction, all in flight. Some of the boots had sprung open, spilling chandeliers and blenders and videocassette machines and plastic vials of washing-up liquid. In the backseat of one car Patrick found a spilled cache of family photographs—a Pakistani family, not

Iraqi at all. Carefully he trod past carbonized bodies curled like fetuses as if to protect themselves, others clutching automatic rifles, their blackened heads thrown back.

Out of the silence, he heard something. A wavery voice. At first it unnerved him completely. High and frail, it sounded almost like a child's voice. It seemed to be singing. He had no idea what kind of voice—the voice of who or what—would be singing in that place. Perhaps he should turn back—but he didn't, couldn't. He kept walking, watching for unexploded bombs. It was, he realized as he drew closer, a female voice, high pitched and nasal, singing in Arabic. In front of him was an army pickup truck. Across the front seat lay a charred body. Although, so he implied, he was usually gruff and taciturn in the face of disaster, his stomach was beginning to give out on him. The truck's radio had burst from its dashboard casing and hung in the air, still held by wire threads. Out of this the voice unwound itself like a silver skein. He came closer. Keys still hung in the ignition. Yet how could the battery, two days later, possibly have any juice left in it? He reached out one hand to switch it off but didn't. Couldn't. He drew his hand back again.

Across the table from Basra Alale, who sang, so Lux had said, I swallowed a sip of tea. "Maybe this is presumptuous," I said. "But do you mind if I ask you—this may seem like a crazy question, but I was curious how you got your name. It's an unusual name, isn't it?"

"Yes," she said, with a little laugh. Her high forehead, her round eyes shone. "My father gave this name to me. Yes, it is the city. Once he visited many, many cities and this one, he says, is the most beautiful. Not now, no. But long ago. In that time there were many flowers and fountains and hanging gardens."

"What does your father do?"

"An engineer. He was a water engineer."

"Perhaps my father," I said, "is a little like your father. Lux and Arcadia aren't ordinary Canadian names."

"They live in Canada? Still? Your family?"

"In Toronto. My mother, my father, and Lux."

Basra's hands lay flat upon the table. "Ah," she said. "Toronto. Where there is the world's tallest building."

"Not building, exactly. Tallest free-standing structure. A cement tower doesn't count as a building."

"Ah," she said again. "And the underground is called the subway." I nodded. "And there is a hospital not for *children* but for Sick Children." Her face remained impassive as she spoke.

"Your father's been there?"

"No," she said. "My father is dead." She shook her head, as if shrugging off sympathy.

"And the rest of your family?"

"My mother also, but long ago. My sister remains in Kenya. My brothers did not wish to leave Mogadishu."

"If there's anything more you should need . . ." I was going to open my wallet and pull out my card, but Arcadia Hearne, Centre for Contemporary War Studies, seemed somehow inappropriate under the circumstances, as if I had come with flagrant ulterior motives. Instead I ripped a corner from my paper placemat. "You can ring me on either of these numbers."

"Thank you," Basra said, and tucked the scrap of paper into her palm. "You are most kind." Her high forehead made her look almost placid, but through her eyes ran—what? A flicker of fear? We kissed—one cheek, then the other. I shook hands with the man named Amir, who rose deftly to his feet, and with Wahid, who led me back down the aisle between the tables, unlocked the front door, and released me into the street.

I CAME TO LONDON, carrying one blue vinyl suitcase, believing it was possible to escape the past. There was history in London, but it was not my history. My mother's parents had lived in England during the Second World War, but in Manchester, not in London, and they weren't English. Married at seventeen, they had grown up together on the island of Malta. (A love of islands, my mother said, and a desperation to escape Europe had taken them at war's end to New Zealand.)

I'd left no note behind me in Toronto. Emptying my bank account, I'd paid for my ticket in cash, lied to the immigration officer and told him I was visiting. In London, there were friends of friends I might have called, but didn't. I wanted a blank slate. No traces. *Terra nullius*.

In less than a week, I found a room in a shared flat in Turnham Green, miles west of Central London. Nor was it as hard to find work as I'd feared—the sort of work where you can get paid in cash under the table. I answered an ad propped in the window of a tea shop run by a Polish couple and began making sandwiches, slipping them into little white paper bags and twisting the corners into ears for customers to take away. Through a

THE RULES OF ENGAGEMENT

boy I met at the tea shop, I found a second job in a pub near the
law courts, one that barristers frequented, their hair flattened or
sticking up in twigs after being squashed by a wig all day. I
copied the voices I heard around me. *Right,* I said. *Brilliant.
Ring me.* I doused my new *London A to Z* in the bathtub to make
it look more weatherworn once I'd discovered that everyone,
not only tourists, carried about maps of the city. There were
times when I could even pass as English, partly because of my
name, which here people assumed to be simply a sign of English
eccentricity. Standing under the trickle of a cold shower in the
cold bathroom of the shared flat, I burned with desire—for
transformation, to create a new life.

Yet, like anyone who lives somewhere illegally, I was gripped
by the temporary. I could not shake my fear that at any moment
the life I'd fashioned could be taken away. I kept my suitcase
under the bed, my books in piles on the floor. I avoided the
sharp gazes of policemen. I barely left the city and did not leave
the country in case I could not get back.

A year and a half after I arrived in London, I met Martin Cale
in a basement vegetarian café just off the Tottenham Court
Road. As he maneuvered, tray in hand, between tables, his coat,
slung over one arm, knocked over my sugar bowl. With our
fingers, we scooped the cubes—of raw sugar, naturally—back
into the bowl. When I offered him my extra napkin, he sat down
across from me: not much older than I was, tall and bony, with
a bony face. He crossed his arms over his narrow chest. "Are
you all right?" he asked, and leaned forward with such concern
and sympathy that something opened wide inside me. This was,
at that moment, exactly what I wanted—to be stared at as atten-
tively as he was staring and asked, "Are you all right?"

And again, the first night that we arranged to meet for drinks.
In Brixton, not far from Martin's flat. "Are you all right?"
Beneath his coat, he wore an unironed shirt. His dark hair stood

up in tufts. I felt as moved by the words as I had the first time, though a frizzle of caution zigzagged through me—as if something had been exposed that I didn't want to be, some glimpse of disarray, some hint of what I'd abandoned when fleeing Toronto, which simply made me want to hide this all the more, and prove that, yes, indeed, I was all right.

Three weeks after we met, I moved in with Martin Cale. Four months after that, I married him.

It was not his Englishness that attracted me. Not exactly. Though he was English. While still a teenager, he'd played bass in a band called the Poisoned Lollies, which had cut two albums and had two singles reach the charts before the group fell apart. Now he wrote freelance reviews for music papers and composed for small dance and theater companies. He toyed with the idea of forming another band.

"Call it Tube Alloys," I said. "It's the British version of the Manhattan Project. It was—in the race to build the bomb? Really, the British team called themselves that. I always thought it might make a good name for a band." Did he stare at me strangely?

Just as, when I asked him if he'd ever been to Sellafield, the nuclear power plant in the north of England, on a school trip, for instance, he peered at me oddly.

Most of Martin's income came from his work as an electrician, on building sites, on warehouse or flat conversions. And in those days, when everything that could be converted was being converted, there was a great demand for the work he did.

He fixed things. In his small, rattly van, he brought home

chairs, a lamp on a wrought-iron stand, a discarded chandelier, a section of metal mantelpiece—objects he'd salvaged from tips or building sites. Planks with which to build bookshelves. He seemed ingenious and eager and practical. An easier love. He comforted me. He would fix me.

When I left my job at the sandwich shop, Martin found me work two days a week helping out a friend of his who cut hair. I learned to cut hair. Sort of. He came home one day with a bag of wigs for me to practice on. Through another friend, I began proofreading two days a week at a magazine on country homes.

We threw dinner parties. Standing at the cooker, shoulders sloped toward the flame, Martin fried fish in butter and sloshed it with white wine so that for days at a time the flat swam with a briny, buttery smell. I bought him flowers and baked a three-chocolate cake. At night, when we slept, he tucked his knees against mine. I drank in his warmth. When he took off his glasses, his eyes had a sly, almost feline cast. He chewed his fingernails, only the tips, and never in front of me.

We got married in April in a registry office. Afterward we piled into the van with friends and drove to Hampstead Heath, where, in blasts of wind, we paraded over the hills and on top of one of them drank champagne out of plastic glasses and ate Moroccan strawberries.

I said yes when Martin asked me to marry him because I wanted to start anew. (And for immigration reasons.) To escape the sense that everything could be taken away from me. The impetuousness of the gesture appealed to us—we were too young (as people kept telling us), we'd known each other for such a short time. Perhaps he thought he was rescuing me. Yet it wasn't really impetuousness on my part. I wanted to prove that grand romantic gestures were still possible. This was calculated. I needed to prove that I believed in them. That love

did not have to lead to destruction. It could save me. Or offer
safety.

I began to send postcards home. I wrote that I was fine and not
to worry. I wrote to say that I had gotten married. I told Martin
I'd had a falling-out with my family, which was why I'd run
away to London. That my father worked in the nuclear industry, nothing military, but we'd had our differences. (Martin and
I had both come of age beneath the cloud of possible nuclear
cataclysm, and we'd met soon enough after the Chernobyl reactor fire that people in London still stared dubiously into their
milk before they drank it, and radioactive sheep roamed the
Welsh hills.)

I never gave a return address and mailed each postcard from
the same central post office, and since there was no telephone
registered in my name, I assumed it would be difficult for
anyone to find me. Should anyone have tried to find me.

Yet at night I still woke out of dreams that I couldn't shake
away. I dreamed a body split open on the ground, blood—the
body of a dark-haired boy. I dreamed myself on a rooftop, leaping between the slanted gables from one slope to the next, closing my eyes as I hurled myself across the chasm between them.
I grabbed the latticed wood trim that ran along the peaks of the
brick houses and when I glanced down, Evan was there staring
up at me.

I saw them on the street. My heart raced at the sight of a
young man in a brown leather jacket, whose dark hair made a
thick dip at the back of his neck, who lurched along with a sharp
limp. I shook when a smaller, sand-blond figure blazed around
a corner ahead of me. I'd be stalled by a body glimpsed entering
a bookstore or a blur of lips framed by a black cab's window.

Out walking by myself, I grew convinced that someone with

a gun was following me. He would leap out of a phone box or trail me through the retractable flaps of the ticket turnstiles and into the stations of the underground, onto platforms where smoky winds blew. Walking home by myself at night through the streets of Brixton, I carried fear and a certain fatalism with me—past the boarded-up market, reduced now to a jumble of cardboard boxes and shifty incense sellers where during the day an automated loudspeaker blared, *Beware of pickpockets*; past Beauty Tandoori and the Oh So Keen Chinese Takeaway; past the cheap cosmetics shop on the corner where you gathered what you wanted in a plastic basket and the owner gave you a boiled sweet when you paid. I waited for explosions, to walk around the corner and see our building going up in smoke. No disaster would surprise me.

In the dark, as I pressed my arms around Martin, a little voice—a voice I tried to squelch—went, *Look at me*. Even as I tried to vanquish the past through touch. An arm. A leg. A nipple.

As Martin's long-limbed body slept beside me, I felt my father's hands on my shoulders, my father furiously shaking me. I imagined my mother curled on the sofa in the shaded green living room of the house in Toronto, staring up at the ceiling; skinny Lux, earphones clamped to her ears, bolting from the front door to her room at the top of the stairs. I rolled onto my back, hearing voices: Martin and I in the van, driving north and east out of London, past fields smelling of fog and peat. We were on our way to visit Martin's parents in Norwich. Martin's father, a solicitor who worked for the County Council, stepped out of their red-brick house to greet us and kissed Martin on the cheek. *Are you all right?* he asked. Martin's mother, who taught in a comprehensive, held out both hands. *Are you all right?* The next day, outside the local chemist's, we ran into an old high-school girlfriend of Martin's, a girl with a voice as bright and sweet as jam, and I listened as the two of them greeted each other—*Are you all right?*—the way, where I came from, we ask *How are you?* and expect only the most cursory answer.

In the dark beside Martin, I swallowed and touched my fingers to the hollow at the base of my throat. I felt like a girl in a fairy tale who has something stuck in her throat and does not know, when she opens her mouth, what will come tumbling out—frogs or stones or pearls. I slipped from the bed and poured myself a glass of water. In front of the bathroom mirror, I stretched my mouth open wide.

A MAN WAS WALKING toward me along the canal path. He came around a curve, from under the arch of a bridge, face in shadow, then burnished by light. I recognized his features before I could quite place them—but I was thinking about other men, and how the world is full of odd propositions.

Only that morning, as I'd walked, swinging my soft-sided briefcase, past Camden Market, a young man had come up to me and asked, "Do you need a secretary?" I'd stopped, intrigued and startled, by a stall that sold pink windup somersaulting dogs side by side with handcuffs and miniature plastic Kalashnikovs. Standing in front of me, the young man was slim hipped and sloe eyed and wore a tight white T-shirt. I glanced at the handcuffs, then back at him—and almost said yes.

The day before that, in Covent Garden, an even younger man had tapped me on the shoulder. "Do you know any jobs?" His voice was whispery and accented—Eastern European, I guessed. Presumably he wasn't here legally. He wore a sweet cologne. I didn't know of any jobs. What should I have done? I shook my head.

A dark-haired man in a café, a tweed-jacketed man unobtrusively watching . . .

"Amir!" I called when he was mere feet from me, eyes on the path ahead of him. He was squinting a little, even with the sun behind him, for the light was very bright. I'd heard from none of them since that night nearly a month before in the Good Grub Café—other than Lux, to whom I'd spoken briefly after her return from South Africa. Nor had I expected to, though I had wondered what had happened to Basra Alale.

As he turned, his face—in that first instant, before he had a chance to hide it—flared with discomfort, even alarm. Was it the wrong man? I would have stepped back into invisibility, but there was nowhere to step. Already the muscles in his cheeks and around his eyes were transforming, reassembling themselves into a sort of welcome. Guarded but cordial.

I pushed back my sunglasses. "Arcadia Hearne," I said. "Do you remember? I met you that night—"

"Yes, yes, of course. How are you?" He was smiling now, politely extending his hand, which I shook.

"I just thought I'd see if you had any news. About Basra." For I was curious, and felt a tangential pang of responsibility for her. "Are things all right? Any word I could pass on?"

He glanced around him. In daylight, he seemed almost boyish, wrapped in an air of casual self-containment. He was perhaps as tall as I was, but no taller. His black hair was trimmed short over the ears, left longer on top but razored neatly at the back of the neck above the collar of his blue shirt—perhaps the same shirt he'd worn the night I'd met him, sleeves now rolled to his elbows. He carried nothing—no bag, no knapsack, no newspaper. "She's quite all right." He dipped his head and slung his arms around his chest. "Thank you. Thank you for what you did."

"Really, it was nothing."

A man in skimpy shorts and fluorescent trainers jogged past. On the far side of the canal, the gardens of tall row houses looked nearly Venetian. Worn stone steps, green with moss, led down to the brackish water where a narrow rowboat drifted at the end of an algaed rope. In the west, two bridges away, beyond Amir, rose the emerald haze of Regent's Park.

"Do you live nearby?" He indicated my briefcase and net bag of groceries.

"Not far," I said vaguely. "A little way north. Do you?"

"No, no." He shook his head emphatically. "East. In Hackney."

"Are you just out for a walk, then?"

"I work not far away."

"You do? Doing what?"

"In a copy shop."

Coffee? Copy?

"A printing shop."

"Yes. Right." Shielding my eyes from the sun, I stepped back from the center of the path, away from the lime-green water, toward the brick wall at the far side and the wrought-iron bench at its foot. "Are you in close touch with Basra?"

"Not so much. Not anymore. But from everything I've heard she's doing well."

Not so much. Not anymore. Which meant what in terms of the unspecified relationship between them? He didn't seem inclined to elaborate. I was only the courier, after all. "And you," he went on, "what do you do here in London?"

The *here* was a subtle touch. I noted it. It implied an elsewhere. As if to say, you, who have come here from elsewhere, or you who, like me, have come here from elsewhere. As if there were other places in the world either of us might conceivably be. And it was true, if I listened closely—while his voice sounded quite unaffectedly English, every so often, in the shape of a

vowel or a distinctive rise and fall, it revealed a trace of foreign-
ness, a little continental drift.

"I work for a place called the Centre for Contemporary War
Studies."

He looked surprised and—this, too, was just visible—mildly
amused at his own surprise, readjusting whatever he had imagined, whatever he had so far presumed.

He ducked his head again, looked up. "And that is?"

"We're a research organization, quite small. A resource
center. Occasionally we're quoted in the media, but there's no
reason you'd have heard of us."

"What do you do there?"

"I'm an associate director, though we're not terribly hierar-
chical. We have a director, then there's the rest of us. I'm a
researcher, a theorist. I'm writing a book, actually."

"About?"

"Intervention issues. Military interventions, but also humanitarian interventions insofar as they're related to the fighting of
contemporary war."

"And how do you come to this area of specialty?"

"Well, it's one of the defining features, isn't it, of wars these
days."

"Mind." His fingers nudged the air beside me, just above my
elbow, as a woman hurtled past, speeding out of the darkness
and cooler air of the bridge at my back—a woman on a unicy-
cle. We both followed her in amazement, watching her feet
manically pedal as they held her in teetery balance, while a little
white terrier galloped in her wake. A white ruff jiggled around
its neck, its stubby legs caught in the velocity of her extraordinary momentum. Then the next curve, the darkness under the
next bridge swallowed them, as the bends in the canal are wont
to. But this is how the canal seduces you, seduces me into walk-

ing from Camden to King's Cross, from Islington all the way east to Limehouse, or from Regent's Park all the way west to Little Venice, and beyond to Paddington, with geographic curiosity, a longing to know what lies hidden beyond the next bend, and the next, and then again one more.

Something—a spell—was broken. I set down my groceries, butter and muesli and a box of tissues visible through the net bag, and shifted my briefcase into my other hand. "It was lovely to run into you," I said. "I'll pass on word that Basra's fine."

He nodded, stepping once more to the middle of the path, veiled and self-contained.

"I'm sorry," I said. "I don't remember your last name."

Did he hesitate for just a minute? "Barmour." He held out his hand. "Amir Barmour."

Sunlight glinted on the turgid water. From the west, the direction in which the unicyclist had disappeared, an old, dun-brown, badly weathered canal boat slid into sight, heaving eastward, its engine relentlessly coughing. A scavenger boat, its deck was open—not like the brightly painted touring boats, which had small decks and long, narrow interior galleys and names like *Helix* or *Galatea* or *Clairvoyant*. This boat was nameless. I watched it come hacking toward me, loaded with derelict appliances—a washing machine, a crazily tilting toilet—and among them there was, mysteriously, no sign of human life.

"Best of luck with the book," Amir said.

"Right." I picked up my bag. "Thanks. So—unless we meet by chance again by the canal. Or, if you're interested in this sort of thing—have you ever been to the War Museum?"

He shook his head.

"We could meet there for lunch, if you fancy. Some day next week. The café's quite pleasant, and the food's really rather good." A little seizure of longing shook me.

Panic blew across his face. Once more his expression rapidly disassembled and reassembled itself. His lips tucked upward in a smile, as if something deeply amused him. He cleared his throat. A blond boy, small and muscular, surged past, footsteps thudding down the path.

"Yes, all right," he said.

I SHOULDN'T HAVE DONE IT. Shouldn't have given into the whim, the folly, whatever it was, of inviting Amir Barmour to have lunch with me. A ridiculous proposition. At the War Museum, of all places. But having forgotten, in the flurry of embarrassment that succeeded asking him, to take his phone number, I couldn't ring him up to cancel. Either he would be there or he would not.

I was not looking for love. Of course, this had nothing to do with love. The thing that also made me uneasy, I suppose, was my history of bad romantic luck.

Two years before, in Geneva, at a conference on the Bosnian war, I'd met an American journalist named Daniel Jacobsen, who, over drinks, had asked me to come with him to Venice for the weekend. He offered to pay for my flight, all gallantry, if I helped pay for the rest, and in the exhilaration of the moment I said yes. He'd just returned from three weeks holed up in Sarajevo, which I could feel on him: a strange superabundance of energy pouring from his skin. He asked me first if I'd been to

Bosnia. I told him no. Nor had I been to Venice since a family trip the year I turned fifteen. I longed to return and dreamed sometimes of Venice. Definitely time to go back, he said.

Mere miles across the water from the dark smoke of that war, we roamed arm in arm through a maze of Venetian canals, breathing in dank and watery air, and I told him about the London canals, and how they sometimes made me think of Venice. "Ever been to Dubrovnik?" he asked. "In Croatia?"

"No," I said. Daniel jerked his head, as if to span the fifty miles or so that separated that country from us. "Once called Little Venice." He chopped his arm through the air in front of him. "Now bombed all to fuck."

In the tiny green room of an old pensione (like a fishbowl, Daniel said, a tiny aquarium), we peeled off our clothes. With mouths and tongues, we provoked, we surrendered our bodies to a frenzy of touch, shouting out in release or in celebration of our own escape. Because we weren't at war.

At dinner, as we ate *linguine al nero di seppia*, linguine with black squid ink, which dyed our mouths glistening purple, and drank wine as red as blood, I asked him questions about Bosnia. Then we argued about Bosnia.

"There should have been an intervention," Daniel said. He seized the edges of the table with his hands. "Earlier. Before the bombing. Okay, that ended the war. Sort of. But on what terms? Everyone knows Dayton's a flawed agreement. Before I went in, I didn't necessarily think I'd feel this way. But when you go—if you write about this kind of thing, of course you'll go— there were such clear grounds for intervening, moral reasons, in defense of a multiethnic state, to stop ethnic cleansing, the government even asked for help." He shook the table a little. "We could have invoked the Genocide Convention."

"You mean a clearly military intervention," I said. "On the ground."

"Yes," he said. "I mean troops. Nothing quick or safe or easy. Troops ready to fight. And die. Mandated to attack. To actually defend people."

"And how do you think we'd ever have got an international mandate to do that?"

"Because there's clearly a hostile aggressor." He looked at me as if he couldn't believe what I was saying. "Look. All the talk about simply trying to contain the conflict is bullshit. Sorry—even all that humanitarian aid—I know individual workers who've been heroes in Bosnia, in Croatia—but what's the point if you're not going to defend the people you're trying to save?"

"But to have a successful military intervention with ground troops, you have to be able to establish a viable endgame, and there's the risk that you end up becoming a participant."

"I'm for robust rules of engagement, war management, whatever you want to call it."

Later that night, as we lolled once more amid the damp sheets, flushed in the red glow of the blown-glass bedside lamp, I turned toward him. "Daniel," I asked. Arms behind his head, he lay with legs spread languidly, though his neck cricked up. "What would you be willing to risk for love?" He froze, limbs stiffening. "Don't worry," I said. My heart sped and settled. I kept my eyes on him. "It's a purely hypothetical question."

"You mean diseases?"

"No—no, I really wasn't thinking—" We had taken all the usual precautions.

"Would I throw myself in a raging river if my lover was drowning?"

"More that sort of thing."

"Would I settle in some city I couldn't stand, say some disgusting, polluted, midsized, middle-European city like

Düsseldorf, just to be with someone? Have a kid just because she wanted one? Why?" He had regained some measure of self-possessed inquisitiveness.

"Curious."

"You?"

"Not sure."

But something had shifted between us. If I closed my eyes I felt molecules of fear radiating from him. And, sometime in the dark of early morning, I awoke to the sound of his breath—no sleeper's snore, but a liquid, asthmatic wheezing. I sat up. He was up before me, hunched over the far side of the bed, inhaler gripped in one hand, feet on the floor. He began to pace back and forth in the tiny space between the bed and wall.

"Daniel." My own body began to shake. "Shall I call a doctor?" Though another part of me wondered how, in Italian (the language of my grandmother but one I barely spoke), in a watery city filled with sleeping people, was I going to do that?

He shook his head, his face slippery with sweat. He wouldn't let me near him, wouldn't let me touch him. "In Sarajevo," he whispered, "no matter how bad the shelling was, in all that time this never happened."

By dawn his breath had quieted. I listened to it, and to the ragged passage of my own breath—his body pulled away from mine, as if this other fear had, in the course of a single night, sped us through some crazy, time-lapse version of a relationship. When the light brightened a little more, I rose and dressed and wrote him a brief note. He did not stir. Bag in hand, I slipped out the door and rode the ferry to the airport, eyeing the line where water met horizon and its rim of invisible smoke. By ten, I'd caught the first plane back to London.

One Friday night, out dancing in a club, I pressed my mouth to a man's ear and told him what I did for a living. Without warning he grabbed me by the wrist. *You like violence, do you?* Before I could pull free, he laid my palm against his chest, against the hard curve of a nipple ring protruding through the gauzy fabric. *There are things you could do to me.* Yanking my hand back, I excused myself and barreled through smoke and bodies toward the door. Out in the street, I turned back—stupidly—to see him standing in the doorway, shouting down the block, audible to anyone for miles. *You want to hurt me, I know you do.*

And of course there was Martin, roaming the streets in his van, rebuilding homes, living with an artist in Whitechapel, the last I'd heard—married again, for all I knew.

Not just bad luck. I was tainted, I sometimes thought.

When the clock in the upstairs research room read five past one, there was no help for it but to close up my notepad, check my lipstick in my compact, and swing out through the soundproof glass doors into the melee of the museum itself. Rockets whistled. Something exploded with a thunderous boom. I descended the stairs to the ground floor, where the anti-aircraft guns and searchlights lurked, where schoolchildren dodged and tourists wandered among the camouflage-painted tanks, past the model of the Little Boy atom bomb.

Amir Barmour was inside the entrance vestibule, at the bottom of a short flight of marble steps—not where I'd expected him to be. His dark hair looked distinctly combed, a sign of—what? Expectancy? Some sense of propriety? Something in me rattled. He wore a light cotton suit jacket. Leather satchel slung over one shoulder, a folded newspaper tucked under one arm, he wandered up and down, looking about with an air of absorbed nonchalance, as if to undercut the impression that he was waiting with any urgency for anyone. At the clatter of heels—my heels—on the marble steps, he turned.

"Hello," I said, distractedly holding out one hand. "Did you buy a ticket?" But he must have, to have entered past the ticket collector and security guard.

"Yes."

"Oh, but I didn't mean you to pay. I was going to meet you outside and bring you in." This seemed particularly mortifying: he had paid for a ticket simply in order to have lunch with me.

"It's really all right," he said.

"Would you like to look round now? Or after lunch? I can give you a sort of mini-tour, if you like."

"Why not after lunch?"

We made our way back up the marble steps, through the small domed vestibule that led into the main galleries.

"This place used to be Bedlam, hospital for the insane," I said.

"That's the one thing I *have* heard about it, actually."

I tripped. I felt as if I'd tripped.

In the cafeteria, lemony sunlight beamed through a screen of leaves and in through the tall, elegant windows. A woman in a metal hard hat, who worked downstairs in the simulation of the Blitz, stood in line ahead of us. There was no more chicken with apricots and olives but there was grilled plaice and potato salad with bacon and cream. *Where's my plaice?* I heard a woman say. When I tried to pay for both our meals, Amir wouldn't let me.

I managed to snare a table by one of the windows, toward the back. I did not, I realized, want to be disturbed or observed by anyone I knew. Watching Amir from across the table, I imagined leaning forward to kiss him—but I would do this with anyone. The collar of his white shirt was open at the neck. He ate, lifting the fork to his mouth, with a kind of eloquent thoughtfulness, as if each mouthful were an extension of gesture or speech. At the same time, simply looking at him, I felt felled by emotional exhaustion, as if my strongest urge was in fact to get up and run.

"Where exactly do you work?"

"Upstairs." I pointed to the ceiling. "In the research rooms. I'll show you." I wondered why he'd come. Simply to be gracious? Because he was amused by the strangeness of the invitation, or thought it rude to refuse, or as a form of thanks for my helping Basra? Or to satisfy some curiosity of his own?

"How long have you been in London?" I asked. This was a question I'd been longing to ask him. It left room, I thought, for many variables.

"Twelve years."

"I've been here ten." I touched a finger to my hair clip, swallowed. "And where before that?"

"Paris. For one year."

"And before that?" The fist in my stomach opened and closed.

"Frankfurt. And before that, Karachi. And in the beginning, Tehran."

I pressed my fingertips to my hot cheeks. "I'm from Toronto."

"I know that," he said calmly. "Basra told me." He leaned back in his chair, but it was not a gesture of withdrawal: he shifted focus, not engagement. "Do you like the city?"

"Which city?"

"Toronto. I have friends who tell me it's quite pleasant."

"I suppose."

Once more his expression altered, something slotting down over his face: a return to graciousness. "I wondered if I might have seen you this past weekend. Just beyond the Victoria Park stretch of the canal—"

I shook my head.

"It's quite far east, I know. I was walking toward Tower Hamlets. And, for the very first time, I saw someone actually catch a fish. You see fishermen, you know—of course you know—all the time, with their tubs of worms—"

"And corn niblets. And cat food. And maggots."

"—but this was the first time I've actually ever seen anyone catch one. There was much general jubilation. Though it was a very little fish."

"Two weeks ago," I said, "I was walking just west of Tower Hamlets and I saw a boy floating slowly downstream on a little styrofoam raft." A black-haired boy with twiggy legs. "He was holding a stick and waving it and I shouted at him, did he need to be rescued, but he shouted back no."

"Once," he said, shifting forward again, "I was walking by the canal when one of these old work boats, you know, went slowly past. Then it slowed even more and a little man's head popped up from among the cargo of old refrigerators. Did I want a lift, he asked. At first I thought, No, no—this was shortly after I'd arrived in London. Years ago. But I said yes and climbed aboard and he took me quite a long way, actually, along the Lee navigation. Though I had to find my own way home."

"But still," I said. "How lovely."

"Flowers you won't find anywhere else in England grow in Kingsland Basin. Did you know that? From seeds they reckon came in on cargo at Limehouse, that blew off the barges."

"I'd heard that. Did you know Alfred Hitchcock made his first film in a Hackney film studio that stood by the canal?"

He nodded and rose abruptly to his feet. "Coffee? Tea?"

"White coffee, please," I said, caught off guard by the jagged acceleration of my heart.

We walked through the galleries of the War Museum. We stopped in the Gulf War Room, with its video sandstorms and model night-vision glasses, and the Balkan War Room, where the sound of sniper fire cracked with alarming sharpness above our heads and where you can pick up telephones and listen to whispered testimonials from citizens of Tuzla or Vukovar or Sarajevo. We came out beneath the Ongoing War pixelboard, whose bulletins are updated every day (Chechnya, Liberia, Algeria), and made our way through the Contemporary War Room, where the interactive computer terminals ask visitors, among other things, *Why do people fight wars?* and you can write your own answer or read other people's responses—*ethnic cleansing, biological imperative, because they're bored*—on the scrolling screen displays.

Downstairs, on the lower level, we cowered in a mock underground station while simulated German bombs dropped above us, walked through the black-and-white footage from Hiroshima that was part of the Atom Bomb Victims Memorial, stumbled on hands and knees in semi-darkness along the model of a World War I trench.

"I know it's hardly exhaustive," I said to Amir, as we collected ourselves at the bottom of the stairs. Embarrassed, I couldn't read his response at all. "There are horrible gaps. But then how could it be—"

"If it were the size of a small city perhaps, and even then—emm, I suspect you'd need several cities. Very different cities."

"Often people think a museum about war will somehow, inevitably, be pro-war."

"So." He gave a fleeting grin. "You devise your own strategy to convince people to come."

Outside, the first blooms of the roses tumbled to the ground in a cascade of petals, soft as earlobes, releasing a thick, fermenting odor—a tang like that of the rose perfume that Lux and I used to make at our grandmother's (our father's mother's) house in

Toronto. We'd stuff petals gathered from her garden into old jam jars, add water, and leave the mixture to stew on her kitchen windowsill. Weeks later, we'd open the jars and gorge ourselves on the scent.

I stopped beside Amir on the path, below the naval guns that jutted toward the city, where a chunk of the former Berlin Wall rose eight feet high.

"Monument or ruin?" I asked, clasping my hands behind me, a breeze scratching at the back of my neck.

He ran his fingers through his black hair. A little broader across the shoulders than I'd first thought, he peered toward the graffitied wall in front of him. "Do you think it's all original? That it came here with the wall? Or might some of it be more recent?" He pointed to the outline of a swastika, bright black on the pitted surface.

"Are kids climbing in over the fences at night with spray cans? They could be, couldn't they?" It was like a barb: something I'd been oblivious to—never considered, never noticed. What I saw, whenever I looked at the wall, was the huge mouth yawning wide in agony, like a hell-mouth in a medieval mystery play, words pouring out like a tongue, exhorting all of us. CHANGE YOUR LIFE.

"Thank you," I said, holding out one hand. "Thank you for coming. I wasn't sure you would. It was very good of you—"

"You didn't think I'd come? Really?" He seemed touched with mock outrage, or genuinely shocked.

"No, I didn't know. It's a long way, relatively speaking. And it's not a place that everybody wants to come."

"It was my pleasure, Arcadia." He shook my hand with a quick, benign smile, as if his curiosity had indeed been satisfied.

Neither of us said any of the usual things. *We must do this again. Do you have my number? Shall we meet for a drink sometime?*

However insincerely they are generally proffered. "Cheers," Amir said, with a little wave, as he turned.

Even this felt excruciating: the sight of the back of his jacket, newspaper folded into a pocket, retreating steadily toward the street.

I MET EVAN when I was eighteen, the autumn of my first year at university in Toronto. I chose him. I picked him out by sight even before we'd introduced ourselves.

One afternoon, as I walked along Hoskins Avenue, I spied a figure bolting up the steps of Strachan College in the rain. At the top of the steps, he heaved over breathlessly, hands on his knees, feet in orange running shoes—oblivious to everything but the residue of his own propulsion. His hair was matted to his scalp, sweatshirt drenched, the skin beneath his flimsy gym shorts— the sinuous muscles of his exposed thighs—wind chilled and red.

Two days later, in sunshine, I saw him again. This time he was kneeling, locking a bicycle to a wrought-iron fence outside Strachan. Light caught in his hair, turning it wheaten, then even brighter, nearly white. A yellow canvas knapsack rode up his shoulders. What caught my attention was his hands, as they shunted the lock around the fence and clasped the bike frame to it—how small they were, how birdlike. What touched me was some suggestion of vulnerability in the way he moved, some-thing not quite balletic, grace mixed with abruptness. He gave off a sense of compressed energy, honed purpose, as if each gesture carried the weight of some interior thrust.

The first week of October, I went with some friends to a party at Strachan where I searched in the semi-dark for the wheat-haired boy but didn't see him.

I left then, quelling disappointment, escaping the wa-wa of amplified music, the frenzy of people away from home for the first time, let loose on their own in Toronto. I lived at home, not in residence, because, in my college, Alexandra, there were only enough rooms for those from out of town.

A stone archway led into the central courtyard of Strachan. There was dew on the grass. Falling leaves smelled like smoke. Voices rose faintly from the wooden benches—the murmur of couples, perhaps. More music wailed from a room upstairs. Lit windows shone like tender, mysterious beacons, swollen with longing or love.

I made my way toward the far side of the courtyard, where the wooden door that led to the main entrance hall stood open, propped ajar. Inside, the smooth floors were flagstone. Corridors led away in either direction beneath glazed lanterns hanging from the ceiling. The bulletin board beside me was scattered with posters for FRENCH LESSONS PRIVATE GROUP AFFORDABLE! TORONTO-MONTREAL BUS TICKETS CHEAP!! SWEET BIRD OF YOUTH AUDITIONS THE GODFATHER ONE SCREENING ONLY!!! FRIDAY 7 P.M. MEDICAL SCIENCES AUDI-TORIUM. Across the vestibule a light shone in the porter's lodge.

The outside door rattled, swinging open. From his shoulders hung the same yellow army-surplus knapsack. His hair lay scattered across his head like straw. Beneath a tight wool bomber jacket, he wore gray flannel trousers—not the sort a former private-school boy might wear, but old, pleated ones, from the forties perhaps. Over one thin wrist he'd shoved a pair of bicy-

cle clips, which clinked like bracelets. No doubt I looked startled. I scrambled for purpose, a way to funnel my own ricochet
of yearning—any reason to be in the hallway other than what
I'd intended, which was to slip out the door through which he'd
just entered, down the front steps, and into the night.

Before I could say anything, he came to a stop, not unfriendly.
"Do you know what a blue moon is?" His voice had a nasal
twang. His manner was blunt, but there was in it also a note of
genuine appeal—and something unabashed, as if he were daring
me to find his question strange.

"What a blue moon is?"

"Not what the expression means, not like 'once in a,' but what
it actually refers to, as in the scientific phenomenon."

"A blue moon." As if spinning out the words a few seconds
longer would offer me something—a missing piece of information. "I've probably read it somewhere, but I don't . . . sorry."
My stomach gurgled weirdly. I listened to the slap of his shoes
over stone as he bounded upstairs to the second floor.

I found him ten days later in the library. Now and again I'd
seen what I convinced myself was his bicycle locked in one of
the jammed racks outside, although it was practically impossible to distinguish one scuffed red ten-speed from another. In
any case, I trawled the reading rooms in search of him, the
banks of plastic chairs in the ground-floor cafeteria, the floors
of stacks, the wooden benches by the Xerox machines where
people gathered to chat. This had become my quest. Which
wasn't to say I didn't study. The plague in medieval Europe.
Plato's *Symposium*. Heaving my books around in my own
canvas knapsack.

I found him at a table in the current periodical room, beyond
the shelves of periodicals. A chemistry textbook was propped

open in front of him. He looked up as I seated myself in an empty chair. "I found out what a blue moon is."

One of his cheeks was flushed—from the rampant heat of the building, from having a palm pressed against it. His lips had a delicate, roseate plushness. He seemed to remember me. "Just a sec." He stood briskly, slipping the metal cap of his fountain pen back over the nib.

Outside the doors of the reading room, we found an empty corner in that odd-cornered, cement-walled building. He leaned back against the concrete pillar behind him, arms crossed.

"If there's a second full moon in a single month it's called a blue moon."

He looked down at his scuffed running shoes before he spoke. "It's funny. That's not even an *old* old wives' tale, it's actually very new. What's interesting is, why is it circulating now, and where did it come from? But if you look in a good astronomical dictionary, that's not what a blue moon is. For a start, you need something much rarer. There's a second full moon in a month every couple of years. That isn't rare enough. But every so often, say once in a lifetime in a particular place on earth, dust particles, maybe from a forest fire or volcanic eruption, dust particles barely longer than the wavelength of light, filter the light of the moon. They filter out the red light and leave the blue. And you have a blue moon."

Dust particles barely longer than the wavelength of light. "Why did you ask me if you already knew?"

"To see if you knew."

Baffled, I was convinced, somehow, that he wasn't mocking me, that what he'd issued was a challenge, or that he'd performed a peculiar act of faith or trust: in this way, I would come back to him.

"I'm Arcadia Hearne," I said. I held out my hand.

If my name surprised him, he didn't show it. "Evan Biederman," he said.

Evan and I went for walks together, heading north, away from campus, across Bloor Street, past the old red-brick mansions of Bedford Road. Neither of us had come to Toronto to go to university and we shared this bond: the disjunction between those of us who already slipped like old hands through the streets and those who'd just arrived. We traded the maps of the city that we'd made for ourselves, their layerings of personal history.

"Tell me things," Evan would say fervently. "Tell me things about yourself." I told him I'd been born in Ottawa, and shortly afterward we'd moved north to Deep Creek. He nodded, as if it were somewhere he had heard of. I told him that my father had grown up in Toronto, off St. Clair West, and that he worked in the nuclear industry. Usually I just said my father was an engineer, as if he built roads or bridges. It seemed simpler. But I was curious to observe Evan's response: this was, in its own way, a kind of test. I told him my father worked for Ontario Power but was also a member of an international team working on the development of an experimental fusion reactor.

"Using tritium," he said. "By-product helium." So he knew, without my needing to explain to him, the differences between nuclear fusion and fission. This filled me with relief. It saved me from complicated explanations, a conflation of my knowledge with my father's knowledge. Nor did Evan act shocked at the thought of what my father did, or try to launch me into argument, as if my father's work were somehow my fault or responsibility, arguments in which I sometimes ended up defending my father simply because, when it came to nuclear energy, many people had so little idea what they were talking about.

I told Evan that I was planning to major in history, and thinking of becoming a medievalist (as far from the domain of nuclear science as possible). How, the autumn we moved to Toronto, the year I turned ten, I would take my sister, who was two years younger, and ride the subway for hours, from Islington to Warden, St. George to Finch: we'd leap off at every station to run upstairs, punch the transfer machine, and grab the paper transfer that it spat out before racing down to the platform again.

"Your mother let you?"

She'd traveled halfway round the world, I said. Geographic exploration didn't frighten her. At any rate, she thought this city seemed safe. "Yours wouldn't have?"

"Oh, sure," he said.

I told him, when we moved out of the forest, down to Toronto, my father had promised my mother a house on a ravine, a house surrounded by trees, and we did live in a house on a ravine, north of Eglinton, even if it was a small tributary with a drainage culvert running through the middle of it.

"Tell me about yourself," I said.

Born in Toronto, Evan had grown up here, although now he was the only one in his family left in the city. His sisters, twins named Karin and Maya, had moved away two years previously to go to university—Maya to Boston, Karin to Vancouver. As we sat over cappuccinos in a Yorkville café, Evan told me about the day in March, seven months before, when Peter, his father, had appeared on television. It was the middle of the month, during March break. Maya was home from Boston, the two of them sprawled on that particular evening on the lumpy old sofa in the sitting room just off the kitchen, Maya idly flicking channels on the cable box. So it was just chance that she happened to hit that particular local news broadcast at that particular moment—just as Delia, Evan's mother, appeared in the doorway, cat draped like a stole around her shoulders, a gin and tonic in one hand. A car had burst into flames on the 401 near Islington. And there was Peter, in his beige overcoat, arm around the young, dark-haired woman they would come later to know as Isobel Melo, a Portuguese investment analyst, the pearl-gray Scirocco a pyre of flames behind them, the two of them too flagrant in the ecstasy of their twin survival to be aware of anything else.

Evan heard no arguments, but the next morning, when he came downstairs, pieces of furniture, books, records were marked with little red dots that Delia had placed on them, like auction items. It was Peter who moved out, who now lived in Philadelphia, teaching in the economics department at the University of Pennsylvania. Delia had held onto the house, although in July she had rented it out and run off to Montreal with a Buddhist art dealer named Gabriel Ferrari.

Evan took me to see the house one afternoon and we stood outside, on Alborough Avenue, while leaves swirled at our feet and a brisk wind buffeted us. It was bigger than our house, dark brick, the thick skeleton of a wisteria vine climbing up the front. "Gondwanaland," Evan said in a clipped and desolate voice, and it took me a moment to recall, right, the enormous proto-continent from which all the current, drifting continents had broken off. He said the cat's name was Eddypuss. He'd named the cat. His mother had taken him. (He showed me a photo of Delia, rangy and dark-haired, told me he thought she was beautiful.) "Get it? Eddypuss?" He gave a sharp, bleak, nasal laugh.

It amazed us that we hadn't met before this. We knew people who knew people, even if we'd gone to different schools. As if we'd been held back by what—fate? luck?—until the right moment. Our own blue moon.

Evan took me to secondhand clothing stores—Tresor, Tango, Lovers & Madmen. He pulled out elbow-length kid gloves for me to try on, tight satin dresses. He lingered over opalescent cuff links and antique collar pins, which he collected and actually used to fasten detachable collars to old-fashioned shirts. Showing me these things, he flushed with pleasure—a kind of magnanimity, I thought, as if he'd been waiting for me in order to share these things. He didn't seem foppish; there was something too focused and purposeful about him for that. Fastidious. A little odd, perhaps, but in a way that I found glamorous. He made me feel glamorous. In his company, the world grew newly luminous.

In the afternoons, after class, we'd sit sometimes in Queen's Park while oak leaves fell from the sky around us. And afterward Evan would invite me back to his residence room, where we'd lounge on the goatskin rug that he'd taken from the house when his mother packed up her belongings. He'd make tea or pour brandy into two snifters of fantastically frail glass. He lit candles in twin brass candlesticks. Flames flickered over the bookshelves above his desk, over the chemistry texts, his Greek dictionary, the volumes of Wordsworth and Shelley, William Blake's engravings and poetic cosmology, for Evan was double-majoring in chemistry and English, specializing in the English Romantics.

Other days, we descended into the ravines—the wild regions, the unobserved places, leaving the rest of the city behind. We carried buttery croissants and brioches in paper bags stuffed into our pockets. From the forest floor, I picked up shiny conkers that had tumbled from chestnut trees, smoothing my fingertips across their casings, silky as Evan's skin. *Duff*, I taught him, cradling a handful of pine needles and rotting compost. I pointed out birds: *pileated woodpecker*, *phoebe*, *nuthatch*. The ravines were rooms, great green rooms expanding around us.

North of St. Clair, beyond the skinny men who lurked and eyed each other at the entrances to overgrown paths, we unlatched the wire-mesh gate that led to the Mount Pleasant Cemetery and let ourselves in. Some days we roamed even farther north through the ravines nearer my house, tree-filled crevasses that wound behind back gardens. We talked of houses we'd like to own, old brick houses, with fireplaces—summoning possible futures for ourselves.

We kissed goodbye outside subway stations. At dusk, under a fading sky, we leaned over the edge of the Glen Road bridge, arms dangling, and Evan told me how from this spot, years before, he and his friend Fergus had tossed long fluorescent tubes down onto the roadway below—tubes stolen from the garbage Dumpsters of the apartment towers to the south.

"Did you hit anyone?" I asked, eyeing the speeding cars below.

"No," he said tersely, "of course not."

The press of his lips, when we kissed, was velvety soft. The touch of his fingers made my spine burn. Love, I thought—the particular taut, sharp ache through my limbs to the pit of my stomach that I identified as love. Leaning close, he ran the tips of his fingers back and forth across my mouth, as if reading something through the skin. "Don't mess with me, Arcadia," he whispered. I breathed in the yeasty tang of his breath. "I'm not interested in frivolity. You have to be prepared to be serious."

Everything ticked: the sky, the bridge, the trees, his fingers, my pulse. "I'm serious," I said.

TO RUN INTO SOMEONE amid the spreading ganglia of a vast metropolis is randomness, pure chance. To run into someone more than once is luck, serendipity, destiny. Or randomness once more. You have your pick.

One June afternoon, I came over to the Edgware Road to have lunch with my friend Hanna Sargeant, who *is* a war correspondent. Red-haired Hanna, who, when she tips up her head, sends the frizzled wildness of her hair sweeping down her back, who smokes unfiltered cigarettes, who gives little snorts of impatience when vexed, who leaves messages on her answerphone that begin, "This is Hanna, I'm in Bosnia at the moment." And gives a number there.

At the end of lunch, she stubbed her cigarette into the ashtray. In a week, she was going back to Bosnia to cover the exhumation of bodies from mass graves. "You should come with me," she said.

"Hanna, I don't need to go to Bosnia." I took a long swig of wine, which refused to go to my head. "I'm not a journalist. And we *are* in constant touch with people. People here, people there. And elsewhere. Constant global communication. I would just be an extra body. A gawker. In the way. I don't see what's to be gained by my becoming a spectator of atrocity."

"Witness," she said. She lit another cigarette, inhaled, coughed once. "It's different. And not just any body. You're in the war business."

"In any case, there are plenty of other wars. Less visible wars. East Timor. Sudan. Sri Lanka. Why that one? What's the criterion by which you choose your war?" With Ray, at the Centre, I'd simply sidestepped the issue: I went to conferences, often enough in Europe, twice to the United States. I had other useful qualities, and the thing was, there were always other people eager to go to war.

"All right then," Hanna said. "Go to some other war."

Yet we kissed goodbye as always. I hugged her hard (for I worried about Hanna out in the field) and told her to look after herself. As always.

Out on the Edgware Road, just beyond an Oxfam shop, I glanced up midstride to see Amir Barmour approaching down the pavement. He wore a white shirt. The same leather satchel hung from his shoulder. The sun beat down. He looked surprised. Probably we both did. But this time he knew exactly who I was. "Have time for a drink?" He gestured neatly toward a Lebanese juice bar across the road. Traffic bellowed past. I nodded, and we dashed into its melee, dodging black taxicabs and swallowing diesel fumes.

Inside, at a silver counter, Amir ordered two glasses of fresh-squeezed mango juice, paid for them, and carried them to a row of stools against the far wall. Mirrored walls surrounded us.

"Day off?" I asked him. He seemed less guarded somehow, more openly cordial than I'd yet seen him.

He shook his head. "I work nearby." Rubbing the edge of one sideburn with a knuckle.

"In the copy shop?"

"No, no." A flicker of annoyance passed and vanished. "On Tuesdays and Thursdays I teach." He pointed through the window. Across the road, a sign hung from the upper story of a building: THE MODERN ENGLISH LANGUAGE SCHOOL. And turned back, scrutinizing me with faint amusement, watching all the assumptions I might have made about him jostle and shift. "I translate, too. Farsi to English. English to Farsi. Business manuals mostly. Indescribably boring, but the money's all right."

"How do you know Basra Alale?" I asked him, as I'd wanted to know from the beginning.

"Through Wahid. I've known Wahid for a while. He rang me up, reckoned I might be able to help out Basra. She was having some troubles with her uncle. Help her find her way around. Because I've done that sort of thing before for other people."

"Does she live with her uncle, then?"

"She did. Not anymore. We found her somewhere else to live."

He glanced over his shoulder, where three teenagers chattered at a silver-topped table. A girl with her back to me deftly slung back her black hair, an action repeated in mirror after mirror. Arabic music pealed out of little speakers hung high on the back wall—a woman's high-pitched voice rose, caught at the edge of a moan, above a rhythm like a heartbeat.

He turned back. That sense once again of a conscious shift of focus. "May I ask what brings you round here?"

"Meeting a friend," I said. "Who's gone off now to do some sort of political commentary for the BBC."

"Ah." He stretched the fingers of one hand out across the countertop, then drew them close together. "How's the book?"

"Fine," I said. "I'm writing at the moment about the problem of moral equivalency. Making both sides in a conflict equal rather than acknowledging one as the aggressor and attempting to disarm him. Or them."

"You could disarm them both, could you not?"

"Well, yes. Though that's even harder. I mean, yes, one wants to attempt that diplomatically, but in a military situation, the question is really what your strategy's going to be—to try to manage the war, let the opponents fight but in a controlled way, or try to stop them." I tasted mango juice, aware of the line of skin where Amir's cheek met his sideburn. "Obviously it depends on the specific circumstances. But that's one of the larger issues, isn't it—does one want to establish peace or aim for justice?" I was conscious, as always, of the composed intensity of his attention, the way he listened with his whole body, limbs stilled, but articulated in my direction—yet not in weird avidity or judgment.

"And it has to be one or the other?"

"No, no, but it usually is. And then of course there's the question of whether to intervene at all. There's always the risk that by intervening you'll simply prolong the conflict." I adjusted a hair comb, felt the twinge of its teeth against my scalp. "On bad days at work," I said, "we joke that there's nothing civil about civil war."

He nodded, and I bit my lip. Hopeless.

One night, the last night that I had spent with my war-journalist friend Patrick O'Daire, we had gone back to Patrick's room in a hotel on the southern side of Hyde Park, not all that far from where I now sat. Patrick would ring me up sometimes when he passed through London, back from war-torn Kabul or the ravages of Nagorno-Karabakh or the refugee camps at Goma. That night, in bed beside Patrick, I woke suddenly. Dry-mouthed, for we'd been drinking, I rose and wrapped myself in one of the plush bathrobes that hang in the closets of such rooms. When I seated myself in the single armchair, littered with the clothes that Patrick and I had abandoned, something hard protruded underneath me. Harder than a wallet. I patted the cloth of Patrick's jacket and drew a pistol from his inside pocket.

Cupping it in my hand, I eyed the shine of the metal. How smooth it was. I wrapped my hand around the pistol and pointed it at the glass, at the dark expanse of trees in the park below and the ribbon of headlights from cars on the road that led through the park, though what I saw was the green of other trees, pale shavings of sunlight. My hand shook.

I heard Patrick shift in the bed, his voice through the dark. "What the fuck do you think you're doing?" A glaze coated his forehead. The grizzled gray of his sideburns floated like specters. Deep creases formed on either side of his mouth, beneath the white glint of his corneas. I tasted my power, his fear, my fear. Was the pistol loaded? I guessed it was.

I called out to him then. "Why do you carry it, Patrick? Why here?"

"Wherever I am, I have something." I could feel him willing me to put it down, although he would not ask me to do so. As a matter of principle. Because some notion of self-interest or self-protection (or bravado) had failed him, and to admit this would be to betray himself.

I laid the pistol on the doily-covered chest of drawers. Then I dressed in the dark and bolted, which was beginning to feel like a habit.

———

Tugging back the cuff of his shirt, Amir Barmour glanced at his watch, made a quick shrug with the corners of his mouth. "I must be off."

I took out my card, scribbled my home number on the back, and handed it to him. "Give me a ring sometime," I said.

I DID NOT START OUT writing about war. Nights when I cannot sleep or in the very early morning when I roll from bed and stumble into my study, my eyes veer toward not only the books about war, but another row of books, books I'd first gathered one by one and stored on the wooden shelves that Martin had built in the flat in Brixton.

Lermontov, Turgenev, Chekhov. Pushkin's *Eugene Onegin*. Russian authors weren't the only thing these works had in common. Also Pirandello's *Collected Plays* and Thomas Mann's *The Magic Mountain*. A collection of Joseph Conrad stories. Beside these were stacked another collection of books, which, in my Brixton days, I'd stored behind the works of literature— among them *A Short History of Dueling* and *The Duel in England*, which included a brief chapter on the transplantation of dueling practices to the colonies.

In those days, I had no official accreditation that would have allowed me to present myself as a researcher at the Reading Room of the British Library, so I traipsed among the second-hand bookshops on Charing Cross Road and made friends with a bookseller named Tom Frane, a beetle-eyed man with skin of vampiric paleness to whom I finally confided exactly what I was looking for. "Books about duels," I blurted. "For research. Anything to do with duels." *Ah*, was all he said, as if this request were, after all, not so unusual.

During the day, if Martin wasn't home, I pulled the books out. I bought myself a notebook. Between haircuts, I sat at the kitchen table, chewing a pencil and taking notes. Some days I went out walking—through Islington, where two seventeenth-century court favorites had slaughtered each other in a duel; through Covent Garden and Lincoln's Inn Fields, which had once both been popular dueling locales; as far as the doorway of the blue-domed Reading Room, built on the grounds of another dueling site. I could have drawn up a duelists' map of the city of London.

I read about duels fought over points of honor, lies, women, an Angora cat. I read about French duels, Russian duels, Italian duels, the barrier duel, the back-to-back duel. In turn-of-the-century Germany, three levels of insult could lead to a duel; the insult of seduction (of wife or daughter or other female dependent) was graded at the highest level, as fierce a violation as landing someone a physical blow.

I learned how to prepare for a duel, and how to stand so that a pistol shot stood the least chance of hitting you. I practiced, positioning myself in front of our bedroom mirror. (Keep both right and left shoulders in line with the object one wishes to hit, feet close together, stomach drawn in, right arm—the hand in which, if right-handed, one holds the pistol—raised at the elbow, upper part of the arm held close to the side.)

In England in the 1830s, it was considered essential for a young man to know how to fight a duel properly, to know the rules, since, when traveling to the Continent, one never knew what young, hot-blooded men one might encounter. Not only was it essential to train to shoot, but to withstand without flinching the terror of being shot at.

Once a duel had been fought from balloons. The last recorded duel in Toronto was fought in 1817. An eighteen-year-old had died, although the words on his tombstone, still visible in the entry of St. James cathedral, read simply A BLIGHT CAME.

I read until my eyes grew bleary, took notes until my hands ached.

One afternoon, grabbing my jacket, I bolted in a frenzy from the flat, from Brixton, north through the city, first by underground, then on foot, across the hump of Primrose Hill, where an army colonel and a navy captain had once fought a pistol duel over the merits of their Newfoundland dogs. Hands bunched in my pockets, I stopped at the summit and squinted up at the sooty English sky.

What does it mean to dream more of the city left behind than the one inhabited? To run toward the thing you think you've fled?

AMIR RANG. I came home one evening to find his voice on the answerphone and at the sound of it, achingly civil, I switched the ring mechanism on the telephone off. *Amir Barmour here, for Arcadia Hearne. I shall try you again.* Whatever had I been thinking, giving him my card? He didn't leave a number.

After pulling the venetian blinds shut tight, I stepped out of my sandals, one after the other. In the kitchen, I stood in front of the electric fan I'd left running and shivered, feeling its warm breeze flutter my face and the damp skin beneath my armpits. I opened the refrigerator, a swell of cold air pressing against me, a breath of emptiness, longing merely for emptiness. I was not lonely. I did not need romance. Yet I swam in a sea of contradictions. I squeezed the last sliver of lemon into a bottle of water and drank from that. Outside, the delphiniums, the daisies, the cosmos wilted in the golden light; the grass looked desiccated.

The morning sky was blue and cloudless. How many days in a row can the sky over London bloom blue and free of cloud? More than two weeks by now, and I was losing count.

One cup of coffee, then another—even three did not seem enough. What I needed was to slosh my face with coffee in order to shock myself awake. I had stayed up late to watch *Mundo*, Lux's show (this week, she was in Iceland, touring the clubs of Reykjavík), then more Lux, episodes I'd taped, not out of simple fandom, though Lux's work did interest me, but because it was so far from what I did that watching her qualified as pure entertainment.

The file on my computer was labeled simply "Forms of Intervention."

Before we can talk about interventions, we need to provide a context for possible intervention. To discuss the conditions of contemporary war, in other words, particularly the prevalence of so-called ethnic wars, or civil war.

In the paper that morning, I'd read about the latest casualties in Algeria—more journalists, more villagers shot by fundamentalist extremists. Hutu border incursions into post-genocide Rwanda. A ceasefire in Chechnya had been brokered. Analyses of the failure of the global call for a land-mine ban, though there was some hope for its resurrection in the future.

Some describe civil war as a form of societal self-mutilation, or a deadly family quarrel, or a duel to the finish between brothers. Some characterize war itself as a contagion: if you're faced with an armed antagonist, it's hard to ignore the threat if you don't want to die.

Rules of engagement exist not only to create just wars, or fair conditions, but to level the playing field. And in the late twentieth century, low-intensity conflicts, such as civil wars, have created the levelest playing fields, if not the fairest. Some describe these conflicts as the revenge of developing nations against the most industrialized, or simply a way of making it possible to go on fighting wars instead of committing instantaneous collective suicide.

I scraped back my chair and made my way to the garden, where I sliced a rose blossom with secateurs, trimmed the stem under running water, and set the flower, in a porcelain vase, on my desk. Then I sat back down.

Some argue that increasing environmental pressures have led to many of the newest round of wars. That such pressures lie beneath the ethnic strife in Africa and elsewhere, beneath wars ascribed to so-called "ancient tribal conflicts."

War over land, over food, over water. War over what a colleague of mine calls the transformation of difference, which he insists is subtly distinct from Freud's narcissism of minor difference—between people who practice the same religion, drink the same beer and smoke the same brand of cigarette, for whom the difference between a coffee and *un café* grows to a chasm.

Then there's the war of surgical strikes, of so-called surgical strikes, the supposed future of war, or non-war—characteristically one form of intervention practiced by the West, where forms of aggression now go hand in hand with a terror of casualties.

What kind of wars can be fought by countries who collectively fear death, whose first concern is the safety of their own personnel, who'll do anything to avoid bringing home body bags?

For most of the world, wars have grown fiercely personal again— devastatingly intimate. (While not precisely the return of history, often this feels like it.)

Civil wars may begin in political agenda, such as the propaganda of tribal conflict, but gain momentum when the woman down the street is raped, when rape itself becomes an instrument of war, when neighbor takes a machete to the skull of neighbor, when blood flows freely and no longer merely the politicians and nationalists are implicated.

Late in the afternoon, Amir rang once more. Although the telephone made no sound, I heard, from my desk, the click and whir of the answerphone on the little chest of drawers across the room. There was a crackle of blank air—of hesitation?—before his voice came on. *Arcadia, Amir Barmour wondering if you might like to meet for a drink.*

I should have picked up, I should have, but I couldn't. What, in the end, was the point? Once again, he left no number.

Some civil wars are being privatized. Mercenary armies are on the rise. Fewer and fewer wars are fought <u>between</u> states.

The number of child soldiers grows larger and larger.

Though the question of course is why? When the slaughter of fellow civilians begins, what part of the impulse is mass hysteria, what part grows from some twisted collective need for recognition, a drama born of humiliation or the desire for self-destruction, what part is fear, what part a craving for power?

What part of the child soldier has been anesthetized?

Why fight at all?

I buried my face in my palms. There's a seductiveness to knowing things that other people do not necessarily expect you to be familiar with. I've grown to depend on this. Being able to identify a Hawker Harrier in flight. Or an F-16. Being familiar with the perils and challenges of crack-thump training. That a TM62 is a Russian antitank mine. There are times when the work I do exhausts me, truly. Or fills me with horror. Yet I've worked hard to get this far. There's a kind of power to what I do. And I thrive on this. I won't deny it.

I took four aspirin with codeine and lay down in the bedroom, waiting for the buzz of codeine to dull the ache across my forehead.

Brain runs through muscle tissue, my friend Tim, the doctor, has told me. We know this now. Memory lurks throughout the body. There are days when I can press sharp nodes and feel the muscle twang—Evan, here. Neil there. Martin. Lux. My mother. My father.

"*Galaxy,*" Evan whispers in my ear, *is derived from the Greek word for milk—think of it, Cay, a sky full of spilled milk.* He licks my cheek. *And "sky" comes from the Latin word for skin.*

Pain travels, Tim says, it migrates through the body. Where it originates is not always where it ends up. We're only just beginning to understand this.

At times, without warning, I'll press my palm and hear the roar of a Toronto subway train, the hum of a streetcar's metal wheels singing in their metal tracks. I'll touch a point beneath my shoulder and see myself in Toronto racing toward the street-car stop at Queen and Bathurst, or College and Spadina. Or I'll be back in Brixton—Martin rattling down a staircase, slamming shut the old van's door.

Some days I feel they're with me always, carried within me as neurochemical presence, encoded in peptides and combinations of proteins, impossible to escape. An interior war.

Some days loss, pure loss and the longing for what's lost, for what I failed to do, grows nearly toxic in my blood.

WHEN I FIRST CAME TO LONDON and walked its streets, I grew ever more aware of the way a history of war was mapped upon the city as scars are mapped upon a body. I hadn't sensed this in Toronto. In London, new towers, modern blocks of town houses rose like hard pink flesh upon former bomb sites. I lived in a city saturated by war culture. There were still bombs, of course—it was just a different sort of war. I learned to fear not rockets or sniper fire but suitcases, briefcases, brown paper packages. Domestic war. Phone booths. Rubbish bins. Letterboxes. Buses. Cars. War in transit, a transitory war. One afternoon, I ran, in a crowd of others, past an abandoned suitcase in the corridor of the underground. I sat in trains as they whizzed through stations emptied of all but white-suited disposal squads. On entering museums or department stores, I grew accustomed to being searched for incendiary devices. There were also days when I longed for armfuls of incendiary devices.

I would go to a club where, from the wooden seats of a small, old amphitheater, I could watch fencers, clad in white, androgynous and anonymous behind the metal grill of their masks. Squeezing my fists between my knees, eyeing the thrust and parry of their foils, I wondered what drew them to their swordplay. Yet I could see the appeal of order imposed on violence, violence transformed by elegance and control. How each forward movement became not just a gesture of attack but one of intimacy, of ardor, the foil an extension of the body, as with each thrust, you seek not to wound but to touch someone.

I read about the culture of German university duelists, which continued through the First World War. The aim, by then, was not to kill one's opponent but to wound him, scar him (scars being a badge of pride, though killing happened). Before that, though, the culture of duels was one in which men were prepared to risk their lives for honor. *Honor.* Wars, too, had once been fought for such things—wars, like duels, like the jousts between knights that preceded them, were once conceived as a way of determining who was right, who was upholding the truth, before God. And if two knights fought over a woman's honor, she would watch them, be compelled to watch her fate being decided, from the stands.

One afternoon, eleven months after marrying Martin, I entered the British Library and asked at the main desk where the international phone directories were kept. Pulling the Metropolitan Toronto white pages from the shelf pointed out to me, I heaved the volume onto a wooden table and seated myself in front of it in a high-backed chair. I glanced around, then pressed my ear to the phone book, as if to the city itself in compressed form, as if a whisper of voices might seep from it.

I looked for them and couldn't find them. I ran my fingers

through the tissue-thin pages—*B* for Biederman. No E. Biederman. No Evan. *L* for Laurier, Neil. No trace. If I had found them, what would I have done? I wrote their names on a scrap of paper as if I might summon them this way, then, as if guilty, scribbled *apples apples apples* over them, a trick my father had once taught me. If you want to cover up something you have already written, write the word *apples* over top of it. He said this was something his own father had taught him, learned during the war, by which he meant the Second World War. Why apples? Something about the arrangement of letters, he said, some particular potency.

H for Hearne. For Herne the Hunter, who used to roam the forests of England's Windsor Park, tracking his ghostly hounds and ghostly quarry. This, too, was something our father had taught us, inventing a lineage for us. Samuel Hearne, explorer of the western arctic. Lafcadio Hearn, nineteenth-century adventurer, whose leapfrog life took him across multiple borders from Greece to Ireland to America to Japan, where he married a Japanese woman and tried to turn himself Japanese.

Hearne, B., which, like a palimpsest, hid the presence of the other Hearne, A. Both still in Toronto, on Glenmaple Avenue. Hearne, Lux (a gust of longing swept me), now had a different address and phone number.

I rang her. Stomach percolating, I left the library, gathered two pocketfuls of chunky one-pound coins, and slotted a handful into a phone box on the far side of the street.

"Cay," Lux said, no answering machine, two years dissolved by her live, dizzyingly familiar voice. "It's so totally, totally amazing to hear from you." My heart swam at the sound. My lips stung. "Where are you?" she shouted.

"In London."

"I know, okay, but where in London?"

"A phone box. Outside the British Museum."

"Is everything all right?"

"Everything's fine."

"Are you coming home?"

"Not yet," I said. I told her a little more about Martin. The line went *pip-pip-pip* as I shoved in more coins. I told her I was going back to university. I didn't say in what. "War Studies" didn't yet come rolling off my tongue. "Tell Mum and Dad I'll call them soon." I asked her if anyone in the last couple of years had tried to get in touch with me, had left any messages for me at the house.

"Like who?" Her voice gave a queer little catch. "Like Evan?"

"Anyone." I knew I'd been the one to leave but silence, their absolute disappearance from my life, all that I did not know, felt as violent as anything.

There was a sudden lull in traffic, through which coursed the intimate, transatlantic quiet of her breath. "Is that why you called, Cay?"

"No," I said, I shouted. "It isn't."

Martin told people. After I confessed to him why I'd really run away to London.

In the middle of one night, I rose and poured myself a glass of water and came back to kneel by the bed at his side. I told him because I'd decided that confiding in him seemed safer than silence. Perhaps it would release me or offer me greater protection from the past. Perhaps the dreams would stop (in a wind, I stepped out of a train onto a subway platform, one of Toronto's outdoor ones, Rosedale, say, or Davisville, to find Neil sitting hunched on a bench, in a trench coat—spilling blood when he opened the trench coat wide).

I told Martin that two boys had fought over me. Their names. I'd been involved with both of them. Sort of. They'd called it a duel. Not with swords but pistols. I waited in fear for some sign of disbelief or outrage or fury or sudden estrangement. Over what I'd done. And what they'd done. He'd reject me. In the mottled half-light of our urban dark, Martin stared at me, teeth shining; then his gaze veered away, toward the ceiling, toward the side. "Kiss me," he whispered, so I straddled him, pressed my lips to his, and felt his mouth surge open, as if he would swallow my story, claim it, make it part of our own romantic history. Was a duel that strange? Perhaps it wasn't that strange, and even if it was, my embrace was proof that I had, after all, chosen him over the two of them.

Yet at dinner parties, I began to notice people, friends, looking at me in new covert ways. As we sat, one night, by candlelight over the dregs of our wine and the remains of a salmon carcass in a Vauxhall squat. Across the table, shadows leaped at people's throats, at the lenses of Martin's glasses.

I excused myself. I bumped my way down a darkened hallway to the bathroom, where I locked the door and sat on the closed wooden lid of the toilet. Tears burned my eyes. He'd told people. Behind my back, he'd told people. This was clear to me. I squeezed my palms as a fierce rushing filled my chest, and swore I could hear whispers creeping underneath the door.

People began to ask me questions. In corners, at other parties. A woman named Rose, a heart-shaped strawberry half in her mouth. Had such a thing really happened? In Toronto—*really*? I learned to expect this. I decided it would be better to answer such questions. *Why not in Toronto?* I said to her. *Why not at the end of the twentieth century?*

Only one person claimed not to believe me. An Australian

friend of Martin's, named Jimmy Peddie, who, drunk, in someone's kitchen, insolent and leering, congratulated me on my
great feats of imagination and insisted that I'd made up the
whole story to lure Martin into marriage. I threw the contents of
my wineglass at him.

"Why?" Martin asked, when I told him that at the university, in
the office of the Department of War Studies, I'd met a man who
was starting up a new, small organization, a research center
about war. And that I'd asked if I could work for him. "I still
don't understand why on earth you want to do something like
this."

"Exploration." I stared ahead of me into the glow of sulfurous
streetlamps and felt the curt vibration of his body beside me.
"It's like wrestling with a problem."

At my side, he gave a bony heave of his shoulders, as if he
wanted to shrug off whatever didn't make sense to him, and at
that instant something in his stance reminded me eerily of Evan.

"I don't see why it has to seem so terrible," I said. "Or so
offensive. A human problem. I don't see why we have to leave
the study of war just to military tacticians."

It was early November. Candles fluttered on front doorsteps
in celebration of Divali, and, out of the darkness, beyond the
bulk of terrace houses, came the bright tear and bang of
vanguard firecrackers, for Guy Fawkes celebrations were only
a few nights away. We had come west, far west, to Ealing, to
hear a friend of mine play fiddle in a pub called the Green Man.
The air was damp and dense with a confusion of smells: coal fire,
wood fire, burning leaves, car exhaust, the hot smudge of candle
flame, the acrid tang of firework smoke, death and resurrection.
An old pumpkin, with a smashed-in mouth, lay abandoned on
top of a plastic rubbish bin.

"Is it because of your father's work?"

"No," I said.

When Martin spoke again, his voice had turned mean and accusatory. "I don't see why you can't leave them behind."

"Them?"

"You know who I mean."

"It isn't just them, you know. It really isn't—"

"So why then? Why? When you can barely even watch a bloody violent movie."

Sometimes skin just seems a casing for tumult; if you stretch it any tighter it will burst. My skin prickled in proximity to Martin. My clutched fists prickled. His mouth fell open in a wince.

We were walking across a little bridge. Beads of moisture made a film across Martin's dark hair and lumpy sweater. What if I'd reached out and touched him then? But I was stymied and overwhelmed by the pain I sensed in him and all the ways in which I'd begun furiously to resent him.

A strange smell drifted toward us—sugary, bubblegum sweet. A sign on a small brick building on the far side of the bridge read, in bold black letters, CHANDER'S GLYCERINE FACTORY. In the yard, enclosed by a chain-link fence, lay row upon row of metal drums, lit ghostly blue under a humming floodlight. Glycerine, which was used in antifreeze and as a sweetener and in dynamite.

"You think I'm not good enough for you, don't you?" Martin shouted as we descended the curve of the bridge. "Don't you?" He picked up a metal rubbish bin that had rolled into the gutter and hurled it clanging down the street. Turning, he stood in the middle of the pavement, waving his arms. "Don't you? Just because I won't kill for you or be killed for you."

THE FIRST TIME that Evan and I made love was in neither his dorm room nor my parents' house, but a hotel room. He'd insisted on it—on the room, on the precise hotel, which he called the Hanover Limbs or the Hanover Legs, but which most people knew as the Hanover Arms.

"Won't it be expensive?" I asked him.

"Aren't we worth it?" He seemed nearly angry, as if there could be no limits to what passion demanded.

Yet what I loved about him was just this commitment, his embrace of romance. I'd fallen in love before, of course, or thought I had, and been loved, too, by boys in high school. I'd gone out for nine months with a boy in the drama society (who left me), for a year with a boy who played the saxophone—the first one I slept with (and whom I left). But nothing like this, no one as adamant or ardent or fearless as Evan.

I told him I'd have to lie to my parents. This, too, seemed to upset him.

"What's there to be ashamed of?"

"It isn't a matter of shame," I said. Not shame, but sex. This being one of the things my parents *were* trying to protect me from, and I didn't think they'd understand the hotel room.

I told them I was going to a party and would spend the night downtown at my friend Simone's. When Evan asked, I lied to him, too, and said I'd simply told them I was spending the night with him.

We had dinner first at a little French restaurant on Avenue Road called La Citronnelle. An expensive restaurant.

"I'd starve myself for days in order to eat with you at a place like this," Evan said. "Not because it's expensive, but because the food is exquisite, and the experience of eating it is exquisite, and because I'll be with you, I'll always remember it." He was an aesthete, it seemed to me sometimes, with an ascetic's temperament, a kind of dualist.

We ate *moules* and *confit de canard*. We drank a red wine that spread like velvet over my tongue, that tasted of earth and moss and crushed berries and the ripe sweetness of decaying leaves. I kept my elbow-length kid gloves on as I ate, arms bare above them, aware of the folds of my thrift-shop blue satin dress sliding over my legs, thinking of sex, aware of the nervous fizz at the core of me.

"Imagine," Evan said, reaching out with his fingertips to touch mine, "if all flames were blue." His cheeks were flushed pink, but his face, apart from this, was very pale. He'd slicked back his hair. Little silver studs held his antique detachable collar in place. "How would that change the way we see the world?"

"Would it?" Blue embers, cool blue coals.

"Of course it would."

We'd be blue with happiness, the world as I knew it transformed.

The week before, he'd beckoned me out of the library and

handed me a little white box in which were gingerbread men he said he'd baked himself in the residence kitchen. On top of them lay a little slip of paper on which he'd written the words EAT ME.

"If I eat them, will I shrink or will I grow?" I asked.

He winked. "Find out for yourself."

We drank thick, dark coffee. We ate *tarte aux abricots*.

On the way south again, Evan looped his arm around my waist. When I wore heels, as now, I stood a little taller than he did. Out of his jacket pocket (an old tuxedo jacket, he wore no coat), he scooped a hotel-room key and dangled it in front of us. He told me, pocketing the key again, that he'd signed us in as the Clouds.

"John Cumulus," I said, bumping my hip to his. "Anna Cirrus." When he grinned, I knew he hadn't acted out of furtiveness, desiring secrecy, but as an expression of private whimsy, which was different.

I was frightened, despite my excitement, that I would disappoint him. Even as I wanted his intensity, his ardor, his yearning to thrust us both away from the merely collegiate—the groping in skinny single beds, the clasping of stray body parts, fingers slipped under belt buckles or bras in the dark of cars or parks. I would somehow not be able to match him—in passion, in recklessness, in a kind of maturity that I ascribed to him— faced with all that skin, all those bare limbs amid the white expanse of the hotel bed.

Yet he'd confessed things to me, opening himself wide with vulnerability. After his mother had left, after the house had been rented but before he'd had to vacate it, he'd slept in the back yard, wrapped in a sleeping bag, for five nights in a row— through rain and starlight—and cried himself to sleep each night. When he was thirteen and the girl he loved had failed to love him back, he'd swallowed a full bottle of aspirin, waking the next morning, groggy but all right. His admissions left me awed and moved. He told me his father had wanted him to go to university in the States, but he'd refused.

In the elevator riding up to the hotel room, I kissed him, and when we pulled apart, as the sixth floor chimed, I used my palm to wipe the smears of lipstick from his lips.

Like a benevolent magician, Evan unlocked the door to the room and ushered me in.

Evan liked the Hanover Arms because it was old, because the rooms weren't antiseptically cleansed of character or synthetically gussied up. There was a white chenille spread on the bed, a closet in one corner, a desk made of real wood. On the bedside table, a spray of orchids arced from a bottle. In the bathroom sink, on a bed of melting ice, lay a small bottle of Veuve Clicquot.

I dropped the shoulder bag in which I carried my supplies, sliding my arms out of my brown suede jacket and letting it fall to the floor. "It's lovely," I said, opening my arms. In the bathroom, Evan knelt on the tiles, swiveling the taps on the bathtub until water gushed out.

"Look in the closet." When I pulled open the door, what I saw were milk jugs, six of them, spilling out of an old gray duffel bag.

"I want to give you a milk bath," Evan called from the doorway, sleeves rolled above his elbows. "Milk and hot water. We could have tried milk alone but I didn't know how you felt about cold baths. This'll be better. It's something I've always wanted to do."

I was amazed, I suppose. "Cleopatra bathed in milk," he said.

When he'd filled the bath partway with hot water, he poured in the milk, jug by jug, a sweet-sour odor drifting up, while I stood behind him. He touched a match to the candle he'd set on the back of the toilet and switched off the overhead light.

Backing away from him, into the room behind us, I stopped

in the middle of the carpet. Candle in hand, Evan switched off the light here, too. "Undress for me," he whispered. I didn't see how I could refuse. Love had never required anything quite like this from me before, but perhaps I had never really known love. I drew my fingers out of my gloves, one by one, sliding the crumpling skin down my arms. I stepped out of my shoes, hitched up my dress at the waist and peeled off my panty hose, one slinky foot, then the other. Working open the long zipper at the back of my dress, I drew my arms free of the cloth and shimmied out of it.

IN MY STUDY, I pressed the playback button on the answerphone. There were messages from Tim, from Hanna. *Cay? Are
you there?* The Australian twang of Ray Farr's voice. Even over
the phone he hummed with the centripetal energy that drew
people to him, his conviction that everyone will necessarily care
about and be fascinated by the issues of contemporary war, his
assumption that those whose help the Centre needs will auto-
matically materialize. *I've a TV gig we may need you for. Oh
yeah, and I've a piece on the Iran-Iraq war that needs translating.
Happen to know any Farsi translators?*

I made myself a drink, dry vermouth with soda water and a twist
of lemon rind, telephoned Lola Race and asked her if she wanted
to see a movie. "Something escapist."
    "You mean some fluffy screwball comedy."
    "No blood and guts. Lola, that's work."
    "Right," Lola said. "What about a meal then? Different sort
of escapism. *Moules frites* and a couple of pints?"
    "Whatever," I said. "Absolutely."

I looked for him in the underground. I looked—despite myself—as I traveled the vast ranks of escalators in King's Cross Station. In the crowds swilling through the streets north of Covent Garden. He'd left no number when he rang and, when I searched the phone book, I found no listing under his name. I knew a few stray facts, but hardly anything about his life. Perhaps by some other stroke of luck or synchronicity, my gaze would skim across a sea of people and alight on Basra Alale, who might be able to help me.

I tried the canal. I walked the towpaths and convinced myself that since this was something I would have done anyway, I was not really looking for him. Or if I was, it was only to pass on Ray's message about translating.

At dusk I left the office and walked the streets east from Islington, through Dalston, toward Hackney, peering into windows—some hung with lace curtains, some with flowered bedsheets. And was filled with amazing gratitude toward those casual exhibitionists who leave their lives exposed to the city streets, open to the peering embrace of voyeurs like me. In one basement, I spied a white armchair plumped beside a white grand piano, beneath a glimpse of a golden chandelier. In another a man in an undershirt hunched over a counter peeling an egg. On the front steps of one terrace house a brown man rocked a pink baby, crooning to it gently, *ba ba ba ba*. Once, across a street, I glimpsed a young woman in a denim skirt and bright white trainers who, for an instant, I thought might be Basra. As I rode the Northern Line north, suffocating in its pungent, grimy heat, my stomach skittered at the sight of a man who might have been Neil (a larky boyishness in the long face, broad hands on knees, head of thick hair) ten years later.

It was just after midsummer: at ten, outside the Chalk Farm

tube, the sky was still awash with pale-blue northern light. I followed a young woman carrying a huge bouquet of lilies as she rounded a corner, and drank in the alcoholic trail of her breath.

In daylight I tried the copy shops in Camden. Quick Print. Print Zone. Jiffy Print. I stared through windows, scanning for Amir's face, then stepped inside and, swallowing embarrassment, asked for him at the counter. In retrospect, it seemed rude and ridiculous to have been trying to avoid him. *No*, I was told each time, *no one by that name. Sorry.*

He hadn't tried to ring me again.

I walked for miles, as I used to do when I first came to London.

Pigeons wheeled through the air above Regent's Park. A woman watched them from beneath a tree, a thick wool coat buttoned chest to knee over her sky-blue sari, as if she were yearning for some far more blistering heat. On her feet there were only the thinnest of gilt sandals. I thought of my mother, once upon a time, claiming Canada with her field guides to the wildlife and her hope and her French-English dictionary.

On the far side of the park, I hailed a Mr. Whippy ice-cream van and bought a grape ice lolly. It was a Thursday afternoon. I made my way down the Edgware Road until I found the sign for the Modern English Language School. I thought, I'm on the verge once more of making a fool of myself. A door led up a flight of wooden stairs to another door. On the far side, a young woman sitting at a metal reception desk glanced up as I entered. What did she see? Traces of sweat on my forehead and in the fringes of my dark hair. The purple stain near the hem of my sundress. My flushed cheeks and moment's hesitation. "Are you here for English lessons?" she asked politely.

"No," I said, "I'm looking for Amir Barmour."

ON OUR FIRST-YEAR ANNIVERSARY, Evan and I rented another hotel room, not in the Hanover Arms but up the street in the Park Plaza.

On Friday afternoons, my last class was at two o'clock. I was to meet him afterward—at the hotel, at five. Evan had made the plans. The room would be under our own names this time. All I had to do was go to the front desk and ask for the number.

When I stepped out of the elevator on the fifteenth floor, the corridor hummed, stretching vertiginously into the distance. Carrying the present I'd brought for him (a jeweled antique tiepin wrapped in a silver box), I counted my way along until I came to the right door. An envelope had been taped to the outside, my name written on it. I was growing accustomed, with Evan, to this sense of playing a game, though what went with it was a feeling of being tipped continually off balance, never knowing quite what to expect, which required a certain mental vigilance.

I ran my fingers along the rim of the envelope to open it. Inside was a gold key—the room key. I smoothed my free hand down my little black dress. Ear tucked to the door, I listened for a moment, hearing nothing, then fit the key into the lock and turned it.

At first I saw nothing. The room was dark—at least, all I could see were spots of hovering candle flame, orange, not blue. I pushed the door shut and stepped forward. "Evan?" There were enough candles that I wondered he hadn't set off some hotel smoke detector—candles in the bathroom, candles on the bureau, candles shaping little bowls of quivery light. The walls shone the color of skin—our skin.

When my eyes adjusted to the light, I saw Evan lounging on the bed, naked, bathed in candlelight, sheets flung back. "You look beautiful," he said. There was a tray beside him (what looked like a dining-hall tray), draped in white linen, and on it lay shucked oysters, opalescence glistening, stalks of asparagus (all this I could now make out), strawberries dipped in chocolate—a display of aphrodisiacs.

We kissed and then, laying the present on the bureau, I padded past him to the window, where I threw open the curtains to let in the sky, a winter sky, at five o'clock already a deep marine blue. We were high enough up that the lights of the city spread out before me—a yellow glaze of cars heading north, the pink tinges of the museum's stone arches below, the mass of Queen's Park visible like a dark star sucked of all light, the scraggly towers of the university beyond that. A bird billowed toward the window ledge, then dove away again.

"Pterodactyl," Evan called, although I had seen a pigeon. What everyone else called digestives, he called suggestive biscuits.

I turned back and sat down on the edge of the bed beside him. "When Krakatoa erupted in 1883," I said softly, "the sky in the south Pacific was dark for five days from the volcanic ash, and it caused a blue moon."

He touched my lips. "I love you so much, you know."

I buried my head against his bare shoulder. "I love you, too." And I did, I told myself, I did, as if telling myself this would make it even more true.

He fed me an oyster, tipping it up so that it slid whole, in its tiny saline sea, down my throat. And then I fed him one, watching his eyes close.

The flames of the candles on the bedside table rippled. I knelt beside him and traced the smooth slide of his pectoral muscles, the silky curve of deltoid below his shoulder, his swelling biceps. He was small, slim but solid, and more muscled than anyone else I'd been with. Sometimes, lying in bed, I'd point to muscles and he'd name them for me: latissimus dorsi, rhomboid, trapezius. He could be so gentle. When I was sick, he'd made me chicken soup from scratch and a cheese soufflé. Once he'd brought my mother flowers. Now he pushed my dress up my thighs, over the top of my stockings—I was wearing old-fashioned stockings attached with clasps to a garter, which Evan had bought for me at one of the old-clothing shops. With his other hand, he unsnapped the clip and tugged out the pins holding up my hair. "You're my Arcadia," he whispered.

As he turned me, lowering me to the bed beside him, I lost my balance. Bumped something, glimpsed a teeter of flame. Inhaled the sharp, unmistakable odor of burning hair. Out of the corner of my eye, Evan blew past; a white pillow mashed beside my head. The smell grew smokier, more acrid—scorched hair, scorched cotton, singed feathers.

When Evan lifted the pillow, I sat up tentatively and patted my scalp. Shriveled hair fell away. "Burnt offering," he said. With a grin, he picked up a clump of hair that began to dissolve in his fingers. Pulling the housekeeping envelope out of the drawer in the bedside table, he dropped a few strands into it and licked the envelope shut.

I rolled from the bed, and, in the bathroom, flicked on the

light and stared at myself in the mirror. I looked wan and startled. I fingered the place beneath my ear where my hair had burned. Another hank fell away.

When I stepped back into the room, Evan was on his knees on the bed, gazing toward the window, a gesture not of supplication but one that suggested infinite patience. A spasm rocked me—some new kind of longing. Gratitude and fear and fear overcome—and the sense of being bound to him more tightly than ever because of it.

AMIR MADE ME DINNER at his flat in Hackney—as thanks, he said, for the translation work, though I insisted I'd done nothing but relay a message. We sat at a round wooden table, in front of a tall window shoved open wide so as to let as much westerly breeze as possible waft over us like a balm. What once must have been a single high-ceilinged room had at some point been subdivided into a sitting room, with space cleared by the window for the table, and, separated by a partial wall, a narrow galley kitchen. He lit two candles already lumpen and dribbly from use. In the breeze, more wax spilled onto the crumpled linen tablecloth, but he didn't seem to care. He served a salad of tart white cheese and radishes and jungle-sized portions of watercress, whose spindly ends, if I'd been by myself, I would have picked up and eaten with my fingers. Chicken with pomegranate sauce, which he said he'd made from scratch: sweet juice and pulp and ground walnuts and a dash of rose water. He poured out two large glasses of the wine I'd brought, gracious and cordial as ever.

I asked him if he'd heard Basra sing and he said, yes, once, and that she had a haunting, spectacular voice, but didn't add anything further.

"I caught you on television," he said. "I didn't realize you did that sort of thing." Three of us on a panel discussing the contradictions between the rights of state sovereignty and the rights of individuals to be free of oppressive states, this being the justification used to support most interventions. "You looked very glam."

"Rubbish," I said, wiping my mouth on a creased cloth napkin. "Anyway, that's not the point."

When I asked if he still had family in Iran, he nodded. "My parents. My sisters." He said he had grown up in a house built around a courtyard in the middle of which stood a tiny fountain, its basin filled with goldfish.

"Have you ever been back?"

He shook his head.

"Would it be possible, these days, to go back, if you wanted to?"

"These days, if one wanted to, I reckon it might be possible."

"Did you serve in the army?"

"Of course. Briefly."

"Did you fight in the war with Iraq?"

"No, I left before that. Otherwise I'd be dead, more than likely."

He lived in a small row of terrace houses, like blocks of terrace houses all over London, on the third of four floors, high enough that the windows gave a view across the city. As we sat, great floods of copper light poured across our arms and shoulders. A loose flap of cloth or paper vibrated somewhere across the room. Reggae music chugged below, as it had, so often, when Martin and I had lived in Brixton.

While Amir made tea, I prowled the sitting room. A single dried rose lay on the mantelpiece. I crouched beside the fireplace, in front of the shelves where, beneath a sleek black sound system, his collection of CD albums lay—Persian music, European classical music, American jazz.

When the phone rang, he picked it up in the kitchen, and I listened as his voice rose in delight—in intimacy?—pluming away from me, transforming fluidly and familiarly, in intonation, in rhythm, growing less English. *You saw Mariam in Paris? Did you? It's been years, you know. Oh, you must, you must. And Hassan, still in Germany?* Someone Iranian? Though he did not switch into Farsi. Location I tried also to guess: Berlin, or Frankfurt?

He served us tea in glass teacups, glass saucers beneath, setting them down on a glass coffee table. Amir settled in the worn velvet armchair, its arms rubbed nearly bald, a pile of phone books where one curved wooden leg ought to be, and I on the flowered settee.

The phone rang again—a different phone, the muted dweedle of a mobile smothered in a jacket pocket or a bag—but this time he made no move to answer it.

Outside, the western sky turned turquoise. Lights sprang on in other rooms, like illuminated squares of stained glass or the little doors on Christmas Advent calendars that open to reveal other worlds. In the bathroom, my fingertips tweaked: at the sight of the single white toothbrush, handle down in a glass; a branch of dried eucalyptus hanging from the shower rail; a candle set in a china saucer on the back of the toilet. My cheeks were flushed—I was only mildly drunk, but definitely flushed.

When I returned, I found Amir in the kitchen, black hair shining under the bright overhead light, grinding coffee. "Decided I needed something stronger before I drove you home."

I felt a jolt, it's true: of dismay? Of disappointment? "I'll ring for a minicab. Really. If you give me the number of a local service—"

"Of course I'll drive you home."

On the back dash of his battered, dun-colored Fiat, as in the car of almost every London driver, lay a ragged *A to Z* flung open to some pink quadrant of the city. The first time I'd told him where I lived, he'd raised his eyebrows as if to say, Primrose Hill, how posh. And I suppose it is, it was, though I swore the basement flat was small and I'd lived there nearly five years and a friend of mine had lived in the flat for years before that.

Wind blew in through the open windows. Under a sea-green sky, a tribe of tiny children clad in sailor suits crowded around the outdoor patrons of a pub, jangling coin boxes at the adults' thighs. "What are they doing out?" I cried. "It's past their bedtime, it's nearly closing time." Amir simply shrugged. The midsummer moon sailed high and white and full above us.

He ejected one tape and slid another into the tape deck. "Listen," he said. "This is made-in-California Iranian pop. You've probably never heard such a thing. I listen to it only in the car—it's very kitsch, I suppose—but in the car I really like it." A girl's voice warbled, as breathless as any other pop star's, spilling out through our windows. A woman's voice crooned, languid, above a fast, propulsive beat. I felt alert, astonishingly alert, which wasn't caffeine, which was different than vigilance—skin and brain stretched tight. Red cars swooped around us, blood brown under the sodium glare of the streetlights. With a sheepish, infectious grin, he passed me an open box of chocolate-covered biscuits (chocolate half melted), which had been wedged behind the parking brake. I watched his left hand on the gear stick, upshifting, the car lightly shuddering. I eyed the biscuit perched between his teeth, the sharp line of hair at the nape of his neck, the warm and honeyed skin above the white curve of his collar. If I reached out and touched him there, what would he do?

He rang me the next night—from his car, on a mobile, judging from the rush of traffic and air around him.

"Where are you?" I asked.

"In Slough." What was he doing out in Slough? And what was he doing ringing me from Slough? "Wondering what you're up to."

"Working," I said. I was writing about Somalia, about the concept of thresholds. How the failure of the American-led intervention in Somalia affected what happened, or failed to happen, in Rwanda, even though the state-led plans for the genocide were known at the highest levels of the U.N. How the fear of casualties won out, the Americans' post-Somalia policy of "force protection," in which one's first priority must be to protect oneself.

About how the history of intervention is a history of such thresholds, the outcome of one affecting the next, from the Gulf War through Somalia, Bosnia, Rwanda. And how the decision to take action is decided equally by whom you determine to be a stranger. Not only what you are willing to risk but for whom.

Somewhere a siren wailed. "I was just wondering when you might be free," he said. "If you fancied meeting up?"

I rose from my desk, my kneecaps cracking. Phone in hand, I pressed my face to the bars of the venetian blinds, to the blurry streetwide view.

"Come round if you like," I said. "I'm free." You can't spend all your time writing about war, after all.

I let him in and locked the door behind him. He encircled my face with his hands as I kissed him, opening his lips with my tongue. Stumbling, we knocked over the answerphone on its little table, a string of garbled, speeded-up voices unspooling for a moment, then bleating into silence.

In the bedroom, he came up behind me, undid the clasp at the waist of my skirt, and let it fall.

We lay in a spill of arms, both breathless, bathed in sweat. Naked, I wandered to the kitchen, and brought back two glasses of water. Lit the candle on the bedside table and turned to observe him: skin like dark sand against the pale-olive of my limbs, the darker coins of his nipples, the dark rill of hair that ran from his navel to his pubis, the puckering of muscles in his forehead—the process of thought not hidden, but casually revealed.

The second approach was more languorous, as if we had all the time in the world to begin again, and begin again, to learn by touch the touch the other's body craved, searching for one pulse, then another.

"You're not married, are you?" I asked. We'd pulled the top sheet from the floor and billowed it around us, propped the pillows between the wall and our backs.

"No," he said calmly. "Not now. I was for nine years. We divorced almost two years ago. Why, are you?"

"No," I said. "Divorced just six months ago, actually. Though we'd been separated for nearly five years."

He'd been married to a woman named Claire—English, although they'd met in Frankfurt. She had been his English as a Second Language teacher—Advanced English as a Second Language. She'd taught him when to say *hair*, as in the hair on your head, and when to say *hairs*, as in the golden down on your arm. That *blondish* was not a word in English, only *blonde*. Now she lived in Manchester.

"Why did you split up?" I stared not at his face but at other parts of him: his knees, his fingers.

"I suppose we outgrew each other. Things shifted. After we came to England. I did not need—perhaps I began to seem less exotic. Or I began to talk too much. Mutual, on the whole. You?" He grinned. "Was it a love match or an immigration marriage?"

"Mmm," I said. "A bit of both, really. My mother's parents lived here, briefly, in Manchester, during the war, but they weren't English. I *was* stopped once. It probably sounds quite silly, all things considered, though it wasn't at the time. On a ferry. Martin and I had gone to France, for a week, before we were married, and we were coming back. And a customs officer stopped me and searched my bag and my wallet and found a bank slip from a London bank and an envelope—I'd scribbled some phone numbers on it, that's why I was carrying it—but it was addressed to me at a London address. And he could see from my passport that this was after my six-month stamp had expired. So he wouldn't let me in. He couldn't prove I was working, though obviously he suspected it. I told Martin to go on, and when I got back to France, I used up all the money I had left to take a train to Holland and a different ferry to Folkestone."

He nodded, smoothing his thumb along my right forearm. I rolled onto my side, slipping my arm free to prop beneath my head. He was thirty-four. From Frankfurt, he and Claire had moved to Paris, where she had also taught English, and then to London—to West London, to a flat in Hammersmith, where things began to fall apart.

In the morning, shirt untucked and flapping, he wandered out to the newsagent's on the corner and came back not only with the *Guardian* that I had requested, but with two other papers as well.

"Three?" I said. I couldn't help myself. "Why three?"

He'd combed back his hair, but the new nicks of a beard were beginning to shade his cheeks. "To follow the world's wars," he said.

"There are better ways."

"I didn't say it was the only way."

I'd made two cups of coffee and set out yogurt and a plate of toast, beside a pot of honey. I stared at him as he read his paper, folded in vertical sections, unlike my habitual sprawl. Though by now I wanted him to go—or part of me did. He drank the coffee, politely refused the yogurt and the toast.

"Sometimes I'd like to believe," I said, licking my sticky fingers, "that being informed, that knowledge is an end in itself, that one is justified simply in knowing what's going on in the world. Of course we spend a lot of time in intervention studies thinking about how one determines appropriate spheres of action. For individuals. For countries. Where to act, and when, and how. In an age of global vision and moral opinion. When we see so much, and know so much. Too much, possibly. When we're all these global voyeurs, really, watching endless television clips of atrocities—how are we to make sure we don't all collapse into utter passivity?"

"You could call it impartiality."

"Not if you're going to act."

"If one's going to act, one has to choose when and—"

"Yes," I said, "but the question is, how do you choose?"

Two days later, he rang again.

At dusk, we lolled on the tilted flagstones of my patio, legs entwined, refilling our glasses from a bottle of chenin blanc. Delphiniums swayed in mauve spires. Pillars of gnats spiraled through the air above us like complex molecular structures. We'd thrown on approximations of our clothes: my skirt and barely buttoned shirt, no underwear.

"Do you think war's inevitable?" he asked me. "I mean, that sort of violence." His fingers traced the outline of my breasts through thin linen, then slid beneath it.

"I'm not an advocate of war, just an investigator of it."

"I didn't say you were, just, do you think it's inevitable?"

"Depends what sort of inevitable."

"Right, then, biologically. For a start." Really, he made my work seem quite normal—the object of genuine interest, but not the kinky fascination of some men I had known, nor a source of barely suppressed judgment. And this touched me, and was a better way than most to seduce me.

"Well, aggression has a genetic base, doesn't it," I said. "In the limbic system, though that doesn't necessarily mean violence does. And it's not absolutely clear that aggression is the source of war—or that one can collapse war and all other sorts of violence. Brain chemistry's affected by early childhood environment, and that can predispose people to violent behavior. But genetically we're also nomads, aren't we, and migrations lead to conflict—"

"Do they? Always?"

"Well, they have, haven't they, throughout human history, although perhaps that doesn't mean it's genetic, only there's something embedded in the shape of our cultures, our economies, our politics, and it *is* important not to ignore the politics."

"A Clausewitzian."

I opened my eyes to look at him sharply. He had also studied political history. "No," I said. "Not precisely. Only it's important these days not to act as though everything can be put down to the irrational or to the biological or to age-old animosities—especially if one wants to believe it might be possible, somehow, to change."

Eyes open or closed, I could feel the hum of his body close by mine, the vibration of his intent and curious gaze, the occasional quiver of wariness, the pluck of dry amusement. The somnolent heat of him. While my own body burned, achy with exhaustion, stretched taut from sex—my brain singing a bright, electric tune, which he also aroused in me.

"Did you know," I said, rolling onto my back, head on the grass, "I was reading this morning that fear is located in a different part of the brain than any other human emotion."

He leaned over me, drifting a blade of grass across my throat. "But you, Arcadia? Do you believe war's inevitable?"

I frowned and flung out my arms. "I don't know." Soldiers killed far more than they used to. In previous wars, there were far greater numbers who misaimed, or simply failed to shoot. These days, they're trained, and conditioned, to kill more efficiently. "Perhaps that's what I'm trying to decide."

Like this? he asked. *Touch you like this?* Or else I took his fingers and showed him. And afterward, in the dark, my gaze would sometimes trace the row of old vinyl record albums stored high on a shelf beyond the far side of his bed, above some motley rows of books. On the top shelf was the plastic-domed record player on which he must once have played them. I wondered why he kept them: a few old Beatles albums, David Bowie, some mid-eighties pop albums by Madonna and the Pet Shop Boys. Was it out of nostalgia, or sterner reminiscence? Were they an alphabet of who he'd been or tried to be in the years when he first came to England?

There was caution in him: I sensed that. He was my release, I told myself. My summer distraction. I invited him out for dinner. I made him chocolate mousse.

One night as we lay sprawled on our backs in his bed, having kicked free the pale-blue sheet, exposing ourselves to the licks of breeze that were all that reached us through the open window, I turned to him, curved my knees to my chest and asked, "Will you tell me how you left Tehran? And why you left?"

He was a university student when he'd first applied for a visa to study abroad—in London, actually. He'd already studied some English and spoke it, not well, of course, but not terribly, and this in itself was grounds for certain suspicions against him. That he wanted to flee into the embrace of the West, *when really, what I wanted was merely to travel, to be cosmopolitan, which is not the same as wanting to be Westernized, even though people so often act as if it is.* That he'd applied for the visa at all, despite the fact that he was turned down, was also seen as potentially seditious.

There was also the Israeli stamp in his passport. He'd had neighbors, growing up in Tehran, who were Jewish, which was unusual but not absolutely unheard of. And one summer, the summer Amir was fifteen, relatives of theirs from Israel came to visit, including a boy, Ariel, who was two years older than Amir, and Vared, a girl, who was his age. And the next summer, with his father's permission, he went for two weeks to visit them in Tel Aviv. They spoke to each other in English. They wrote letters back and forth, practicing their English.

After his request for a student visa was turned down, he applied for an exit visa—perhaps naïvely, but the borders were still open; it was still conceivable to leave. His application was again refused. Friends were being arrested and beaten up. As Marxist-Leninists. *We were Marxist-Leninists who believed in individual rights and sat around in each other's homes drinking smuggled alcohol and listening to ABBA, or whatever tacky, catchy pop music we could get our hands on. We wanted to be able to walk into a bar and order a drink. We weren't the slightest bit religious.*

A week after his request for an exit visa was refused, he was arrested and jailed for suspicion. He had done three months of army training. His jailers and interrogators seemed convinced he was trying to get to Israel, obsessed with the fact that Vared's and Ariel's father was a career officer in the Israeli army. *A psychologist, actually,* Amir said. Six months later he was released.

An uncle helped him flee the country and came up with the money, but Amir was the one who followed the leads, the whispered voices, met burly men in coffeehouses who talked into their coffee and threatened terrible retribution on all his family if he gave any of their secrets away. He managed to scrabble together enough money for a midpriced escape, which was substantial, but the cheapest sort apparently meant days of walking and was so dangerous you might as well give up anyway. For the price he paid he was told he'd get an escape that involved only a few hours on foot.

You are sick with trust, he said, *because you have to be*. On the nearly twenty-four-hour bus ride into the desert, he knew only that among the other passengers were two who would also be part of the escape party. *Is it the woman in the brown veil who eyes a man's cigarette longingly, or the older woman with gnarled hands hugging a handbag, or the man in the too-tight herringbone suit?* One of the burly men was also there, like a malevolent spy.

From the bus terminus, a van bore them farther into the desert, four of them crouched in the back, in the dark, holding onto metal gas cans.

Their walk, as it turned out, was more than a few hours. All day, led by guides, they trudged through blazing desert heat, the older woman with the handbag crying ceaselessly but silently beside him. The signs that marked their path were nearly invisible. Every so often, one of the guides, an old man, would crouch, listening avidly, ear pressed to the sand.

In the dark, it was not even possible to light a cigarette for fear of being seen, because the dry snap of night air in the desert made even the tiniest flicker visible for miles. *Already*, he said, *you know that whatever happens to you, you have disappeared.*

Feet bleeding, shoes ripped to shreds, they crossed the border through the worn-thin dark of very early morning, within shooting distance of a unit of Revolutionary Guards.

"And there I was," Amir said as a slate-gray English dawn came slivering in around the edges of the curtains. "In a Pakistani border station, drinking bottle after bottle of Coke, smoking cigarette after cigarette, stunned to find myself there, still terrified—after all those hours—that I'd be shot, fighting the urge to do the one thing that seemed more inconceivable and crazy, but only barely, than what I'd just done—racing madly back toward the border and the cocked guns of the border guards."

"But you didn't."

"I did not."

THE NEXT NIGHT, after midnight, we rose from my bed and, grabbing the watering can, switched on the hose and watered my garden, for it is illegal during drought conditions in London to water your garden, though as I listened to the hiss of droplets, I swore I could hear echoes from elsewhere. In a whisper, I pointed out the hollyhock, the lupin, the foxglove. Our skin gleamed in the silvered moonlight. We kissed under the apple tree.

And when, wet footed, we returned to bed, Amir said to me, "Right, now it's your turn."

"My turn?"

"To tell me how you came and why you left."

I wrapped my arms around my knees. "I had a duel fought over me." *It was long ago, it was all so long ago.*

"A what?"

"A duel. With pistols." My head went still. What would he make of this? Though often people responded this way. I'd have to repeat myself when I told them. "At dawn. In a ravine. In Toronto. Two men fought over me. When I was twenty-one. We were all at university."

"Tell me more," he said with that gaze I'd come to recognize, his particular calm scrutiny.

I squeezed my arms. "I was involved with one of them, involved in the long slow process of extrication, really. We'd been together for almost three years. And then I met the other one. The first one challenged the second one to a duel. Do you know how—"

"He found out."

"Mmm."

"One of them was killed?"

"Shot in the groin, in the iliac artery. It's a major artery. He lost a tremendous amount of blood, but they managed to get him to a hospital. The one who was challenged. They did it the way they used to fight duels—you know—in the nineteenth century. Very formally. In secret. With seconds—friends with them as their representatives. And a medical student."

"They fought for love."

"Presumably."

"Was the one who shot him charged?"

"I'm not sure. Because I fled, and after that I had no further contact with them."

"Why did you flee?"

"I was devastated. When I found out. By all of it, by what they'd done. It seemed like the only thing to do."

Long after Amir had fallen asleep, slipping across that border, lost to me in the foreign country of sleep, I slid my feet to the floor and, pulling my arms into the sleeves of my robe, made my way into the hall. One arm pressed to the lintel, I stood staring through the doorway into my study. Wands of pink light from the streetlamp outside stole through the venetian blinds and banded across the bookshelves. What I sensed but could not see lay hidden away behind the books: my fencing foil, a brown envelope crammed with old notes and photographs that I'd brought with me from Toronto. A tiny windup superhero figurine. A single brass candlestick.

In the bathroom, the electric light above the sink flickered when I switched it on. I leaned toward the mirror, pulling my hair back in one fist, studying the tracery of lines at the corners of my eyes, the ghost of a sharp line forming between my eyebrows.

Neil in the grass. All that blood. Neil's body twitching on the ground.

I'd once asked my friend Tim, the doctor in Hammersmith, if one could indeed die from a wound to the iliac artery. *Depends what sort of wound.* A gunshot wound, for instance. *Shot right in the artery? Yeah, if you didn't get medical attention fast, very fast. If you lost enough blood, of course you could die from it.*

Amir found me lying in the hallway: I was following the path of the moon as it moved through the kitchen window, as it grazed the rooftop chimney pots on the far side of the garden. Moonlight slid over me, moonlight pouring along the walls and the floor. I was thinking about a man I'd met at a party. Drunk, in the middle of the room, he'd unbuttoned his shirt and pointed to the tattoo inscribed across his left breast. *No One Gets* was what it said. The pain had been so great, he told me, he'd never been able to finish it. *Out of Here Alive*, he added.

When I tell people about the duel, I choose my moments carefully, and I do not tell everyone. Yet I've grown to yearn for this instant, for all that is exposed in people's faces when I tell them. This, too, has become something I need to know. For there's power in my revelation. I've watched women's faces transform into something like envy; others grow cool. Men start back or draw forward, tugged by danger, the possibility of dangerous behavior. And there are times, I admit, when I have used the duel as a lure. Nights when I've felt restless or curious or lonely, I have confided in men in bars, in an opera box, in bedrooms, and waited to see what they would do.

I've looked at men (yes, even Amir) and wondered, Would he be willing to fight for me? Scarred or a fool.

Once, as I walked arm in arm with a man (a man I had not told) across the Waterloo Bridge, he turned to me and said, "The opposite of love isn't hate, it's fear." A strange burning crept along my side.

In the hallway, Amir lowered himself to a crouch.

"The first recorded duel in America was fought in Plymouth, Massachusetts, in 1621, between Edward Doty and Edward Leicester," I said. "There's no reason you should know this."

His breath rustled across my knees. "What are you looking for, Arcadia?"

The moon was gone, all moonlight vanished from the hallway. "An explanation," I said. "Expiation."

I MET NEIL LAURIER one ragingly hot summer day in a grimy tavern on Yonge Street. It was late July. I was working for the summer in the university library, in the social sciences department, while Evan painted houses with his friend Fergus. He was living with Fergus, too, in a basement apartment on Bedford Road, in the house of a man who raised pythons, *round as a woman's thigh*, in Fergus's words. The man kept them in large glass terraria, upstairs, above their heads. Evan showed them to me once. The three of us often ate dinner in the apartment together, the two of them regaling me with painting stories— the wild exploits that someone, usually Fergus, had got up to. Nearly pulling down the diamond-cut chandelier in one living room. Underestimating the amount of time it would take to do an exterior job by so much that they were out desperately painting three-story walls at two in the morning by the glow of high-beam flashlights. Evan would giggle into his pizza.

Or we went out for drinks, Fergus and I drinking whiskey sours and Evan, vodka gimlets.

A few times a week I spent the night. I was living, now, in the basement of my parents' house, which had become my apartment and from which I could come and go pretty much as I liked.

I had decided to walk from the library over to Yonge Street to look for shoes. I was searching for a pair to match a turquoise dress I'd bought two weeks before in New York City, where Evan and I had flown for the weekend to celebrate his twenty-first birthday. We'd stayed in the tiny studio of a friend of his sister Maya's, sleeping on sofa cushions on the floor. On my twenty-first, a month before, we'd donned straw hats and elegant clothes and picnicked *sur l'herbe* on the Toronto islands.

The heat on Yonge Street was so thick that I was frightened the rubber soles of my sandals would melt beneath me. Black tar blistered in strips between the slabs of pavement. Water leaked in rivulets and streamed across the sidewalks from dripping air conditioners. Sweat bled across my shoulders, mingling with suntan lotion, salty and sweet.

Exhaust, from the low-slung cars of American tourists or the souped-up American cars of suburban kids, flooded from tailpipes as they trolled the city's main drag, past the tacky head shops, the leather parlors, the house of heavy-metal bouffant hairdos, tiny chrome-filled cafés. My head ached from the shock of contrast—heat addling muscles still in the grip of the library's arctic air-conditioning. I longed for northern forests: if I kept walking north, up this the longest street in the world, one day I would reach the cool enclosure of ferny boughs of pine, though I craved as much the quick slide of a glass of any sort of water.

Dashing across a side street on a red light, I pushed open the heavy doors of the Olde Yorke Tavern, which would stink, I knew, of cigarette smoke, the dim air awash with a gabble of voices from the sports channel, but offer pure anonymity and the blessed sanctuary of frigid air. A dry chill met the slippery heat of my skin. The interior dimness, after the bleached sunlight, was blinding, a flare of deep pink seared against the inside of my eyelids.

When my sight cleared, I noticed a figure sitting at the bar. Neil Laurier, who had been in my Hegel lecture class the previous fall semester. He was reading, denimed legs looped around the metal legs of his bar stool, neck crooked over the pages of Kierkegaard's *Either/Or*. I noted the title when he flipped shut the cover, and that there was a tiny hole near the collar of his worn-gray Joy Division T-shirt.

"Hey," he said, and, lifting the chilled curve of his beer bottle, pressed it to my forehead. He held it still. The bartender, seeing us, no doubt assumed what anyone seeing us might have assumed. That our intentions toward each other were clear. The surprise of it, the ease, the release—I surrendered to the sense of something relaxing deeply in me in a way I never felt with Evan. Nothing premeditated.

I closed my eyes. I sensed but could not see Neil's legs spread wide on either side of me, was aware how easy it would be to reach out and touch the fray of denim, the bumps of his knees. Everything swam across that open shore, some liminal place between heat and cold. He pulled the beer bottle away, a small gasp of skin, and I leaned forward, seeking the cool, until my forehead met his forehead, noses casually bumping, and my lips brushed his cheek. I touched my fingertips to his temples. He did not pull away or stiffen.

I had never before felt such purity of desire, the casualness and immediacy of every gesture, the sweet bright taste of danger. Every breath seemed contagious, reckless. Pulling away, I signaled the bartender, asked him for a glass of water. Neil offered me his beer. I took a swig. When the bartender brought the glass, I downed the water, wiped my lips hurriedly with the back of my hand. "I have to go," I said.

THERE WERE DAYS at a time when I didn't see Amir—when he'd be juggling extra private English lessons with needed-it-yesterday translation gigs, not to mention his regular hours in the copy shop. The Copy Copy Shop. And I, too, was busy, immersed in work. Ray Farr had flown off to Angola. Thousands of bodies had been exhumed from the mass graves in Srebrenica. The expulsion of Hutus from the massive camps in Burundi had begun, thousands upon thousands on the long, forced march back to Rwanda. (Could one legitimately call these refugee camps? Were people refugees simply by virtue of being outside their own borders, even if thousands upon thousands were also murderers? Did one have an obligation to help them, to feed them? Because they were guilty, should one let them starve? Should they be compelled to return?)

My hands ached from typing. People kept calling the office, asking for opinions, for information, for answers, and I believe it is important for people to know, to think about such things.

The world was heating up.

But then he'd ring me. Or I'd ring him. And we'd meet for iced coffee, sit in glorious, Mediterranean sunshine outside one of the cafés on Inverness Street. Or I'd pick him up at the Modern English Language School and we'd head to Holland Park, walk arm in arm along the wooded paths, among the shrieking peacocks. Leaving work, I'd find him slouched on a bench in Highbury Fields, under the line of trees near the Oasis Café, scanning a newspaper, glancing up to see if I'd appeared, munching from a paper bag of takeaway pakoras.

Sometimes he'd ask me questions about Toronto. How green was it? Was it true there was an intersection of streets named College and University? How many subway lines were there? Did I have a favorite café?

"Planning a visit?"

"No," he said with a shrug, "just curious."

"In any case," I said. "I haven't been back in ten years. All this is history."

As lovely as he was, as the time we spent together was, I told no one about him. Not Lola, not Hanna. Certainly not Lux. And the day when Amir came by the Centre to drop off his translations, I made sure I wasn't there. I wanted some privacy, I told myself.

He had a degree in economics from Tehran University. At sixteen, he'd longed to own a red sports car. I didn't ask him any further questions about Basra. He didn't mention her. I suppose I no longer wanted to know exactly what the nature of his relationship to her had been, if his interest had been at all sexual.

One Friday afternoon we rode the underground together out to West Kensington, to pick up Amir's car from a garage run by a friend of his. Radiator trouble, he'd said. As the train doors opened, we stepped onto the aboveground platform into a hurly-burly of noise—the thwack of a helicopter slicing the milky sky overhead.

Nothing else seemed out of the ordinary, although when we hurried up the stairs to the street we met an entranceway jammed with people. Outside, beyond the crowd, the street was cleared except for the white capsules of police cars, a flashing ambulance, fire engines, police officers standing guard in their lime-green safety vests. A bomb? It had all the look of. Across the road the windows of the Gandhi restaurant were cracked. Sand lay piled in the street outside, beside a gaping hole, a man's abandoned hard hat, a row of toppled red plastic safety pylons.

"Gas explosion." A woman with a loaf of bread tucked under one arm turned toward me. "Can't be too careful, though, can they?"

We sidled past people toward the street. Dashed hand in hand away from the stalled block, into a zoo of diverted traffic. People sat leaning on their horns. In front of us, a delivery van—Flora's Bouquets for All Occasions—swerved from a side road, cutting off a little red Peugeot. As if all this were routine, really, both drivers leaped out. The driver of the Peugeot sprang to the back of his car, unlocked the boot, and pulled out a tire iron. Whirling it above his head, he lunged in pursuit of the delivery driver, who set off along the street he'd just driven down, ducking behind parked cars like a nervous rabbit, and only when he realized nothing had shucked off his pursuer did true terror seize his face, as he glanced back once more and began to flee in earnest.

On the corner, a man outside a launderette garbled into his mobile, pointing after the disappearing men. All this sluiced from us. We shook our heads as we ran, evading violence, as if dispersing droplets of water.

Outside Bahram's Luxury Car Garage, a man in blue cover-alls loitered, wolfing a hamburger. Inside, the air was thick with the pungency of oil and other car excrescences. A man in a worn suit jacket, grease dabbing the cuffs of his shirt, leaped from a chair in the windowed interior office and headed briskly toward us, wiping his hands. Mustached, long faced, but hardly mournful. He grabbed Amir by the shoulder. When they broke their embrace, Amir introduced me. "Arcadia's from Toronto," he said, offering this as if it were an explanation.

In his office, Bahram made us tea, which had a unique, car-flavored oiliness. We sat on chairs that swiveled at wonky angles and threatened to expel us. On the wall at Bahram's back was taped a photo of a bikinied girl, ripped from a tabloid, brown skinned with age. The garage hung suspended in quiet. A single sleek blue Jaguar was jacked on hoists in the work bays. The Fiat, Bahram said, waving one arm, was fine, *fine*, and parked across the street.

"Why is it," I asked, cupping my mug in both palms, "that the English drive so many red cars? Have you noticed?"

"Do they?" Bahram said.

"They do."

"Perhaps they're more visible at night." Amir leaned one elbow comfortably against Bahram's desk.

"Like fire trucks, possibly. Though white would be more visible, wouldn't it?"

"Perhaps they like this color," Bahram said. Had there, I wondered as his gaze traveled across me, been other pale girls—other pale girls whom Amir had brought to visit him—between me and Claire?

We told border stories, and I'd been in this situation before, hanging out among the wanderers, the continent jumpers, in which this becomes the point of convergence, our common language. We all easily assume it.

Only last week, Bahram said, his nephew—*he works for British Air*—had gone to Toronto—here he flared me a quick look—for the weekend, because an old school chum had moved there, and he got free standby travel on the airline. And when he came back, he'd been strip-searched and held for hours by British customs officers, despite his British passport, because no one would believe he'd hopped across the pond for the weekend merely to visit a friend, especially not a brown boy like him.

Setting my mug down, I told them about my American friend Nina, whose lost passport had just been returned to her by the FBI, ten years after it had gone missing. Although what was even more remarkable was that no attempt had been made to expunge its altered state: the mustache drawn over her photograph, the darkened eyebrows, the amendment of her name from *Nina* to *Nino*.

Did they look at each other then? Did I imagine that? Do I— now—imagine that?

"Why won't you go back?" he asked me.

"Because I have no desire to."

"Though you could, if you wanted to."

"Yes, if I wanted."

"Are you estranged from your family?"

"No," I said. "Yes. Sort of."

He taught me words. *Seeb*. Handing me an apple. *Darya*. Pointing to the sea on a day we drove there. *Seeneh*. Breast. *You know, when I first began to speak English one of the hardest sounds was the 'th' sound. Say 'thought,' Claire would say to me, and I'd say 'troth.'*

Paradise, he told me, derived from the Persian word for garden.

When he came, he buried his lips against my neck and whispered *Joon*, my love, my darling, *Joonamun*. Or *Fuck*. Tossing his head back. *Fuck*.

I was working at home one morning when Amir rang and asked if he could drop round. Not for long, he said. He was driving up to Birmingham to meet a translation client. In fact he'd be away overnight.

Perhaps half an hour later I heard the distinctive putter of the Fiat's motor, the sudden accelerated whine as Amir reversed into a parking spot. After a moment, the front gate clanged and he was waving at me as he strode along the front walk, then from the top of the outside stairs.

I met him at the door. We kissed. He swung one arm around my waist, delicious man. He wore a cotton suit jacket over his shirt, satchel slung over one shoulder. He'd cut his hair again, razored short over the nape of his neck. "Sorry I can't stay," he said, sweeping into the room.

"Do you have time for a coffee? Tea? A glass of water?"

He shook his head. Dragging the armchair until it faced my desk, he seated himself and began to unbuckle his satchel.

"Are you going into town at all today?" he asked.

"Not to the office. Why?"

"Anywhere central, though? I just wondered if you might be able to run an errand for me."

"What?"

"Deliver a translation job to someone in a bookshop not far from the British Museum. On Gospel Street. It's rather urgent. It can wait, though if you thought you might be able to—"

"Could do." I twisted the felt-tipped pen I held between my

fingers. "I have a meeting at two near the American Embassy."

"I'll pay your tube fare."

"Really, Amir, don't be silly."

Laying a brown padded envelope on the corner of the desk, he took the pen and paper I handed him and wrote down a name, an address, a telephone number. "Right," he said. "Ask for Aliya. I'll ring her to say you'll be dropping round. She said she'd be there till half-six tonight—is that all right?"

"Should be."

"And if she's not there, by any chance, don't leave it, will you, just bring it back. All right?"

"All right."

He stood and, leaning over me, kissed me warmly. "Thank you, my darling." Glancing across at the screen—*breakdowns in the distinctions between war and crime*—as he rose. "I'll ring you as soon as I'm back. I ought to be back tomorrow night."

And everything might have been all right, if my meeting had not run terribly late. Five of us—a French specialist in international law, American and South African political scientists, a Danish conflict-resolution expert—were supposed to be compiling a policy paper on the potential for a global rapid-reaction force, but all we seemed able to do was argue: Would it have a mandate for aggressive "peace enforcement"? Could it be used to pursue war criminals, even within their own jurisdictions? And, above all (I heard my own voice in the fray), who would lead—who could claim the moral authority to lead it?

It was past six by the time I said my goodbyes and fled that airless, windowless, biliously fluorescent room. Downstairs, beyond the gunmetal-gray doors of the lift and the double set of glass doors that led out to the street, rain teemed down. No light sprinkle, either, but a true deluge, as if steamy weather fronts and wind currents swelling and circling in strange new configurations had finally burst. Cars swam past, jetting wet plumes. The gutters roared with water. Silhouettes bobbed in the back of every single taxi. Bag over my head, in a sort of mad shock, I dashed north toward Oxford Street, where a row of buses inched along like lumbering bottom feeders.

If the underground had not failed. That's what the voice over the intercom said: *Eastbound service on the Central Line has failed.* That's all it said. If the telephone on the platform had taken coins, not phone cards. If there had been a machine that issued phone cards. If I'd been able to get anywhere near one of the working phone boxes out on the street, but there were already queues of drenched souls and luckier bodies under the domes of their umbrellas.

It was not quite half past six when I dove into the back of a black cab, even before it had come to a stop at the curb and its dour, pin-striped occupant had paid the driver. Traffic was slow, of course, horribly slow, but I settled for the semblance of any movement at all, lulled by the rubbery, unfamiliar slip-slip of wipers across the windshield. I wrung out my hair. I checked the contents of my carry bag.

By the time we pulled up in front of the Old Fidelity Bookshop, it was past seven. Even through the smeared cab window, I could see that the blinds over the door were drawn. Books shone in the unlit shop front like pallid faces. I asked the driver to wait while I dashed to the front steps and knocked, peered into the interior, then knocked again. When no one answered—I'd tried, then, hadn't I?—I darted back toward the dry cocoon of the cab, counted my money, and asked the driver to take me home.

———

After peeling off my sodden clothes and making myself a cup of tea with brandy, I sank onto the love seat in the study and picked up the telephone to ring Amir's mobile. Presumably he'd be out of its range. If so, I'd leave him a message. Only, after the first ring, an automated female voice cut into the line and told me the number was not in service.

I set down the phone, then picked it up again and keyed in his number at home, where the line rang, nine times, ten times, and no machine picked up.

Rising, I made my way to my desk and sat, chin pressed against my fists. Water gurgled loudly in the downspouts, though the ticking of rain against the glass had stopped. I rang the copy shop, because I knew they were open late, not because I thought he'd be there.

"I'm trying to reach Amir Barmour."

"Amir?" said the voice who answered—Rachel? Wendy? " 'e's on 'oliday this week."

"All week?"

"Yeah," she said. "Can I 'elp you?"

"Do you know by any chance where he's—"

"'oo's this?"

I switched the telephone off.

Birmingham, he'd said, which was not all that far from Manchester, where Claire lived. Where he'd told me Claire lived. Though he'd given no indication of having much of any sort of contact with her. I sat very still, listening acutely, as if trying to pick up some new frequency shifting through the air, the ghostly outlines of foreign objects.

Beyond the garden and the garden beyond, above the shaded silhouettes of chimney pots, apricot clouds billowed into the west. When I opened the kitchen window, the sharp, sweet vegetable exultation of the garden surged in. Chilled air. At any moment he might ring, of course. Tell me he missed me. Ask me if I'd delivered his package.

There's no excuse for what I did. No, there *are* excuses, there are always endless self-justifications.

Better to know. To see. That's what I told myself.

After the evening sky had dimmed to urban purple, after the television crackling for hours through the walls had at last clicked into silence, after the footsteps of Colleen, my upstairs neighbor, had skittered across the floor to reach her ringing telephone, her voice spiraling upward in delight once she'd said hello, after she'd clattered down the stairs, banging the front door shut behind her, I swiveled the venetian blinds in the study completely shut, which I almost never do. In the kitchen, I drew the curtains.

Removing Amir's envelope from my bag, I pressed it gently with my fingertips, as if testing a fruit for ripeness. A translation job. When I lifted the envelope to my ear and shook it, something shushed about inside.

I could have taken a knife and sliced the envelope open. Replaced one envelope with another. If I delivered it in the morning, no one would be the wiser. But I didn't. I switched on the kettle, waited for it to boil, and steamed open the adhesive seal.

How still everything was—not a silence that cushions and embraces, but one that rubs and chafes against the skin. I sat down at the table in the chair where once, three months ago, Lux had sat, sunlight glinting off the little red heart tattooed on her shoulder.

Out of the envelope I drew something in a clear plastic baggy. I knew instantly what it was, for nothing else looks quite like it. Sliding one fingernail along the Ziploc, I pulled free a passport. Riffled my burning fingers through the stiff, multicolored pages.

A Canadian passport. On the identification page was a black-and-white photograph of a black-haired, mustached man. Michael Manera. No one I recognized. Born: Palermo, Italy. Citizenship: Canada. I balanced the passport on my palm. Gently, I laid it on the table, skin alive to the pulse of dangerous information, to something that at any instant might explode.

A TRANSLATION JOB, he'd said, only not the kind I'd thought of. As the night grew lean and long and quieter still, I sat and stared and stared at the blue booklet, as if this way it might reveal itself to me. Goose bumps pixelated my arms. At my wrist, my watch ticked.

I buried my head in my arms and thought, I've allowed myself to be seduced, seduced into trust, seduced by his lucid attention, his courtliness, when all he's seen is my potential usefulness. Pure delusion to think I was ever more than the courier.

And now what was I going to do? What if there are things you decide you'd rather not know? It's too late, of course. Once you know them, you're in, you're implicated.

No more distraction. Or safety. The stakes had changed.

I could reseal the envelope, deliver it in the morning to Aliya at the Old Fidelity Bookshop. Say nothing. Let the secrets keep multiplying.

Or I could get rid of the passport. Toss it in the dustbin. Cut it up and flush it down the toilet. Burn it. But I was leaping to conclusions. I sat up. What if there was some perfectly ordi-nary—*ordinary?*—explanation for its presence? If I got rid of it, there would be questions. The need to come up with some sort of explanation if or when, and presumably when, Amir reappeared.

I could expunge him from my life. Refuse to answer his phone calls, refuse to answer the door if he rang the bell, keep the blinds shut tight if he tried to peer through the window. Not wanting to know any more. Dive back into work with a vengeance, because there would always be work, there would always be conflicts ready to escalate into war.

Just one more wrecked romance. Put it down to that.

Perhaps he'd wanted me to find it. Perhaps he'd believed somehow that I'd do exactly what I'd done. Set it up. Set me up. Acted out of some perverse notion of self-revelation. A sort of undercover trust.

Although it was my curiosity that had got the better of me, my thirst for knowledge, there was no escaping that.

As the sky outside turned passport blue, I staggered up. I paced back and forth—down the hallway, past my white, invaded walls. In the study, I stared at the blank screen of my computer, the hapless, useless shelves of books, the maps with their shifting, thumbtack-stabbed, contested borders.

(No wonder he was so solicitous about my work, so interested in the world's wars.)

I sank into the armchair and wondered who Michael Manera was. Was the photo in the passport truly a snapshot of him? Or of someone else? Did Michael Manera know that his passport had embarked upon this independent journey? Was it destined for someone in London or elsewhere? Refugee or criminal? Someone fleeing a public or a private war?

I must have slept then, or grazed sleep anyway, drooling a little, mouth to the green fabric of the chair. Aware at the same time of a pillow squashed beneath my cheek, the murky breath of another, Neil's whisper, *Love makes its own morality*, as he had once whispered, as we lay in the mess of his ground-floor room, that last month, in the Grace Street house. I'd been half asleep then, too, dozy from sex, a little blue, or I might have heard him better, rather than wondering if he'd said *mortality* or *morality*, then registering Martin Buber, the German-Jewish philosopher whose books he'd lent me, and how Neil, constant kidder, never liked to say things straight. *No,* I'd whispered back. *It's love that makes morality possible.*

At dawn, I locked the passport in the bottom drawer of my filing cabinet, dropped the key into my desk drawer, laced my feet into my walking boots, and set off on foot for Hackney. There were people about, but then, in a city this size, there are always people about, bodies jostling endlessly against other bodies as they pursue their hidden missions, their double lives.

The sky was a soft dove gray. By the time I reached Dalston, fleets of red buses were already swooping toward me. In the Ridley Road market, merchants heaved boxes of papayas and guavas onto their stalls. Clusters of bananas hung from thick hooks. I walked past the fresh kill—pigs' snouts, pigs' feet— breathing in the scent of blood, past a sudden billow of women's silky undergarments, a froth of long white wedding gowns.

It was not that I expected to find Amir's car parked on Amir's street, and I didn't. I stopped for a moment, staring up at his closed windows, his still and listless curtains. What if he wasn't coming back? People disappeared, I knew they did. A girl crouched on the front stoop, on steps I'd run up numerous times. She strained toward a quivering kitten. *"Boy, boy, boy,"* she called.

In a smoky caff, where I felt as much a tourist as any tourist among tables full of East End blokes, I nursed a cup of tea, and, once it was past nine o'clock, headed out to the street to find a call box. When I rang the Modern English Language School, the receptionist answered, and when I asked if Amir were coming in this week, she said no, he'd booked off. Confirmation was all I was looking for, really.

I didn't head home, I walked south, toward one of the entrances to the canal. Here, brick walls lined the waterway. The water itself looked particularly turbid, dank brown and still, nothing one would choose to throw oneself into, and in any case, as far as I knew, the water was too shallow to drown in. I turned east, toward the sun, which rose ahead of me, lurking behind a pale yellow miasma of cloud. Toward the rose gardens of Victoria Park. In the distance ranged wasted fields and the bleak apartment blocks of Tower Hamlets, while close by gnats danced and crickets hummed in the long grass.

There were a few anglers, hunched like herons, none of whom turned as I passed. At the terminus of the path, by Limehouse Basin, a policeman in a lime vest swished a stick through a patch of weeds on the far side of the water, where crushed beer cans and puffy polythene bags like bloated heads bobbed against the bank. Yet he didn't have the urgency of a man searching for a body, and, in any case, I refused to believe this was the fate that had swallowed Amir.

West, beyond the point where I'd picked up the path, in Islington, I had to re-enter the city and hike through the streets—past wide glass-walled shops, pizza takeaways, video-rental outlets—while the canal threaded through a tunnel beneath my feet. North of King's Cross, the towpath grew once again more derelict. The great iron rungs of the old gasworks loomed. A rope hung like a noose from the scaffold cladding one warehouse. Graffiti emblazoning one sooty bridge read: BRUTAL ATTACK and IT COULD BE YOU.

Beyond the Camden Lock, a tourist company's fleet of painted boats lay moored side by side. I kept going, west past the Peterborough Avenue bridge, which led toward home. Past Regent's Park and the cries of the trapped macaws in the zoo, past Little Venice, and on, along the Paddington arm. The farther I walked, the more questions strode through me. What exactly was Amir engaged in? Was he, too, a sort of courier? Was everything he'd told me about himself just feint or filigree, a screen for secrets? Were there other clues I'd missed?

In the heat of the sun, I collapsed on a wrought-iron bench, pulled off my boots, and slapped sticking plasters all over my blistered feet.

Late afternoon, I turned and headed back. The rush of water in a weir, the quiet passing of occasional strangers were in their own way soothing. And, if you are walking east by the canal in the later afternoon, it is impossible for anyone to surprise you from behind—their long shadow will rise up across your path, will slide coolly across your shoulders, before they do.

I didn't stop at the Peterborough Avenue bridge, though, I kept going, eastward once more, scanning about, and it was on the stretch north of St. Pancras, beyond the St. Pancras Lock, that I found him. Across the water, at the near end of a small basin where canal boats were moored. There was no doubt in my mind—the blue shirt, the neat energy with which he leaped from the stern of a canal boat onto a floating dock. "Amir!"

He froze, as if he would deny once again that my voice calling his name had anything to do with him, horror or fear or alarm coursing through him. Then he turned, peering with one hand propped to his forehead, and waved. As if all this were utterly normal. "Hang on just a minute!"

He loosened the mooring ropes of the boat from which he'd leaped. Painted black and white, it had no colorful whirligig of trim as some boats did, just a bright azure belly and the name SWALLOW written in block letters along its prow.

Standing at the tiller on the stern deck, he started the motor and guided the boat out of its mooring, directing it fluently across the canal—perfectly adept, it seemed, at what he was doing. Sweat gathered between my shoulder blades and in my palms.

When he had drawn the boat close along the bank beside me, he cut the motor, knelt, and fed the stern rope loosely through a mooring ring. "Could you?" Indicating the prow, so I walked along the body of the boat, wove the rope I found there through a second mooring ring, fashioned some snarly version of a knot, and walked back.

"Out for a walk, then?" He looked so mild, so cheerful, so gallant.

I punched him.

Tottering, he doubled over, arms flung round himself. Not into the water, thank God, I'd had no intention— "Amir, I'm so sorry." The reverberation of the gesture traveled up and down my arm, which I clutched in horror, as if I could stop myself from any further— Shock swilled through me, and yet, on top of it, a distilled note, a guilty adrenaline rush of satisfaction.

I thought he might tug free the ropes and float away forever. But he didn't. Chin stiffly raised, he folded the creases in his shirt back into the waist of his jeans.

"I'm so sorry." I continued to clutch my fist. "I found the passport." That was one way of putting it.

He nodded. Taking hold of my arm above the elbow, he lifted me, not so delicately, aboard. Nudged me down the steps that led through a tiny door into the narrow galley of the boat. "Wait here." And pulled the door closed behind me.

Inside, with the door drawn, lay a world of honeyed wood. Two slender beds, one to each side, one with a nylon holdall thrown across it and the indentation of a head upon the pillow. The floor swayed as Amir leaped once more to shore. Behind an accordion door, a toilet. A snug kitchen, a small table latched to one wall, two stools, two cooking elements beside a tiny sink. All of which I would have delighted in if we'd simply been setting out on an adventure. I followed the path of his feet along the bank through a row of miniature windows. On the tiny kitchen shelves were crowded tins of tuna fish and baked beans, packets of spaghetti, biscuits, bottles of water, a small bottle of Scotch. A crumb-covered plate lay on the table. Mooring rings clinked, the boat shaking a little. Then, from behind me, came the putter of the engine. When I tugged on the closed door that led up to the prow, it opened.

We began to move. He steered us in a semicircle back toward the mooring basin, but used its width only to change our direction—from west to east.

I could have leaped into the chest-deep water, waded to shore. Or waved my arms and hollered, hoping someone might hear me in one of the warehouses along the bank. But I didn't. Instead I sat down on the small bow deck.

Behind us, a railway train surged past, percussing along its tracks. Above, cars sped obliviously over the Caledonian Road as we slid into the darkness of the Islington tunnel, the coughing of the motor growing huge, the green light at the bow illuminating the curve of slick bricks overhead. Once a steam tug would have pulled a canal boat through this tunnel, while the canal man's children wound their dray horse through the streets above. Whole families used to live on canal boats, slipping through the city like aliens, no home other than the water, bearing their hidden, mysterious cargo. Before the era of steam tugs, canal men would lie on their backs on the flat roofs of their boats, feet to the invisible stonework at their sides, and walk their way out of the dark.

We broke into the light again on the far side of Islington, a blackbird burbling somewhere. At the first lock, I made no move to help Amir—but then he did not seem to require my help. Having opened and shut the first gate, he paced back and forth along the edge of the lock as the water gushed through its sluices and the boat on which I sat sank slowly, the stone walls of the lock rising on either side. An inventor of military rockets had designed the canal's first locks: I decided against telling him this, though perhaps he knew it.

He moored us finally in the east—far east—beyond Victoria Park, by the opposite bank from the towpath, adjacent to a ragged field, near more gasworks. How different the view looked from here, from the deck of a boat, as if I had never seen this stretch of the canal before, although I had walked past, to and fro, only that morning.

The door at the far end of the boat clacked shut and Amir's footsteps approached along the galley. As I entered the kitchen he plucked a bottle of water from a shelf; two glasses; the bottle of Scotch. Fading light bled through gaps in the flowered curtains that he'd pulled across the tiny windows.

"Thirsty?" And I was, I was parched, though a kind of depression also scoured me.

We seated ourselves on the two stools, facing each other across the table.

"Perhaps you wouldn't mind closing the door behind you." I pushed it shut.

"I tried to deliver it," I said. "But my meeting ran late. Then I got stuck in the rain. By the time I got to the bookshop it was closed. So I tried to ring you. Neither of your lines appeared to be in service. Which seemed odd. So I rang the copy shop. They told me you were on holiday."

"You might say that."

"Did you go to Birmingham?"

"No, I didn't go to Birmingham."

"Where does it come from?"

"What does?"

"The passport."

"From Canada."

"That's not what—where is it going?"

"To Turkey. A Kurdish man in Turkey. Who desperately needs to get out of Turkey."

"And how will it get there?"

"Someone will take it."

"Not you."

"Not me, no. That's not my job."

"And your job is?"

"The documentation. Mostly. Though not entirely."

"Documentation."

"I adapt them. Amend them. If they need it. Give them second lives, you might say."

"Where do you get them?"

"Passports? People lose them, or sell them. There's quite a traffic in such things, as I'm sure you know, though I try to be very careful about where I get my supplies."

"You're a passport forger."

"Among other things, as you also know. But that's the most apt word for it, yes."

He remained very still, glass in hand. Stillness pervaded him. He did not look in any obvious way transformed. Same lips. Same fingers. A bit sallow around the eyes, as if he had not slept that much, although he had shaved in the day and a half since I'd last seen him.

"How long have you been doing this?" Parched in a way that no amount of water, or Scotch and water, would quench.

"I'm not sure I really feel comfortable telling you just at the moment, which has nothing to do with you—though I will tell you, I don't do it for Hong Kong businessmen or wealthy Rwandan *génocidaires* or—one could go on—I do it for refugees. Naturally, I can't always be sure. I do my best. As you know, there are all sorts of reasons people want to flee one life for another." He rubbed the side of one hand quizzically against his cheek. "You look appalled. I'm surprised, actually, that you look so appalled."

I stood then, and began to pace, though, in the tiny kitchen, there was very little room to pace. "For a start, it's criminal." And dangerous.

"Right. And the conditions under which some people are forced to flee are equally criminal under international law."

"What if you were caught?"

"I'd say exactly that. And that there has been a history of this sort of action in wartime. In Europe, I'd point out, during the last World War. And that some of the people who provided such documentation were afterward declared heroes. And it is *not* a crime, if you are a genuine refugee, to travel on false documents. According to the Geneva Convention. And that we live now, also, in wartime. At least some of us do. So surely the same sort of rules, or allowances, ought to apply."

"And if you were charged?"

"Prison if I were convicted. Particularly if they had clear evidence. I presume."

"Could they throw you out of the country?"

"I'm a British citizen. So, no, not so easily."

"This is what you did for Basra, isn't it?"

"It is."

"Where is she?"

"In Toronto. And I know she made it in, because a friend, a colleague of mine, met her, and told me."

"I thought that organization, Rights Now, was helping her."

His hands moved as he talked, touching things: his glass, the table, the air. *Toronto.* "They were, they did, they brought her here. I believe originally they were trying to arrange for her to go to Canada, but there was some trouble, or the case was simply moving very slowly, and there was some risk at the camp in Kenya—the government was trying to resettle people elsewhere or send them back. She had, she has, an uncle in London. Who agreed to sponsor her. But he wanted to marry her off. He's very traditional. And that wasn't at all what she wanted. She's vulnerable, you know, because of the trouble she'd been in back in Somalia, because of her notoriety, because of those songs—no clan, no extended family is going to support her, wherever she is. And, of course, she wants to sing. She was singing in the refugee camp, putting on occasional concerts. This man reckoned she'd be grateful—he'd forgive the past and she's beautiful, so—he reckoned she'd just shut up."

"And?"

He rose, pulled open the little fridge and extracted a package of cheese from it. He ripped the plastic from a packet of crackers and brought both crackers and cheese to the table. With a paring knife, he began slicing the cheese in quick, deft cuts. "She wouldn't shut up. She sang. Quite literally. He locked her in the house and she kept singing. And when she wouldn't marry the man he wanted, he threatened to turn her in. She escaped from his house, and so we decided to try for Canada. It would have been risky having her claim refugee status, because she was traveling from here, and they would have just said, why didn't you claim in England? Or, since you're arriving from England, you're hardly in danger. Sorry. Though the visa route's tricky. It involves quite a lot of preparation. D'you know all this? I'll take a client shopping to make sure they have the right clothes, make sure their haircut matches the photograph in the passport as closely as possible, prepare them to answer quite specific questions about the place where they're going, where they're claiming to live. It's a lot of work, frankly. But if an immigration officer's at all suspicious, they'll ask very, very particular questions."

"And she made it in."

"Yeah, she's in."

"She's safe, she's—" He offered me a cracker, but I shook my head.

"I know she made it in," he said. "That's all I know."

"What do you want from me?"

"Want from you?"

"My passport? A few more tips about Toronto?"

He rocked back his stool, wiping his palms across his thighs. "Frankly, there isn't much value in your passport, not in this sort of trade, though if you had a Canadian passport with a Somali or an Algerian name in it—"

"Oh, fuck off."

"Arcadia, I don't want your passport."

"Perhaps you'd like me to run a few more errands for you."

"Well, I don't know." He righted his stool, the muscles of his face quickening, offering, as so often, the appearance—the *illusion*—of trust, of accessible thought. "I shouldn't have asked you. I was going to tell you. I really thought, because of the work you do, that you would—though perhaps that's a ludicrous assumption. Then there was the matter of deciding when to tell you. And how. Because it's a rather difficult thing to consider confiding."

I said nothing.

"Right," he said. He cleared his throat; arranged the crackers on a plate, set olives and radishes in the middle of them. "The other day someone rang me. I try, needless to say, to be extremely careful. And said that I ought to move my office and all my equipment as swiftly as possible. And myself. I may have to leave the flat as well, but I ought to be able to stay here for a while. The boat belongs to a friend, in case you're wondering. And what I simply thought was if I could get that last one off—"

I stood mere inches from him, my stomach looping itself in a sequence of snaky knots. The room felt even closer than before, as though, if I moved, I would bump against the wall or ceiling.

"Does Claire know?"

"She knew. Toward the end. It was not, I might add, the reason we split up."

"There are other ways of helping people."

"Right—give money to some aid society? Support some humanitarian organization so they can keep themselves in business, maintaining their refugee camps? *Areh*, Arcadia"—he threw up his hands—"someone helped me, I'll help someone. I didn't get to Europe on my own bloody documentation."

"*You* make money off them."

"Not very much money, let me tell you. And it requires money. And I'm a very small-scale operation. You *know* the conditions under which people flee, how they flee wars. You write about intervention. You're the specialist, aren't you? Right, then—why not think of this as my private act of intervention—or my small gesture in an era of globalization. Free up the transit of people. Make borders a little more porous. Why not? If there's free transit of goods and free traffic of information, which you're always going on about—"

"It would be chaos."

"Oh, the terror of those in industrialized nations as the hordes descend, which they wouldn't."

"People aren't just fleeing from something, they're fleeing *to*. They *want* borders, safety, government. States. Which is not an argument in favor of nationalism—"

He leaped to his feet. "Is that what all this is about? *Really?*"

"No," I said as my voice rose. "It's the risk. It seems so crazy when you've—"

"How can you, the theorist, possibly judge me?"

"I'm not judging you!"

"Shhh." Finger to his lips. "I've chosen this risk. Chosen it." I'd have backed away from him if there were anywhere to back. "Perhaps if you took a few more risks yourself. Isn't that the question, really, Arcadia? It is, isn't it? What are the risks that you'd be willing to take?"

II

LIGHT GLINTED along one shifting wing. Above my head a nozzle spewed a small, relentless wind drier than desert air, while the vibrating walls around me heaved and roared. Outside the bubble of my window, the sun burned down, nothing to intercept its rays at thirty-seven thousand feet. Far below swelled humps of cloud.

I had not pulled down the window flap, as the flight attendants had requested, in order to simulate womblike darkness, the better to watch the movie and numb the frantic restlessness that characterizes any long-haul daytime flight, to obliterate the fact that we were indeed in flight and hurtling through the air.

The effect was not of darkness, exactly, or not true darkness, but—if I stared through the gaps between the windows and seats ahead of me—of a row of eyelids lit pink, as if we were inside a head glimpsing a ferocity of light through closed eyes. A brilliant aurora speared through any exposed chinks.

At my feet, on the floor between the two rows of seats, lay a girl wrapped in a thin airline blanket, smacking her lips softly as she slept. The middle seat, which she had occupied, was empty, while on the aisle, the woman whom I presumed to be her mother stared at the desperate shadows on the screen in front of us. Her grunts and chuckles, the garbled mutterings that drifted through her headphones, became my soundtrack.

Through dark glasses (which I wore not only to hide my red-rimmed eyes, but because I was not inclined to talk to anyone), I stared down at the clouds, ribbed now, in an expanse of tighter undulations. Somewhere below lay the North Atlantic. Shock percolated through me, as if, after two days, my body was lost in its own sea—nothing but exhaustion and now momentum mixing alchemically with shock to create some new element.

How easy it had been in the end. To pick up the phone. Wait for the ticket agent's voice. Name my point of origin, repeat my destination. When did I wish to travel? As soon as possible.

And there was a seat—by chance or luck. I didn't wince at the price, though at any other time I would have called it astronomical, just gave the woman the numbers on my credit card.

It had been two in the morning—the middle of my second night without sleep. My drenched and smelly clothes still lay on the floor of the bathroom, the clothes I'd soaked some hours before, leaping from the deck of the canal boat. I'd heard Amir's voice behind me as I leaped, his shout—but didn't stop, just spat out a mouthful of murky water, boots sliding over the muck of the bottom.

It was true the water did not reach above my head and I could wade, after a fashion, to the far bank, grasp its cement cusp, and drag myself onto the towpath. "Arcadia," he called again—it was not yet dark, not fully dark, but I did not turn around to look at him, just spat again and scrambled to my feet and sloshingly began to jog.

Beside the path, empty crisp packets scudded against great lobs of concrete. There was barely an overhead lamp in sight. Ordinarily I would never have considered being on this stretch of the canal by myself, or with anyone, at dusk or after dark. My keys and the change purse I'd brought with me were still in my pockets, thank God, Amir's words like a trail streaming out behind me. *What risks,* though what I heard was not only *risks,* but *What borders are you prepared to cross?*

Ten minutes later, I stood on the platform of the Mile End tube station, stared at surreptitiously by other figures, breathing hard and dripping.

Rising from my airplane seat, I stepped carefully over the sleeping girl and squeezed past her mother into the aisle.

In the middle of the plane, by the emergency exit, a woman in an emerald sari stood waiting for a vacant toilet. I poured myself a paper cup of water from the wall dispenser and tried to imagine what Basra Alale must have felt traveling this same route with the forged passport tucked in her cloth money sack or some interior pocket. On this very flight there could be someone, no doubt was someone, more than one, making the same sort of journey. Who knew, in any case, what desperation others carried with them, what crazy sorrow, vertiginous loss, feverish yearning? What dreams of haven?

I thought, too, of the girl who'd traveled the reverse of this route ten years before, who'd clutched sunglasses even though it was nighttime, when windows reflect nothing but your own reflection back at you (seeing red, seeing green, blood on the grass, trees closing in), who'd believed in the fantastic properties of escape and her own capacity for reinvention. Had that act been truly riskless?

Once, Lux had told me, she, too, had been in the midst of a transatlantic journey—to somewhere or home from somewhere, I couldn't remember which. She, too, had risen from her seat and made her way toward the toilets at the back of the plane. She'd poured herself a cup of water and was on the verge of taking a sip when the plane bucked in a spasm of turbulence. Losing her footing, spilling water, she fell toward one of the lavatory doors—fell into it so hard that she pushed the crease in the middle of the door open.

It couldn't have been locked properly. There was a woman inside. Not sitting on the toilet. When the door folded open, the overhead light in the cubicle flicked off, although a dim glow still emanated from somewhere. The woman stood inches from Lux, flattened against the opposite wall. Lux began apologizing profusely. Then she noticed that, cupped in her palm, the woman held something, pieces of something, and that, though the woman's mouth was closed, her jaw and the muscles in her throat were working rapidly.

"She didn't move or speak," Lux said, "but I could tell she was eating her passport. She must have torn it up somehow."

Her passport, or perhaps not hers. She might have flushed it, real or forged, down the toilet. Many did. Perhaps she was frightened that the toilet would clog (it often happened). Perhaps she had been warned of just this possibility. Perhaps she had been ordered to do as she was doing by those who'd engineered her journey, or decided herself that this was the best way to get rid of all traces of a previous life.

"What did you do?" I asked Lux.

She stared at me, as if what she'd done next ought to have been obvious. "Closed the door. Waited until I heard the lock click and the little red 'Occupied' sign slid all the way over."

Far below, land began to reveal itself and I gazed down, uneasy excitement rising as I picked out points I recognized, reconstructing the landscape like a map—a map of the past that I discovered I still knew. Inland from the rugged coast of Labrador, we traveled over pine forest as dense and furred as moss. We flew along the north shore of the St. Lawrence, and over the wide St. Lawrence itself, our shadow darting like a tiny fish over the water. The tin roofs of farmhouses sparked. The island of Montreal, a sudden glimpse of urban aggregation, quickly dissolved into cloud as we steered north of the river again, then out of cloud and over a maze of lakes as small as fish themselves, more woods, our shadow flitting now over land like a swallow.

The width of Lake Simcoe opened beneath us like a palm— no, a closed hand with thumb and forefinger extended. The details of the map grew clearer, the contours of the landscape magnified—the furrows of shoreline, of promontory, the varie- gated green of trees, the floaty, cell-like speed of traffic on high- ways. We approached Toronto in a circle from the north, then from the west, over industrial parks and endless cul-de-sacs and crescents and the blue gleam of pea-sized swimming pools, vast acres of identical roofs of tract homes and two-car garages. Did anything look familiar? But then, it had been years and years since I had made this approach. We kept circling, over the inner city now, its grid intersected by long diagonal roads that marked the ghost paths of old Indian trails. A glimpse of the shore of that bigger lake, Ontario, like an inland ocean, the upthrust of downtown towers, as something rose in my chest, a needle-like spear that rose—

"The CNN Tower," shrieked the girl, who, awake, sat in the seat next to mine. Craning against her seat belt, she leaned across me toward the window.

"It's the CN Tower, actually," I said. "Canadian National." Like a local, and listened, startled, to the shift in my intonation, the slippage of my own vowels.

They were Danish, the mother said. In English. She was bringing her daughter to visit her ex-husband's family. They were planning a day trip to Niagara Falls.

Sunlight tilted in through the exposed windows on the far side of the plane. In London it would be ten in the evening. Where was Amir? Sitting at the tawny table in the canal boat, eating baked beans on toast, drinking from the bottle of Scotch, strategizing on his mobile, preparing to forge more new lives, to penetrate more borders? Had he tried to call?

I came in on a Canadian passport, which I had kept current all these years, for traveling as a Canadian is perhaps the easiest way to find safe passage. In a crisis, everyone wants to be one of us. We're known globally for our innocuousness, our apparent harmlessness. No wonder our passports are the most forged in the world.

I stopped in an airport washroom on my way to the customs and immigration hall. One of the stalls was occupied, another out of order. Clogged with abandoned passports? Could be. The last place to jettison the detritus of escape before claiming refugee status.

In the immigration hall, under a pixelboard sign that welcomed me in two official languages, a woman in a blue shirt asked where I was going, where I lived, what was the purpose of my visit. *Any gifts?* I was frightened that I might begin babbling, say that I barely knew what I was doing in Toronto, that I felt stunned to be here, that I was trying to decide what were appropriate or necessary acts of intervention.

Voices jangled the air, air fraught with nervousness and incipient peril, and I wondered what Basra had felt as she'd stood here, holding that passport. What had the officer asked her? How had she responded? If she'd made it in safely, then what? A black-haired couple with tired shoulders were conducted toward the private interrogation rooms while the hall rang with the metal clatter of officers' stamps.

I walked through unimpeded, though my heart was knocking. Took the stairs that led down to the baggage carousels, handed my stamped entry card to the waiting customs officer, who waved me past. A pair of sliding doors sprang open at my approach, and I ran the gauntlet of arrival—past turbaned men, small girls in frilly dresses, lovers clasping roses wrapped in plastic, the gazes of those on this side of the door looking nearly as anxious. Expectant, disappointed, they stared at me as if I were both alien and emissary. I slipped from them, dizzy but unclaimed and unencumbered.

A bank machine spilled bills at me, my bank card flicking out like a tongue. I looked around and tried to decide if what I registered was something as distinctive as memory or simply the anonymous familiarity of any airport. What felt Canadian? The signs. ELEVATORS/ASCENSEURS. A girl's voice that rose at the end of a sentence like a question? The long corridor of the terminal stretching away to my left felt specifically recalled—as did the view, I thought, as I stepped through another set of sliding doors into the thick humidity of outdoor air. Blunt square columns. Gashes of sunlight falling on the cement tiers of the parking garage beyond. New words, old words grew in my mouth like plums.

"Where to?" the taxi driver asked, once I'd dropped my bags in the trunk and we'd settled ourselves in his huge, plush, air-conditioned vehicle.

"The New Media building, please." I'd thought that far ahead. "It's downtown—"

"I know where it is." He turned to me and nodded. He was young, eager to please. A burgundy turban sheathed his head, his facial hair still wispy. He had switched on the radio, tuned low to a rock station, so that I could just catch the North

American pulse of a deejay's voice, the fast parade of music. Outside, long, wide cars sped all around us—cars that despite their sleek, aerodynamic forms seemed built to take up as much room as possible on the road. The whole dimension of traffic was different: everything made an assumption about claiming space. Monster trucks. We zoomed down what felt like the wrong side of the highway, surrounded by a flock of blue-on-white Ontario license plates.

"You here on business?"

"Visiting."

"Been here before?"

"Mmm—born here, grew up here."

"Yeah?" His voice rose, cracking in its higher register, and he grinned into the rearview mirror, as if we'd been playing some guessing game in which I'd bested him, yet he was happy to be gracious in defeat.

From one of the multiple lanes of the Queen Elizabeth Way, which led into the Gardiner Expressway, the vista of the city opened ahead of us, the blinding sun now at our backs. By the shores of the lake, the dense cluster of downtown towers rippled in hot smog, rose blurrily as if from mist.

On the verge that separated the two streams of traffic on Lake Shore Boulevard, Canada geese blithely cropped at grass. The white domes of the old Sunnyside Bathing Pavilion rose, the lake a metal blue behind them.

We took Spadina north. On King, two streetcars rumbled in their tracks, surging from east and west across the intersection like great tablets striped in white and red and black, the wires that powered them fizzing. Everywhere I looked there were wires overhead, bolts of electricity strung between tall cement trees, cables webbing their way through the air above every street—an oddly small-town sight, as if at some point in the transition to metropolis, someone had neglected to put them underground.

The driver wove through back streets, turned a corner, and pulled up on Queen outside a pair of plate-glass doors. Across the street the bookstore called Between the Covers still stood— Evan and I used to meet there sometimes among the shelves of poetry. Everything registered as a little shock. The tiny printing shop beside the bookstore—where we'd bought pads of brilliantly colored paper in fuchsia, lemon, indigo, lime—was now a shop that sold sunglasses.

I stepped out once more into sullen, steamy heat, paid the driver, grabbed my bags. Two girls in platform sandals made a wobbly dash through traffic. He waved at them. Everything looked very glossy, very sleek.

I felt visible in some peculiar way, or as if some part of me wanted someone to witness my arrival. I glanced about for a familiar face, the electricity of recognition, even though the impulse seemed slightly deranged.

Inside the refrigerated gloom of the New Media's entrance hall, under a bank of television monitors, a young man sat behind a desk, his shoulders thick as logs, scalp shining beneath the delicate fuzz of his brush cut and the wires of his headset, three silver rings in his right nostril—more bouncer than receptionist, I'd have said.

"Who for?"

"Is Lux Hearne in?"

"She expecting you?" He spoke with a kind of tamed aggression, capable of deterring casual fan, riffraff, the uncool.

"I'm her sister, Arcadia." A prickle traveled up my neck. Lux could be anywhere. She could have jetted off on a morning flight—I was offering her less warning of arrival than she'd ever given me. "I just flew in from London."

He stared, perhaps searching for some point of resemblance. My bloodshot eyes? My bags were out of sight at my feet. A woman in stretchy silver pants passed by, gave him a little trill with her fingers as he buzzed her through the glass doors behind him. "Renée," he said, speaking into his headset. "Someone to see Lux. Unh-uh. What's your name again?"

"Arcadia," I said. "Arcadia Hearne." He didn't ask me to sit down, but then there was nowhere to sit.

I pulled my bottled water from my shoulder bag, swilled the rest of the water, set the bottle on the floor. My skin burned. My feet felt tipsy, as if they might slide from underneath me. The whole world had a delirious edge.

In front of me, a young woman appeared, a slice of midriff bared between T-shirt and jeans, her hair a mass of tiny tufts held back by plastic hair grips. "Hi?" she said.

"I'm Arcadia." I held out my hand. Above the bouncer, images flashed: tanks, rubble, a swimming pool, rubble. Somewhere someone was singing. "Lux's sister. We've talked on the phone before. Is she free? If not, I—"

She nodded, tufts jiggling, and reached to take one of my bags. "You just arrived?"

"I did. It's a sort of surprise."

"Right on." She held the glass door open for me. Past a staircase, halfway down a corridor, she pushed open another door.

"Thanks," I said.

"Watch your feet."

Rivers of cable serpentined across the floor, winding between desks and the open spaces between them, toward an arena at the front of the large room where the woman in silver pants stood, one hip cocked, as she spoke to the camera gripped by the roving videographer in front of her. People's mouths moved differently here when they talked.

Behind her, out on the sidewalk, boys pressed their faces to the plate-glass windows—a boy ripped off his T-shirt, exposing the long glide of his torso, jeans slung loose and low around his hips.

Lux's element.

Across the room, angled away from me, Lux leaned against a desk, a coffee mug clasped in both hands and pressed to her stomach. The wings of her shoulder blades made a shadow outline beneath her T-shirt. Little kinks darted up my spine. When the gaze of the dreadlocked man in conversation with her lifted, she turned—mere reflex at first, before her eyebrows and her mouth seized up, and in that instant she looked more startled than I had ever seen her. With a cry, she dropped her mug, scattering liquid and shards of china. "Oh my God," she said. "What are you doing here?"

ONE LATE SEPTEMBER AFTERNOON, Neil Laurier came loping toward me across the Alexandra College courtyard. Slung over one shoulder and diagonally across his chest was a bag I would have described as an airplane carry-on, made of stiff blue nylon. Books protruded from it, and a pad of paper. "Hey," he said, slowing as he approached, and lifted a palm in greeting. He seemed taller than I remembered. Another worn T-shirt, different band this time. Aged running shoes. Already there was a kind of intimacy between us, as if we'd leaped past several stages of acquaintanceship, although I had not seen him since that day in the Olde Yorke Tavern in July.

He tipped the book I was carrying toward him so that he could read the spine. *Raleigh in the New World.* "What's that about?" he asked, as if we were simply picking up a conversation.

I humped my shoulders. "The colonization of Virginia and the rape of Guyana."

He did not respond, just squinted at me, one hand roving over his forehead. "Mind stepping into the shade for a moment?"

He made his request sound so ordinary, not suggestive but practical. Together we made our way across the glistering lawn toward one of the thick stone portals that led out to the street. At each instant, my body was acutely aware of each tiny move his body made. The long, strong bones gliding beneath his skin. His loose, emphatic lope.

Passing out of the sunlight into the dim and silky cool was once again blinding, a flare out of which Neil rematerialized.

His skin was more tanned than when I'd last seen him—beautifully tawny. He stood taller than Evan, a few inches taller than me. A furze of dark hair met between his eyebrows. He shifted the strap of his bag so that the weight hung against his back.

"Did you get out of town at all this summer?" I asked.

He nodded. "You?"

"I had two weeks off at the end and I went north for one of them."

"Cottage?"

"Farm." The farm that Evan's father owned. Not all that far north. With Evan. "Where'd you go?"

"My folks have a cabin in the Laurentians, an hour north of Montreal, so I spent all August lying in the woods reading the complete works of Kierkegaard."

"You did not."

He shrugged. "I finished *The Seducer's Diary*."

"So *are* you an undergrad?"

"Till January. Skipped a semester once. Philosophy major. Then I'm going into the graduate program."

"In philosophy?"

"It's great job training." There was no obvious facetiousness in his voice. "You taking any philosophy?"

"Not this semester."

"Damn," he said.

From his back pocket, he drew a piece of cigarette paper, spat a piece of gum into it, and tossed the little ball into the garbage can in the far corner of the entryway. Extracting a pen from his bag, he began to write on the corner of a flyer pinned to the bulletin board beside us. When the ink dried up, he shook the pen, then ripped off the corner of the paper and continued writing, balancing the paper on one denimed knee, pen marks—numbers—nearly bursting through it. He handed me the scrap. "I'm in Frye," he said. Frye was another one of the colleges. I presumed he meant he lived there. "If you ever feel like getting together, let me know."

"WHY DID YOU COME?" Lux asked. We were sitting in her kitchen.

"I told you," I said. "Because it seemed like time. I decided I'd been away long enough."

"But why now?"

"Lux," I said, "three months ago you were in my garden telling me to come."

She'd made us coffee that she swore was decaf, though it had jittered through me in acid bolts as if there were indeed caffeine in it. Nothing I'd said yet seemed to satisfy her. She'd asked me first as we cabbed it west along Queen toward the tree-lined street where she and Haydee shared an apartment. And again as we set out for the corner to buy takeout food for dinner, past the greengrocer called Square Fruit and Vegetables which Lux pointed out with rapture. *That's why I moved here,* she said. *I went in once and asked if they had any square fruit and the Portuguese woman at the cash looked at me as if I was insane.*

The air was muzzy with the scent of globular peaches stacked in baskets, the musk of cherries, hornets swarming around them. Melons sat in lush piles. In the next shopwindow, behind tinted plate glass, hung shimmery dresses suspended on slowly twisting chains. Refinished wardrobes, faux-aged plant pots lined the sidewalk. A few steps farther and the druggy fragrance of fruit mingled with, then was replaced by the charbroiled flavors of rotisserie chicken. Not all that far from here, though long ago, I used to play pool with Neil.

"Did something happen?" Lux asked.

"Nothing terrible's happened. I haven't quit my job."

"Is it for work?"

"No," I said. "Though there are people I can meet up with here."

She frowned. "Have you told Mum and Dad?"

"Not yet. I will soon. I just wanted to settle a little first. Get my bearings."

We'd eaten our takeout chicken on Lux's back deck, under the shade of a linden tree, shooing away wasps, licking our fingers when we were through. We downed cherries by the handful and spat the pits into a bowl, as we used to do as children. Afterward we moved inside and Lux made coffee, setting two mugs and a carton of milk on her arborite kitchen table.

"I'm sorry," I said. My hands were shaking, the air stirring in low rolls, a susurration of leaves pouring in through the open window, a fanning of green waves. "I think I have to go to bed."

In her bedroom, Lux pulled sheets from the top of her closet, then led the way down the hall to a smaller room where she unfurled a futon mattress across the floor. There was a desk in this room, shelves lined with videotapes, CDs, travel guides. I seated myself in the only chair, gravity pulling me toward the ground, helpless to move any further. Stuffing a pillow into its case while Lux billowed a sheet into the air, I eyed the rough patches of skin at her elbows, the kinks of her dark hair, the blunt line of her painted toenails, and thought how strange all this was—how strange to be the visitor; the fact that I had never before seen her in her own apartment.

Yawning, I swallowed air, and tried to steady myself, to focus. "Lux," I said, "you haven't, by any chance, heard from Basra Alale, have you?"

"Basra Alale?"

"The woman I delivered your package to in London."

"No," Lux said. She crouched as she looked up. "Why? I wasn't expecting to."

"I'd heard she might be here." Cautiously.

"From who?"

"Someone I met through work. Who knew of her a little."

Her forehead wrinkled. "What would she be doing here?"

"She came here. I mean, she left London." I searched her face for clues, for any sign of things she might be concealing. Did she know what the money I'd delivered had been used for?

"How would she have got in?"

"I'm not sure," I said. "I was wondering if any of the people at Rights Now might know."

"I could ask them. I could call them tomorrow." Did she know some if not all of those American bills had been used to buy a forged Canadian passport?

"If she's here," I said, "I just thought I'd try, if I could, to check and make sure she's all right."

I woke, having no idea where I was or what time it was. The blurred dial of a travel alarm clock drifted somewhere in the dark. When I reached out one hand, I touched floor. From somewhere, a *scritch, scritch*—an animal clawing its way down bark? Then, distantly, but approaching, the swoop and roar of a streetcar—a Toronto streetcar—hurtling at night speeds along its tracks. Underneath that, like a ghost stratum, lay London, remembered, conjured London—the grit and sulfur of morning rush hour, the crowds of Camden, litter of handbills, teeming heat. Elsewhere. I rolled onto my side, pulled the sheet over my head, and when I woke next, to silence, the sun was blinding.

I lay on my back and pondered. I felt oddly disembodied, rinsed and out of kilter. Who knew what would happen as soon as I rose and opened the bedroom door.

The rest of the apartment was silent. On the kitchen table, I found a set of keys and a note from Lux saying she'd left for work. It was eleven o'clock. Haydee was dancing in Stuttgart. I made an espresso in the espresso maker on the counter, cooled it with ice, burned two slices of toast, and ate them before wandering out to the deck. I had never planned for a return. I had never planned what I would do upon return. I peered down at the alley that ran between this row of houses and those on the next street, sat in a pool of marbled sunlight, and wondered who Amir Barmour really was and how much of his story I was to believe and what else I didn't know about him. Would I call him—when would I call him? But if he was still on the canal boat, I did not have a way to reach him.

The phone rang and I let it ring, knowing there was almost no chance it could be for me. It stopped; then, almost immediately, began again. I ducked back into the kitchen and, hesitating only fractionally, lifted the portable receiver from the counter.

"Oh good," Lux said, "I was hoping you'd answer. I didn't wake you, did I?"

"No, you didn't. I was up."

"Did you sleep well?"

"Very well. Wonderfully. Though I haven't been lately. Sorry to arrive on your doorstep in such a state of exhaustion."

"I called Rights Now this morning." The din of a television station jabbered behind her while her voice unspooled with uncomplicated brightness, as if she couldn't possibly be hiding anything. "They said they hadn't heard about Basra Alale being here, they said they'd turned her case over to this Somali women's organization in London. The Somalia-England Resettlement Programme. They gave me the number if you want it."

"Sure," I said. I found a ballpoint pen in a tin can.

"Cay—Mum may call me later. If I speak to her, what do you want me to say?"

"Don't say anything. I'll call soon. Later. Really I shall."

"I have plans tonight, is that okay? I'm working late and then I have this dinner, it's kind of an industry thing I have to go to. Are you going to be staying at my place tonight?"

"If that's all right."

"It's fine."

"Lux, really—you don't have to entertain me."

As soon as I hung up, I thought, I should have asked her where their phone books are.

If I were Lux or Haydee, if I were a music-TV journalist or a dancer, if I traveled the world but came home to an apartment on the top floor of an old brick house in downtown Toronto, if I had met my girlfriend when she stopped me in the street to ask where I'd bought my boots (as, four years back, Haydee had stopped Lux), where would I keep my phone books?

Had Lux always slept with girls?

When I left, she was nineteen, in the first year of radio and television arts, still living at home with our parents, and I had no idea then who she'd slept with or if she'd ever slept with anyone. If she went out on dates, she never talked about them. She had friends, male and female, but never gave any sign of *going out* with any of them.

We didn't talk much then. Living in the basement, immersed in my own life, I didn't see that much of her. What I remembered was the pitch of her body—the way she'd stiffen and tilt and bolt, as if never quite at home in her limbs or her clothes, although then, as always, she'd had an arresting and luxuriant voice. For her last high-school formal, she asked to borrow the blue satin dress I'd bought to wear with Evan. Skinny, she somehow looked stuffed into it, wore black work boots beneath, her hair longer then, frizzier, belling about her face. If there was anguish in her (who's more beautiful, the endless internal comparisons), I refused to think about it. And that last year, I was particularly oblivious to her.

Perhaps, when Lux told our parents about Haydee, or introduced her to them, they were relieved more than anything— after what I'd put them through. They weren't upset, Lux insisted, and, it was true, they'd never seemed to be. Always, obliquely there, encircling any familial discussion that edged toward, then veered from sex: the issue of what had happened to me, of what I'd done. Perhaps, in comparison, what Haydee offered seemed relatively simple and safe.

I believe in loyalty, Lux had said once, drunk, in the pub down the street from my flat, and she would not look at me as she spoke. *I really, really do.*

I wasn't sure how she expected me to respond to that.

I found the phone books not in any kitchen cupboard (where I kept mine), not in the hall closet stuffed with boots and shoes, not in their living room, where mirrors were propped along one wall, a purple strip of yoga mat in front of them. Not in the smaller room where I'd spent the night, but in the bedroom, under the bed, swathed in saffron sheets, that Lux shared with her lover.

The white pages, when I extracted it, smelled, I thought, of massage oil. I wiped the cover with one arm and carried it down the hall to the kitchen.

A chain activated the ceiling fan above the table, its wings gaining speed as they sliced through the hot air. Outside, a cicada's cry began to climb—a sound so lush, so thick with memories of North American high summer that I nearly doubled over.

Pen in hand, a glass of water at my side, I cracked open the phone book. I licked the tip of my index finger, as I used to do in the days when I read the phone directories in the British Library Reading Room, and began to flick through the pages, past the Personal to the Business listings. *Soa— Som—* There were five Somali organizations. The Somali-Canadian Friendship Centre. The Somalia Women's Group on Lawrence West. I wrote down the numbers and addresses for all of them on a piece of paper. I could call the number in London that Lux had given me, but I suspected that if Basra had fled here on a forged passport, she was unlikely to have had much, if anything, to do with a resettlement program there.

There were no Alales in the Personal listings.

Soon I would call my parents. But not yet.

All those years ago, in the British Library, I would search not only the Metropolitan Toronto directory but those for other cities, too. New York. Berlin. Paris. Hong Kong. Honolulu. Surreptitiously, I'd pour over phone books like encyclopedias of the heart, like maps of the world. And I found Biedermans and Lauriers, one year an N. Laurier in Rome. I'd write down the phone numbers, stare at them, think about calling, before crumpling the paper I'd jotted them on. What could I possibly say?

Now, as then, I looked for Evan's name, and Neil's. Under B. Under L. Now, as then, I found no trace of them. Not in Toronto.

Little better than searching for ghosts.

NEIL AND I PLAYED POOL. I waited almost two weeks before I called him, and when I did, this was what he suggested—though not in the student union building where I knew there were a couple of tables. On Queen Street, just west of Bathurst, a place called the Corral—if that wasn't too far away. The kind of tavern where grizzled old guys in baseball caps sat at the bar sucking back Molson Ex from bottles. Not unlike the bar where we'd met, in fact. (These were the days before pool tables could be found in the back of every bar or café.)

I told Neil I was a terrible player. I didn't say that I'd learned to play with Lux in the basement of a tract home in Pickering, east along the lake shore—taught by the tall twin sons of a colleague of my father's, a man who was an engineer at the Pickering nuclear-power plant. At night, as we drove home after those visits, I would sometimes turn to look back at the lights on the row of pale, bulbous domes spanning the sky behind us.

"If you hate the place," he added, "we can always go somewhere else."

I suggested four that first time, a Tuesday, because Evan had a class. Rilke's poetry. The *Duino Elegies*. In German. An elective. Because meeting in daytime seemed less compromising some- how, though, naturally, the tavern was dark and windowless. I sat at the bar with my bottle of beer, swallowing smoke, stared at the clock as the old men stared at me, and waited, jumpy. I pinched the skin on the back of one hand and thought, It's my choice to be here. I have other friends. We go out together. Moon over drinks. Go to movies. Not parties, since Evan hated parties. He thought they were a pointless way to socialize if what you wanted was to talk to people. I hesitated before arguing that sometimes the point wasn't simply to talk to people.

Twenty minutes passed. Perhaps Neil had forgotten. I grew furious. Perhaps it was all some joke and he had no intention of showing up.

At twenty-five past, I stood, paid for my beer, and was buttoning my brown suede jacket when he burst through the door, the white globe of a motorcycle helmet bulging under one arm. He dropped to his knees in front of me. "I'm a craven man, Cay. I wasn't sure you'd wait. I got held up. This is the last time I try being honest with the library. I told them I'd lost a book. Well, I told them the truth, that I'd left it on a bus. And the woman I was dealing with freaked. Totally—maybe you know her, I forgot, you work there, don't you, maybe I'd better be careful what I say. Anyway, it was like the whole edifice of learning was about to crumble. I'd just burned the library at Alexandria. Whatever. She said, how were they supposed to maintain a world-class university when people like me insisted—*insisted*—on behaving so irresponsibly. I was convinced I was going to get thirty lashes."

"But you didn't." I stopped buttoning.

"Just a fine." He stood, set the helmet on a stool, and dusted off his jeans, so noncommittally it was as if he'd already forgot- ten the drama of the gesture that had dirtied them. The leather coat he flung off was almost knee length, rather shapeless, the leather old and cracked and shiny.

"Do you want me to lash you?"

"Lash me, Cay, lash me." He jostled me amiably with an elbow. "What can I get you to drink?"

We were unexpectedly well matched at pool. Neil was by far the better player, able to set up shots with mathematical elegance so that the balls would spin and ricochet exactly as he said they would.

"Consequences," he cried out, "think about consequences." As he demonstrated the angle the cue ball would take. "Watch this, watch this." He was lean and tall and goofy. He took silly risks. He was reading Wittgenstein. The *Tractatus* poked from the pocket of his leather coat. His T-shirt split from the waist of his jeans as he contorted himself, head twisted over his shoulder, to jab a backward shot.

I picked up the ball, which had crashed to the floor, set it back on the table, and aligned my shot, warmed by the click of successful contact, the soft *oomph* as my ball hit the pocket.

I told myself I'd come to see if I would feel a repeat of the calm release I'd felt in Neil's presence that day back in July. A smooth settling, which did not preclude excitement. And I felt it.

We did not touch. We were careful not to touch except in the most offhand or businesslike way—Neil adjusting my fingers so that they formed a better bridge on the green felt surface. *Like this, like this!* If we bumped each other, we excused ourselves. *Oops, sorry.*

He told me that he'd had the motorbike for a couple of years but was thinking of getting rid of it. He asked me where I lived and I said a few blocks north of Eglinton, in a separate apartment in the basement of my parents' house. I did not say that I hadn't moved out because I couldn't, because if I did, Evan wanted me to move in with him. My parents didn't know this, and I wasn't sure, anyway, that they would like the idea of my moving in with Evan.

In late August, Evan had returned to the house on Alborough Avenue that Peter, his father, had bought back from his mother when Peter had returned (sans Isobel Melo) to Toronto at the beginning of July. It had shocked me that Evan would move in with his father, about whom he was often scathingly vituperative. About Peter's sports cars (there were a couple, a Triumph, an Audi). His stock trading (professorship just a disguise for being a stock-market weasel). His blond bonhomie.

Yet I knew that Evan loved the house, its old solidity, the gold washes of light through the upstairs rooms. Why else would he return there? He needed, he wanted a home, I realized. He'd even gone so far as to retrieve the cat Eddypuss from his mother in Montreal. The house *was* beautiful, though I honestly couldn't imagine moving into it.

"Is that all right?" Neil asked. Living at home, I assumed he meant.

"It's all right."

We said good night outside on Queen Street.

"I can give you a lift on the bike if you want."

"It's all right."

"How'll you get home? Or wherever you're going."

"Streetcar." A streetcar rumbled past, its twin green headlamps shining like boat lamps. "Look," I said, shifting from hip to hip. Under a fizzing streetlight, the spiky bloodstain on my jacket, from the day that Evan had cut himself in the ravine, had turned brown. A splotch just above my right breast, where I'd embraced him, not necessarily recognizable as blood. I touched the stain sometimes when I was alone. I could have had the jacket dry-cleaned, but hadn't.

"You should know this." I crossed my arms over my chest. "I have a boyfriend—Evan Biederman—we've been together for a couple of years."

"It's okay," Neil said, and thrust his hand forward for me to shake. "I know that."

WHEN WAS THE POINT that I began to think of my father's work in terms of risk? Not as a child, certainly. Early on, I simply thought of him as a scientist. Someone who researched things. He told us his work had to do with energy, with heat and light, and I imagined him soft-shoeing through rooms full of lightbulbs, because even then I was aware of him as an elegant man.

When he came home in the evenings, he would pour himself a glass of red wine. He listened to Rachmaninoff and Janáček. Sometimes, in winter, he would cross-country ski to work, as did a number of the European researchers who were his colleagues. In summer, some of them biked.

One year, in school, we were given a tour of the nuclear-power plant that was part of the nuclear-research facility where our fathers (mostly our fathers) worked. We were told how clean this power was, and what promises it held out for the future, our future, and how Canadians had, in this very place, developed the design for a reactor now in use all over the world. We were given yellow jackets and boots to wear—at least this is what I recall—as we were led through halls, through cooling rooms whose white surfaces seemed so slick and clean as to be sources of light themselves. Naturally, there were parts of the plant that we were not taken to see.

By the time we moved to Toronto and I turned ten, I knew my father to be a nuclear engineer. He told me he worked with tritium, that he and a team of Canadians were known for their expertise in tritium-handling technology, that tritium was used in remote lighting—lights that had to be seen from great distances, such as those on airport runways. He did not say that tritium was a by-product both of the nuclear industry and nuclear weapons, that it was used in bombs and throughout the American nuclear arsenal (and for this reason Americans were eager to get their hands on Canadian tritium), that tritium was extraordinarily volatile, easily breathed in or soaked up through the skin.

When the Three Mile Island reactor fire took place in Pennsylvania, the year I was fourteen, he reassured us, soothed Lux of her fear of dying in a radioactive fire. The Americans used a different kind of reactor, he said, and ours were safer. Yes, there were risks, there were always risks, but, where we lived, they were very, very slim.

He talked to us about nuclear cowboys and nuclear fishermen. Nuclear cowboys, he said, were reckless, cavalier in the face of radiation, believing they could do anything. Whereas nuclear fishermen were careful and approached their source of power as if it were a fruitful but dangerous sea: they took only what they needed and respected its dangers. He and his colleagues, he said, were nuclear fishermen.

Sometimes my parents had dinner parties, the dining room bobbing with nuclear fishermen and their wives. My mother, too, was elegant, though there was a hint of wariness about her that wasn't in my father. She had, as my father loved to point out, beautiful hands, and wore trim pantsuits, and sometimes, if she were dressing for the evening, would gather her shoulder-length hair into a loose chignon.

They had met in Lepreau, New Brunswick. My mother would show us photographs in her album from this time. On a rug flung over the hood of Benedict's bright-red MG convertible, she lounged like a mermaid (a little self-consciously, as if posed?). A ribbon of ocean ran behind her. There was my father, wind-tousled, possibly cocky, draped against the side of his car. Then she would tell us the story of how they'd met.

She was waitressing for the summer in a fish-and-chip restaurant when Benedict pulled up one day. After finishing her arts degree, she'd left New Zealand and traveled through Italy, and was trying to save up enough money to make her way across Canada. She'd come to New Brunswick hoping to see whales. As soon as she opened her mouth to take his order, he was intrigued—what was a girl with an accent like hers doing waiting tables in a little town on the Bay of Fundy? He was no local either, but, just out of graduate school, was researching sites for potential nuclear-power stations. (How soon did he tell her this? How exactly did he tell her this?) One weekend, they drove a day and a night to Montreal to find her the real espresso that she craved.

Two months later, at the end of the summer, Benedict gave her an ultimatum: go off and travel the country, or travel the world with me.

(Did she deliberate long, or did passion propel her? Did she think of her choice as simply exchanging one adventure for another—the road west for this dashing man, this herald of the future?)

They didn't travel. Not then. At least not any farther than Ottawa. Though later they would travel to conferences around the globe—conferences on nuclear-reactor design, nuclear-power policy and waste disposal, issues of nuclear safety.

———

What had pushed my father into safety issues? For this was what he had become in recent years, a safety man. Perhaps it was calculation (he was capable of calculation as well as charm), seeing that the public tide had turned more adamantly against the peaceful wonders of nuclear power. Or a more sober recognition that there were issues of waste management and leakages, cracks in the infrastructure of aging nuclear-power plants, which neither the industry nor his commitment to nuclear power had properly addressed. Only that morning, in the paper I'd bought down the street from Lux's apartment, there'd been an article about closures and what the article called the possible "early death" of some Canadian-designed reactors. On the other hand, my father had never given any sign that he was intending to abandon his passion altogether.

Had my mother said anything to provoke or push him into safety issues? Perhaps she'd been a voice, an infiltrator, insisting on the importance of safety—recently or all along. A voice of reason. Safety for us, for anyone—on her knees in front of us, wiping the hair from our eyes, running her fingers over our skin, in the kitchen of the white bungalow in Deep Creek. Or, alone with him, had she simply been complicit, stilling any worries in the face of his enthusiasm?

When we moved to Toronto, my father left his job with Canada Atomic, and, at Ontario Power, joined the team they had assembled to work on the international experimental fusion reactor. Its fuel source was to be tritium (hence his involvement), deuterium, and heavy hydrogen, three times as heavy as regular hydrogen and much easier to source than the uranium used in fission reactors. Fission split atoms, he explained. Fusion bound them. As animated, as fluent in his descriptions to us, as lit with conviction as ever.

A fusion reactor would not have the same potential for runaway reactions, its waste products would be far less noxious, and thus (if they could only get it to work and agree on which country was to build the prototype), it would be much more inherently safe. He explained all this at our bedside, by the glow of a leaf-shaped night-light.

These days I could follow his career on-line and I did, sometimes, tracking him through his articles, even though doing so aroused such a complex jarring of emotion in me. "Vitrification Processes for Deep Space Disposal." "Safety Procedures for Introducing a Nuclear Source into the Work Environment." This man, this fantastically intelligent man, this fantastically intelligent, potentially lethal man—known for his expertise in leading safety reviews, for drawing up procedures for monitoring radiation-emission levels, for conducting risk-assessment studies—was he as much of a fisherman as he maintained? Or was he capable of covert denial and failing to heed warnings of incipient danger?

One night in April, that last spring in Toronto, before I ran away to London, I had challenged him. It was late, I had not been paying much attention to the news, when I turned on the radio to discover that half a world away, in a place called Chernobyl, Reactor #4 in a Ukrainian nuclear-power plant had exploded.

How can you just sit here?

I'd burst up the basement stairs. He wasn't sitting, he was standing in the middle of the living room, must have started to his feet at the sound of the door. There was music playing. Presumably my mother had gone to bed.

Don't you feel guilty?

"Arcadia," he said with equanimity, gravity, no false cheeriness. He spoke—I wanted to believe—as if to a colleague, at least as if to take me seriously, as I wanted to be spoken to, as a father should speak to a daughter. "Given that I have a particular knowledge and expertise, it's my responsibility not to run away but to ascertain the best possible way to use it."

Dapper even then, glass in hand. Light from the hallway strode along his half-Italian cheekbones. Perhaps he *had* been on the phone all evening with colleagues. What I knew was how difficult it was, always, to be angry with him, to argue with him. *Cool* was how Evan had once described him, which he qualified by saying that there were times when my father unnerved him. It was true my father could be prickly around Evan. Evan thought my father was protective of me, and perhaps he was. They seemed incapable of recognizing each other as differently idealistic men. But then, I'd think, Evan had an equally uneasy relationship with his own father.

In the living room that night, I rocked from foot to foot, the odor of chlorine spinning around me like a second skin, for I had been swimming nearly every day in the university pool. Though what I smelled through the bleach, when I lifted my hands to my face, was the tang of Neil's semen.

I did not call my parents. Instead, I rode the subway north to Eglinton and took a bus north from there. I could have walked in from Avenue Road on the west or Yonge Street on the east. (Did Amir teach his clients that there was a street in Toronto with the tautological name of Avenue Road, and that *Yonge* is pronounced *Young*?) Impossible not to feel that I was traveling back in time—seeing my parents here was not like seeing them in various European cities. The word *nostalgia*, coined by a Swiss doctor in 1678, originally described a soldier's fear that he would never see his homeland again. What was the opposite of nostalgia? Whatever it was, I felt it.

The variety store still stood on the corner, the place where Lux and I used to buy chewing gum and hockey cards and chocolate bars. They sold flowers, too, nothing glamorous, but I assembled a bouquet of baby's breath and dahlias and had them wrapped.

How do you dress for such a return? If your arms are chilled and your heart swings like a pendulum? I'd worn sandals and a dress.

It was a little after six-thirty. By now my mother should have arrived home, commuting north by subway and bus, as I had come, from her job as an administrator in the university's department of botany. Then she would take the dog, her dog, really, a golden lab named Lily, out for a walk. These things I knew. (And that some days—mysteriously—she went canoeing.) There was a risk (a very small risk) that I would meet her striding briskly toward me down the sidewalk.

But I didn't. The house stood as it always had: red brick, two storied, close to its neighbors, in whose drives were strewn children's toys—a fluorescent-pink tricycle, a flounce of skipping rope. When I left, this was a neighborhood of late adolescence, of children recently grown. There was no sign of a car, but then it could simply be in their garage. These days, my father, a free-lance consultant, worked mostly at home, out of an office in the basement, where I had once lived.

No movement at all. No whinnying through the fat leaves of the chestnut, which flourished, taller than ever, on the front lawn. No rustling in the hedgerow beside the short, paved driveway. There was a long moment when I simply observed, and felt nothing.

I couldn't do it. I walked past one way, came to a stop at the end of the block and loitered, as if admiring the cropped lawns and the tall, old trees and the tended flower beds, before turning back. Perhaps if there had been some glimpse of motion inside, but even the curtains in the downstairs windows were drawn. Yet this was something my mother had always done in the heat of the summer, because she didn't believe in wasting energy (nuclear energy) on air-conditioning.

What if they weren't home? I couldn't bear the possibility of approaching the door only to have no one answer.

At the near end of the block, a road ran north, crossing the ravine that coiled behind the house. On the far side, stone steps led down to the bottom of the slope. Here, too, all was quiet. No children were playing, which surprised me, because when we were growing up, except during school hours, children were always racing through the woods or in the grass along the edge of the creek. Wilderness was a place we were let loose to play in. Even at dinnertime, family meals were inevitably staggered so that someone was always in the woods, kicking sticks, patiently waiting. The year I turned sixteen, however, the city buried the creek in a drainage pipe, covered it over with sod, and gated it, because across the city, in a creek similar to this one, a girl had drowned. Now, no doubt, mothers looked out into the trees, the long grass, the tricky shadows, and saw only danger.

Beyond the trees that led up toward the house, my parents were visible, raised, as if upon a platform, radiant in the long light. They had built a deck, which, having never seen it, I'd forgotten about. My mother lounged in a wooden deck chair, legs crossed, sunglasses shielding her eyes, the dog named Lily in a sloppy pile at her feet. Across from her, my father stood at the railing, turned away from me, gazing out. Smoke seeped from the edges of a covered barbecue and wisped around them. I tried to tell, from the angle of their limbs, if they were happy, if, like some mathematical equation, this might be decipherable. Was this the life that my mother, crossing oceans, had imagined? Was this my father's longed-for private paradise?

He'd told me once, in some European city, that his ultimate test when doing a risk assessment in a nuclear-power plant was *Would I let you or Anne or Lux in there? It's the emotional test. And if I'm convinced that you'll be safe, it's safe.*

Why didn't this reassure me?

For years, I'd fought to make his work seem comprehensible; I'd searched for signs, for any sign of ambivalence or torment, and could not find it.

Sometimes, in London, I'd wake, bolt up, and think, I grew up beside an experimental nuclear reactor. When you're a child, whatever life you have seems normal, because you have no other and in any case you have no choice about it. *You faced no greater risk there than anywhere,* my father said repeatedly. *Arcadia, there's more radiation released in radon gas that seeps naturally into people's basements.*

He believed in the exporting of Canadian nuclear technology, that by sending our knowledge out beyond our borders, we were helping other, smaller nations achieve economic independence and energy self-sufficiency. He'd told me this as he poured me a glass of wine in a Copenhagen restaurant. He downplayed the risk—not the risk, the *fact*, as I pointed out in that same restaurant—that our heavy-water reactors were being used in certain countries eager for another sort of power, to process weapons fuel. We were not innocents. We could even be called collaborators.

He was, according to a recent article, a proponent of the plan to accept weapons-grade plutonium from the Americans and Russians for disposal in Canadian reactors, as long, he argued, as there was an international structure in place to ensure that it was indeed weapons fuel that was being converted. Swords into plowshares.

There were times when, despite myself, I'd stare into the mirror in my bathroom, peering at my skin as if it would turn suddenly translucent and reveal whatever traces there were of the risks that he'd exposed us to. Perhaps there were dangers that he hadn't admitted and something *was* growing inside me. Then I'd tell myself it was dangerous even to think like this, better simply to believe him. Despite the nights when I woke out of dreams in which my limbs, sometimes one limb, had turned pale blue and was softly glowing in the dark.

In a pay phone on Yonge Street, I dropped a quarter in the coin slot and listened to the phone at the other end begin to ring. Would my mother raise herself from her chair or my father start from the railing? Whose shoes were making their way across the wooden floor like a pulse, like my own pulse frenetically ticking?

"Hello?" my mother said. Even after all these years, her voice still held residual traces of New Zealand.

"Hi," I said, crushing the flowers a little as I bumped back against the wall of the phone booth.

"Arcadia!" Just at that moment a bus squealed to a stop on the opposite side of the street, by the park, releasing its pneumatic brakes with elephantine gusto. "Where are you? There's rather a lot of noise."

"I'm down at the corner," I said.

I TOOK A BUS from Lawrence West Station, miles from downtown, traveling west through suburban flatlands, through stretches of the city that I was convinced I had never seen before, far, far from the city that I had grown up in. I strained through the gritty window to follow the street numbers, which leaped between squat, bleak apartment buildings—mid-rises, low-rises—and the wide Sahara of malls and plazas. Stepping out at last on the corner of Lawrence and Kipling, I clutched my sun hat to my head, and, bashed by a hot wind, had to dive into a bus shelter in order to pull out my notepad and check once again the address that I was looking for.

The Somalia Women's Group was housed in a building at the edge of a small strip mall. Past a shimmer of cars. Through a steel door, which banged shut behind me. Up a fluorescently lit flight of stairs. Bookended between a dentist's and a podiatrist's office.

I had decided to start with the Women's Group because, it seemed to me, if Basra *was* on her own, a women's organization was one place that she might get in touch with. Amir had said she could not count on the support of any extended family or clan, here or anywhere. She might not want this. On the other hand, perhaps she had her own network of friends and contacts. Lacking proper documentation or working papers, presumably she did need support of some kind. Since I was, in an admittedly oblique way, one of the agents who had helped bring her here, the least I could do was find out what had happened to her. Make sure she was safe. See if there was anything I could do to help her.

Yet this whole train of thought, my whole rationale for action, was based on the assumption, the possibly shaky assumption, that what Amir had told me was true. And I had no way to verify this other than finding Basra—the surest way of confirming whether or not he had told me the truth. I needed to know this— was he what he'd said he was?—as much as anything.

"You are looking for something?"

Behind the open door of the Somalia Women's Group's office, a woman rose from a desk. Her face was rounder than Basra's. She wore a light jacket over a blouse and tailored skirt, her hair pulled tight against her scalp, as Basra's had been. It was difficult to tell how old she was.

I'm not sure what I had expected: more of a drop-in center, a room full of garrulous women chatting in chairs, walls lined with posters; not this two-desk office, not all that unlike the office where I worked.

"I'm looking for someone, actually," I said. "A young woman named Basra Alale. We met in London, England, which is where I live, but I believe she's moved to Toronto, and I wondered if she might have come here, or if you might have heard of her, or know how I might get in touch with her."

The woman's expression did not change: helpful, not unfriendly, though beneath that it retained a diplomatic neutrality. Rolling a ballpoint pen between her fingers, she glanced down at the binder of papers on her desk. To her left, there *was* a second room: full of chairs, its walls lined with posters.

"No, I am sorry," she said. She gave an eloquent shrug. "I do not know of her."

Even if she'd only heard Basra's name in passing, given that it was unusual, she would surely remember it.

"If she'd come here, would there be some record of her?"

"Yes. Probably. But I do not think she has been here. I do not recognize this name."

"Could I leave a message with you? In case she does come. Leave a number. If, by chance, you do run into her, could you tell her that Arcadia Hearne, whom she met in London with Amir, Amir Barmour, is trying to get in touch with her?"

No shift in her expression. No twitch of recognition or cover-up. But with perfect pleasantness and amiability, she handed me a yellow legal pad and her pen.

It was only once I was out in the street again, buffeted by heat and wind, that it struck me what a hopeless way to proceed this was. No one was going to tell me anything. At any Somali-Canadian organization. Why should anybody, taking one look at me, listening to the sort of questions that I was asking, trust me enough to talk? Why *wouldn't* they be suspicious? Perhaps I was some government agent tracking down an illegal immigrant. Even if I thought I hardly looked like one.

In some sense, I thought I owed it to her, to try to find her, although I wondered if this was simply selfishness masking itself as altruism, a kind of mania in which I had ultimately my own interests at heart. Yet I truly did wonder what had become of her.

Raising my arm, I scanned the wide lanes of speeding traffic in the hope that a taxi might materialize out of the chimera of heat. One did eventually, rattled to a stop, windows open, no air-conditioning, the driver nattering on in a language that might be Somali. Which it was, the driver said, when I asked him.

"Where you going?" A box of fried chicken lay open on the front passenger seat, the whole cab pungent with it.

"To Dixon," I told him, for no one who studied contemporary war, who came from Toronto, who spent any time on-line tracking the outcomes of such wars, could fail to know that when the exodus of Somali refugees began, thousands made their way to this city and settled out near the airport in an area that came to be known as Dixon. Throughout the refugee camps of East Africa, people knew where Dixon was, like a country, a hoped-for haven.

"Where you want to go exactly?"

"The corner of Dixon and Kipling." Though I knew this corner as nothing but a point on a map and had no real idea what I would find there.

A complex of frayed white apartment towers, their exterior walls leaching toward gray, rust bleeding through the black metal of their balconies, wind whipping between them. Halfway up one wall, which faced the street, the blackened arc of a fire still scarred the paint above one balcony. Run-down suburbia that has already gone through a couple of generations—although hardly derelict; the grounds beneath the towers, lawns and manmade hillocks studded with stubby pines, were clean and neatly landscaped.

I thought back to London, but could picture nowhere with the same frontier expansiveness—heat and flatness coupled with the constant, shattering reminder of jet-age travel.

Overhead, a plane was approaching, wing lights blazing, thundering in its descent, so close above the towers, it seemed about to shear them. As the ground beneath my feet began to quake, no one other than me looked up.

Not the girl in a red dress, head uncovered, who skipped among the pines toward a metal jungle gym and swing set, called out to by a woman, her head diaphanously veiled, pushing a pram along the sidewalk. I asked the woman if she knew Basra. I asked a man in a T-shirt, with a whistle around his neck, refereeing a gaggle of boys as they chased a soccer ball across the grass. Shouting as another plane began its close approach. I did not ask the men—young men in reflector shades, gold chains around their necks, lounging with cell phones in their palms, a straight-backed old man in cloth cap and thick wool suit—seated on benches in the shade. All Somali. I asked a woman swathed from head to toe in blue, only the thinnest slit in the fabric revealing her eyes, her hands (the only other exposed skin) clutching two plastic shopping bags.

I entered the first building without being stopped, its exterior doors propped open with a piece of wood, perhaps to let what little trace of a breeze there was enter. No one in the lobby or what might have been a game room off the lobby. In the basement I found the laundry room, full of chattering women and children, who, though their faces shone, seemed oblivious to the furnace temperatures while sweat poured from me, women who shook their heads at my questions as they pulled socks from dryers and folded piles of fabric-softener-scented clothes.

Of course I hoped that I might simply spot her, in one place or another, and see her face alight in startled, hazy recollection, as I traipsed through other laundry rooms, as I dashed across six lanes of traffic, as I trawled the aisles of a discount supermarket, my feet slipping in my sandals, feeling my sweat cool to clamminess on my skin. I wanted her to be safe. I wanted to be reassured of her safety. Everywhere, I listened for the sound of singing.

Only men sat in the mall's doughnut shops, nursing cups of coffee. (Most, if not all, survivors of a civil war. Some victims, some no doubt perpetrators.) Somali men lolled inside taxis parked in a row along the curb, baseball caps over their eyes, engines running. Clan loyalties were perhaps as strong here as over there. Perhaps Basra's songs protesting the stranglehold of clan allegiances were known here. Perhaps I should not, in fact, be asking after her.

Perhaps she had got in safely and then something had happened to her. On the other hand, perhaps she had not got in, despite what Amir had said. Perhaps she was being held in detention. Was there a way to find this out without calling unwanted attention to her?

Then again, perhaps I should just give up.

As I sank onto a stool in a doughnut shop, once more Amir's voice went clanging through me. *What risks are you willing to take?* And my own voice, too. *It isn't just a matter of risk. Given that you can't act everywhere, do everything, just as you can't intervene in all conflicts, you have to determine your zones of responsibility. That's what we grapple with in intervention studies. You have to choose where you're going to take your risks, set limits. As you travel from zones of safety into zones of danger. That's what makes risk meaningful.*

Did you act in the place where danger seemed the worst, the moral horrors gravest, or (if you could not confirm the extent of genocidal cleansing) in a place where atrocities were easier to clarify? Or where the possibility for effective action seemed likeliest? Or choose somewhere simply because it was closer (Bosnia rather than Rwanda, say), or because what happened was more likely to impinge on your life? Did you stick to what was happening on your doorstep—though how did you define doorstep, when there was another level of risk, risks that we all ran whether we wanted to or not, global dangers that soaked our lives like fate, that crossed borders with ease. Viruses, the hysteria of nationalism, mutated weather patterns, radioactive clouds, runoff from pesticides.

Understand, I said, *that the risks I choose may not be the risks you'd choose. All right?*

Listen. (Was I talking out loud as I approached the bus stop? Was this why the woman inside the bus shelter stared at me?)

Do you remember the lifeboat dilemma? We discussed it once.
People packed into a lifeboat. Survivors of a wreck. There's not
enough food and water for everyone. Should they try to rescue those
still in the water, desperate to get aboard? Or should they abandon
them? Should they toss some of those already in the boat over the
side so that at least some of those who remain stand a better chance
of surviving? There's a philosophical corollary to the problem, one
they didn't teach us in high school. At least according to certain
schools of moral philosophy. You can judge various courses of
action, but unless you're actually in the boat, actually facing those
particular dangers, trying to decide what risks to run, you have no
way of knowing what you'd do.

I searched for them. Sitting at the kitchen table in my parents'
house, for, after two nights at Lux's, I had moved myself up
there. It felt strange, of course it felt strange, as much for what
had changed as for what had not. I was sleeping (barely sleeping) in the room that had once been Lux's, but had now been
stripped of personality (her stacks of records, bird's nest, stuffed
sheep, spherical baby-blue plastic radio) and neutralized into a
guest room. In the basement, where I had lived for two years
and which was now my father's office, there was no sign of
anything that had once been mine—no trace of the trompe l'oeil
ceiling that Evan had painted the summer I moved down there.

Yet the house felt eerily permeable. From the outside, saturated
by the green of trees. In the basement, behind the blank white
ceiling, clouds scudded across a hyacinth sky—strips of cirrus
met by puffy cumulus. A couple of putti, plump cherubs, gazed
down, coyly winking. Stars blinked out of darkening blue in the
alcove where I'd kept my bed. A wild sky, a baroque sky. A sky
that had made me feel as if I was in a church or a boudoir or out

camping—Evan had bristled when I'd told him this, as if I'd said the wrong thing. *But I love it*, I remember shouting at him.

An hour or so after my mother left for work, my father, too, headed out without a briefcase or explanation. Nor had I asked him for one. We were all still being cautious around one another, their joy at my reappearance matched by apprehensiveness, as if we were each doing a delicate dance across a minefield.

I sat down with a coffee, a notepad, and the phone book. Pulled back my hair. I called the alumni-records office at the university and told the woman who answered that I was trying to trace someone. When I gave Evan's name, my mouth felt full of burrs, milkweed silk, feathers.

"We don't give out addresses over the phone," she said.

"Even to other alumni?" Didn't I count as some sort of alumna, since I'd attended, even if I hadn't graduated?

"Even to other alumni. There's an on-line file of alumni who have agreed to make their addresses accessible to other alumni that we advise people to try."

"Would it be possible to tell me if you have a current address for him or when you last had an address?"

She gave a brisk and disapproving sigh. "Name again?" I spelled it. "Graduate, undergraduate?"

"Undergraduate."

No current information, she clipped when she retrieved me from hold—at least (and this was some reassurance) there seemed to be a record of his name.

"Wait," I said, "wait, there's another one." Philosophy. Undergraduate, then graduate.

"The second degree is incomplete," she said. "Is that the one?"

"I expect."

No current information there either. Her fingers battered

away at some keyboard. "A surprising number of our alumni do not bother to keep us up to date."

Under *M* in the phone book, I found four listings for McConnell, F. None specifically for McConnell, Fergus, who had been Evan's second in the duel. For a couple of years, I, too, had considered Fergus my friend, given that the three of us had so often done things together, given the particular intimacy that can exist between a girl, her lover, and her lover's best friend. Fergus saw girls, too, Evan assured me. There was an ex-girlfriend whom he still obsessed over, but he almost never brought a girl along when the three of us went out. To the art gallery during free evening hours. For dim sum in Chinatown. The day we built a kite (well, they did—Evan's plans, Fergus's construction) and watched it soar aloft from the beach along Ward's Island.

On first meeting, Fergus seemed tough—he had a pugilist's face, squashed nose, cheekbones so high and in such fine relief that they looked as if they had been punched into shape. A stocky build quite unlike Evan's. Yet the art he made—he was a student at the art college—contradicted his appearance: miniature etchings, delicate constructions made of wire. This intrigued me, though when I tried to talk to him about his work, he resisted.

If you know a city well, you can tell from a phone number where in the city you are calling, picture the distance that you are trying to span. I, on the other hand, rusty after all these years, could only guess.

At the first number, a woman named Frieda answered; the second was an automated message from Frank and Uma; the third was not in service; the fourth was a message from an unidentified and unidentifiable male voice, which I decided I'd try again later.

Nothing under new listings.

The art college, like the university, did not give out alumni addresses over the phone. Honestly, the man's voice implied, what did I expect?

"Could you just tell me if you have a record of a graduate named Fergus Dexter McConnell?" From somewhere out of the past, Fergus's middle name flew.

There was one.

"If I wrote a letter and sent it to you, could you forward it?" I was growing dry mouthed and desperate.

"I presume so." Did that mean yes?

Under *L*, I found a Carl Landauer, the name of the philosophy graduate student who had been Neil's second but whom I had not really known. I had never spent time with Neil in a way that would have allowed me to meet his friends—though I would see the two of them sometimes outside the entrance to the library, tall Carl in a baggy trench coat hunched against the wind, both inhaling violently, trying to light up cigarettes. I'd wave with a charade of casualness as I passed.

Carl was an analytic philosopher, Neil had explained, whereas he was a continentalist. Drawn to the precision and scintillation of symbolic logic, Carl also studied the pre-Socratics and the Stoics (through the lens of logic), whereas Neil was more interested in questions of the good life.

Did analytic philosophers believe in dueling? That is to say, how would one justify it? Approach it not as a romantic or existentialist gesture but as strategy, as serving some utilitarian function? How had Carl rationalized it?

Was this the right Carl Landauer? I did not know, but at the tone, I left my name and number.

WE KISSED. But this was all we did. In the alleys behind the taverns or pool halls where we met. Beneath the shadowed overhang of fire escapes. Neil had stopped talking about consequences.

Within the dark contours of back doorways, pressed against pocked steel or the corrugated iron of storage garages, the hot fug of cooking oil and the clatter of restaurant cutlery seeping through the air around us, we opened our mouths, probing with our tongues, wandering within that crazy geography of teeth and gum, our lips growing slippery with saliva. Hungry but not rushed or frantic. We necked—that slang word, teenage word. When we broke for breath, inhaled, exhaled, white tufts of warm air billowed from our mouths. High up, beyond Neil's shoulder, spread the pale nimbus of a streetlamp. Our mouths became the locus of pleasure (the chafing of his chin against mine, the swelling of lips). There is an art to this, when the aim is not to move on but to sustain sensation, find rhythm and variety, feed deeply and be deeply fed.

We met most weeks throughout the first semester, though not

every week. Usually late on Tuesday afternoons, when Evan had a class. During the Christmas break, we didn't see each other, but began again in January when Neil started graduate school and moved from Frye College into the graduate-student residence. We barely spoke by phone—I asked Neil not to call me and I called him only from pay phones. Usually we left messages for each other in the library. I'd devised a system: we tucked the notes into books that had never been signed out. The summer before, bored on the job, I'd begun to compile a list of such volumes. *Sources of Organic Carbon in the Littoral of Lake Gloomier. High Pheasants in Theory and Practice.* I was amazed, actually, that titles like these had piqued no one else's curiosity. On the other hand, I was willing to gamble that, untouched so far, the books were likely to remain so. Mostly we relied on the *Littoral of Lake Gloomier*, grateful for the continued obscurity of Manitoban shorelines. We never signed the notes, just slipped them between cover and frontispiece, a method that seemed virtually foolproof, as long as Evan wasn't spying on me.

Tuesdays I could count on, usually, though Neil hated to confirm plans or where we'd meet until the last minute, so that each week, each time I made my way through the fifth-floor science stacks, there was that nagging note of instability. I hardly saw him around campus—that is to say, he did not seek me out at the library tables or the carrels where I studied, even to say hello. Once, though, he sat down across from me, pulled out Heidegger's *The Question Concerning Technology*, and, brow furrowed, began to read. Then he slid a note across the table. *Is reason or passion the quickest route to the good life? Explicate.*

Why not both? I wrote back. He unfolded the paper, nodded, and left.

Once I ran into him in front of a vending machine in the library cafeteria, cigarette in hand, a new fluorescent-orange courier's sack slung across his chest. A girl in black stockings and high-heeled ankle boots came clacking toward him.

There were other girls—I knew that. I'd seen him in a campus movie lineup, body brushed up against a thin girl with wispy limbs. Indolence streamed from him. On the steps of Frye College, absorbed in conversation with the same black-clad girl that I'd seen in the library, who sat, engrossed, one hand pushed with studied élan into her hennaed hair. What to do with the jealousy that shot through me? Nothing to do, no claim I could make on him. I wondered sometimes if it was the mere pursuit of me that appealed to him, the challenge of trying to wear me down, to—in some sense—corrupt me. How cynical was he? He'd never asked me about breaking up with Evan; then again, I'd never said anything about intending to do so.

Adultery: every so often I would whisper that word to myself. Though I told myself I was not an adulterer. *Betrayal*, I'd whisper, too. What I felt, above all, was a kind of burning curiosity, and a drive toward recklessness, a passionate recklessness, which did not shock me as much as it felt like a seed that Evan had planted in me and was something I needed to pass on. This would not last, I told myself. It was a crush and I would crush whatever it was out of myself. In the meantime, there was something I needed to know, to pursue.

Neil ran late: this was something else I learned about him. Though never as late as that first time. I learned the catalog of his clothing, too: T-shirts and motley sweaters, some with threads coming loose at the cuffs, all of which I must have seen the year before when we were in class together, but which had never registered with the same proprietary acuity as now— talismanic; symbols of intimacy. The scent of his deodorant. The little handknit scarf he knotted at his neck once it grew cool.

Out with Neil, what anxiety I felt about his lack of depend-
ability vanished. Calm reasserted itself. I took to wearing a
black balaclava tugged over my hair when we played pool to see
if that would cut the giveaway odor of smoke: at least that was
the reason I gave to myself. I didn't admit to any attempt at
disguise. In any case, it didn't work. With the smoke, that is. I
began to swim laps in the university pool after I'd gone out with
Neil, a devotion to rigorous activity that made sense to Evan,
when, showered, cleansed, I went afterward to meet him.

One evening, after a game, Neil insisted we go somewhere
else. He wouldn't tell me where, but said we could go by bike.
In a helmet, riding behind him, who would recognize me? I
balked. We compromised: I said I wouldn't ride with him, but if
he gave me directions, I'd meet him. As long as it wasn't too far.
I glanced at my watch.

"The Last Wound-Up," he said.

It was a store that sold windup toys. Tiny, hole-in-the-wall.
Off Yonge Street. A block from the Olde Yorke Tavern. I told
him I knew where it was but had never been in it.

As I approached along the sidewalk from the subway, I could
see Neil there before me, framed in the store's window, lit and
rendered indelibly, hunched over the shelves of toys in front of
him, rocking from the balls of his feet to his heels. When I
entered, he started up, holding out a metal windup cowboy with
an expression of such enthusiastic rapture that I was stunned—
like a trapdoor falling open upon all that I did not know about
him.

To kiss was to court danger but not cross over. We set rules,
established borders. With my leather gloves, I cupped Neil's
cheeks. A place beneath my collarbone thrummed. He buried
his face against my neck, in the gap between hat and collar, and
whispered, *I love the smell of your hair. Smoke* was what I would
have called it.

This was not all we did. We took off our gloves and unzipped our jackets. Wrapping our clothed bodies within this leather casing, we pressed ourselves together. Organic carbon. We let our fingers search through wool and cotton for the pliable gaps that led to skin.

EVERYWHERE I WENT I saw Somali cab drivers. At first I thought it was a mirage, or my desire imposed upon the world. I went downtown. There were towers where there had not been towers before. Condominiums. Shops and movie theaters, gas stations, parking lots that I had once known had disappeared, although the Olde Yorke Tavern was still there. I visited a colleague at the university, a so-called "peace and conflict" specialist. Having no leads, no obvious clues, no trail of pebbles strewn along a path, I strode the streets for hours, as I had done when I first moved to London. With trepidation, I pushed through the doors of the Olde Yorke Tavern, where the same men in baseball caps sat sucking back beer in the frigid dark as if they hadn't moved in ten years. In daylight, then at dusk, as people switched on lamps in living rooms, I peered into windows, looking for one young woman, for two young men.

In two days, I wore out a pair of shoes. And when I grew tired, I hailed cabs, sometimes with almost no sense of destination.

A blue cab, hubcaps jouncing, veered to the curb as I waved to it on Dundas West. I climbed in. The young man behind the wheel blinked his heavy-lidded eyes. The high sharpness of his dark cheekbones shone. There was music playing, which he turned down.

What *was* my destination?

I gave him directions to my parents' house. Viewed from the backseat, his neck was long and slim, his T-shirted shoulders supple. He whistled along to the still-audible song: twanging guitar and drums, a woman's voice whispering hoarse but melodious words, the voice then urgently, rhythmically rising.

"What is this?" I asked.

A tape—because he reached out one hand to eject it.

"You're Somali?" I said. He gave a curt nod, his gaze briefly visible in the rearview mirror. "Is the music Somali?"

"A friend's," he said, after a moment, with the wave of a hand, shoulders undulating. Outside, on the far side of the street, the Park Plaza rose, the dark-brick tiers cloaking shops, offices, the floors of hotel rooms, a swoon of rooms, a room filled with candles, all the way to the rooftop bar.

"Could you put it on again?"

He reinserted the tape and the voice resumed, guitar and drums pressing the beat forward, although it was the voice I listened to, hypnotic despite the scratchy quality of the tape, as it moved between a whisper and a soaring cry, from a sound that opened at the back of the throat to an ululation. It carved out its own landscape, intricate rhythms building a terrain of both pain and beauty. If I closed my eyes, a sky opened inside me, fierce and wide, harsh and tremulously gentle, and I was both pulled beneath it and lifted, as the voice kept circling.

"Who's the singer?" I asked with rising excitement.

He shrugged.

"What's she singing about?"

"Life," he said, "in the country I come from."

"Are they new songs, or old? I mean, traditional—"

"New."

I leaned forward, gripping the plastic cover of the passenger headrest. Could it be? "I know someone who's Somali. Who sings." Should I ask? "Named Basra."

He kept his eyes on the road, the surging traffic of Avenue Road, as we passed the window of an antique shop, which had once been a small French restaurant called La Citronnelle. A new tension gripped his neck and shoulders.

"Have you heard of her?"

He said nothing, just jerked to a stop at an intersection.

I took a gamble. "Is this her?"

When the light changed, he stepped on the gas, accelerating with such velocity that I was yanked back in my seat, as he shifted lanes with impetuousness or bravado, left hand out the window as a signal. Then he glanced over his shoulder.

"*Do* you know her?" I asked. Nothing. So I plunged on. "I met her in London. Through a friend. A friend of mine who knows her. Amir—" Aware of the back of the driver's neck, the sudden bony protrusion of vertebrae, the tautness of his shoulders. "Listen, please, if you know her—could I get a message to her? Could you take me to her? Arrange a meeting?" In my ears, the voice kept spiraling.

"Not now, no," he said, eyes on the road. Outside, a world away: a railway bridge, a lushness of trees. Dense green.

"But later." A crazy tang rose in my mouth. "My name's Arcadia. Arcadia Hearne. You can tell her— Could we meet later, even just to talk?"

"Later. Maybe," he said.

He picked me up at six on the corner of Avenue Road and Glenfern, after coming off his shift. This time, he drove an old brown Chevy, no music playing, though Basra's voice (if it was hers) still rang in my ears. I climbed into the front seat beside him, giddy with luck, and stashed my bag between my feet.

His name, he'd told me, was Yussif. He didn't offer a second name. He'd left Mogadishu four years before. He'd been at the university there. Before. Had he fought, I asked him, when the war, the civil war, broke out? If that was what you wanted to call it. Clan fighting. He was silent for a moment. Then he said: he was in a house, just before he'd fled, that had been attacked. That was all he said. How had he managed to get out of the country? On foot. By donkey. With nothing. Six months later he'd reached a Kenyan camp.

Naturally, I wondered if I should have told someone where I was going. Not my parents. Lux, in some ways, seemed the most obvious person. On the other hand, this would have meant admitting to her exactly what I was doing and risking more questions from her than I wanted. Raoul, the peace-and-conflict specialist? Amir—whom I should, whom I *would* call. Just not yet.

In the end, I'd simply left a note for my parents, for my mother when she came home from work, for my father, wherever he'd headed out to. Saying I'd gone out for the evening, and hoped not to be back too late. Not like a child, I'd told myself, or an adolescent, but like any responsible guest.

We passed a girl embracing the trunk of a linden tree while a woman raced in alarm across a lawn toward her.

"Will Basra be there?" I asked the young man named Yussif, and felt a sweet, sharp pinch—part nerves, part vindication. I'd simply have to trust him.

"I believe so. Yes," he said.

He took me back downtown, swooping east, then south of Bloor, pulling up into a lucky parking spot opposite the St.

James apartment towers, from whose garbage Dumpsters Evan and Fergus used to steal fluorescent lighting tubes.

If she's downtown, I thought, then my own wandering, my on-foot searches, had not been entirely off.

The St. James towers were not unlike the towers of Dixon—as worn, though taller, dwarfing the humans who made their way along the cracked cement paths and tired grass beneath them. Full, too, of displaced lives. On a bench sat two women in saris, one with her head in her hands, the other fanning her with a newspaper. A sprinkler scudded water in a small and hopeful circle. Graffiti in what might have been Tamil script was half blotted out but still visible along one once-white wall.

Beside me, as we walked, Yussif jangled his keys between his fingers—not a nervous gesture, or not obviously so. On his feet, out of the car, he was wiry, moved with a rolling stride. The second building we came to, we entered. In the elevator, he pushed the button for the eighteenth floor.

With another set of keys, he opened the door to an apartment, which on first glance seemed empty, though a second glance revealed a minimum of furnishings. In the kitchen, directly in front of me, a saucepan on the stove. A jar of instant coffee on the counter. Around a corner, two upright chairs. A small TV set. I could not see the bedroom. Perhaps someone, who knew how many people, who did not have the money to buy furniture, lived here. Stayed here. No one seemed to *be* here. He had not said to me that Basra lived here. Tiny bursts of electricity moved through me.

"Sit down. Please." He closed, and locked the door behind us.

I sat down in the chair that faced the door, my bag on my lap.

What's bravery? Was this bravery or simply foolishness?

He pulled the other chair close but did not sit, instead

remained standing beside it, hands in his pockets, close enough that I could see how the light caught the knicks and blemishes of his skin, sense restlessness in him, a kind of leeriness or agitation. Not belligerence, I told myself.

With a sudden bolt of movement, hands erupting from his pockets, he glanced at the metal watch on his left wrist, and, without a word, strode from the apartment, locking the door behind him. Outside, the key turned in the latch. His footsteps drummed down the hall.

I did not move until I heard the elevator ping and the distant shudder of its doors closing; then I rose and approached the door. Although he'd locked it from the outside, I could release the dead bolt from within, which I did, and, opening the door, peered down the empty corridor.

Now what? Was he (as I presumed) intending to return? Why, knowing that I could get out, had he locked the door? Was this a significant gesture or had he acted simply out of habit? Should I make a run for it or wait?

There was a chemical shift in my body; something squeezed against my skull. I closed the door again and waited. Paced. I entered the second room, a bedroom of a sort, where a double mattress was spread across the floor and another one propped against a wall. I listened to the uneasy tock of my own footsteps, the swift fibrillation of my heart. I used the toilet. From the window of the living room I peered down over a narrow balcony across the unruffled city, the guise of any ordinary night, as the sky turned aqua, slowly azure. There was no sign of a telephone. In one of the closets were a man's suit and several pairs of shoes.

What was I doing? If she needed money, I would give it to her. And Lux's number. For Lux would be able to help her in the music business. Then, and only then, would I ask about Amir. I crouched on the floor, hugging my ribs, aware of each sharp line of bone. My head filled with unreachable scenes: the tiled gas fireplace in my study, my garden, Amir's car, the green dereliction of the North London line to Highbury, the faraway wooden stairwell leading up to the Centre for Contemporary War Studies.

An hour passed by my watch. Ten minutes more and footsteps, a single pair, approached along the hall. Someone tried the doorknob, turned it, rather than attempting first to unlock it. Laconic, undistraught, the young man named Yussif reappeared, flicked the overhead light switch and, jangling his ring of keys, locked the door once more.

"I apologize," he said.

"Listen—" I stopped halfway across the room, between the chairs and the door.

"Why do you look for Basra?"

"To make sure she's safe," I said. As long as I remained calm—despite the *thock-thock* of my veins—everything would be fine. "Because I was worried. To help her. I thought you said she'd come, or you'd tell me where—"

"You should not ask for her like this."

He had nothing with him, nothing near him with which to threaten me physically (other than the keys, the chairs, other than what might be in his pockets).

"You will cause trouble for her. Here. If you do this."

"I'm sorry," I said. "Really, I didn't mean—"

"She is good. But you must stop. This, she asks me to say to you." Folding his arms across his chest.

The fingernails of his right hand were longer than those of his left, the way guitarists sometimes wore them. How had I only now noticed this? And that part of the third finger of his left hand was missing.

A new constellation of possibilities burst into view. Did he play with her? Had he played in a band with her back in

Mogadishu? At university, played those songs that had got her (got them?) into trouble?

"Do you—?"

"Leave her alone." His hands threw their weight through the air. Was that a knife? The flash of a tiny blue-handled knife? "Do you hear? This is what I tell you."

"THE PHONE'S FOR YOU," my mother said.

As she handed me the receiver, I wondered what voice I would hear, male or female, a voice that menaced, that came haltingly, that burst across me with a kind of effervescence, that shifted the air, crossing time zones, zinging out of the past?

"Hello?" I said.

"Ah," the voice said. Male and English. "So you're there."

I started to cough. "I'm here," I said. "Hang on just a minute." I called to my mother, who'd stopped (who'd lingered?) in the hallway and, forehead drawn, was scratching the dog's ruff with her long hands. "I'm going to take this in the basement."

Did she look at me with surreptitious curiosity or wariness? "He has two lines," she said. "If you use the desk phone, you'll see which one is blinking."

In the basement, at my father's desk, I sat for a moment, staring at the telephone. I cleared my throat, eyed the darting red light. Then I picked the receiver up.

"Hello," I repeated. To begin again. "Sorry about that." In London, it would be one o'clock in the morning.

"Let me ask you this," the voice said, "were you planning to let me know where you had lighted off to or intending simply to disappear?"

"No," I said, "*no*—I was going to call."

"Are you wondering how I found your number?"

"How did you?"

"I rang your sister at work. Her name's not hard to remember and there are only so many TV stations in Toronto. I suppose I could have tried the Centre, I presume they know where you are, but reckoned I'd feel a bit peculiar asking Ray or Moira for your whereabouts. I did leave messages," he went on, "on your answerphone and E-mail. Perhaps you've received them and haven't bothered to respond. Or decided not to. Though perhaps you haven't bothered to check for messages, in which case, I'll summarize briefly. The tone's fairly consistent in the beginning. I was worried about you. Worried what had happened to you. Let you know how you might reach me. I admit by the end I'd grown a bit frantic."

"It's only been four days."

"Five, by my count."

"All right, five days. I needed a little time. Time to think. I haven't checked my messages. Of course I was going to. Soon. I'm sorry. Really. I didn't think I had a way to get hold of you. Where are you?"

"Where am *I*?"

"Are you still on the boat? Are you—"

"At a friend's."

"Is everything all—"

"Mmm, a bit dicey still. But settling. How's Toronto?"

"Toronto's fine, it's—" On the desk in front of me lay a couple of magazines: *Nuclear Radiation Weekly*, *The Journal of*

Nuclear Engineers. A mug with some mysterious acronym on it: ITFERP. In this very spot, my own desk had once stood, where I had written papers on the French and Russian Revolutions, only mine had been a door upended on two carpenter's trestles, and when I was tired sometimes, I would lie on the floor, spread eagled, staring up at Evan's putti on the blue ceiling, one of whose limbs were oddly angled, the other's head a little over-large.

How to say exactly what Toronto was?

"May I ask what precisely you're doing in Toronto?"

"I decided I had some business to take care of."

"Decided suddenly?"

"And not so suddenly."

Did he wait for a moment to see if anything more was forthcoming before giving a sigh or simply an outrush of breath? "Arcadia, you have something that belongs to me. No, I'll amend that—it doesn't belong to me. But I *do* need it returned."

"I tried to deliver it again," I said, "the next morning, before I left. But Aliya, the woman you told me to ask for, wasn't there. And I didn't have time to wait. I suppose I could have E-mailed you, but I honestly didn't know how safe a message would be under the circumstances."

"So what did you do?"

"It's in my filing cabinet. Locked up."

"Arcadia, *were* you planning to ring me at some point?"

"On what number? I didn't have a number."

"I left you a number. I left a number on your answerphone. There's no point now. Listen, do you think there's any way I might be able to retrieve my package?"

I closed my eyes. "Colleen in the first-floor flat has a key. And the key to the filing cabinet's in the top drawer of my desk. You could go round. I'll ring her to say she'll hear from you.

Do you have a pen? I'll have to run upstairs and get her number."

How perfunctory, how ridiculously and desolately formal all this was.

"Could you ring me back?" That was trust, I thought, with sudden lucidity. If he needed the passport that badly. The conviction that I would ring him back.

But how, given everything that had gone on between us, were we really to restore mutual trust?

When I returned to the basement, I sat for a moment, twisting a pen between my fingers, before I pressed the hard plastic of the numbers he'd given me and called him back. What I felt was turbulence, a deep swill of it, which was not without longing, in addition to an urgency of self-protection, not without desire, and pleasure at the sound of his voice, which returned with its own resurgence of warmth—not just the flat clang of utilitarian need, or irritation.

"Arcadia, listen, I'm sorry, I should never have—"

"No," I said. "Don't. It isn't that."

"I've no interest in taking advantage of you."

"You're not—"

"And thank you for trying to deliver it again. That was really more than I"—I nodded, although of course he couldn't see it—"expected."

"Where did you keep them? Before—do you mind my asking? Did you keep them in your office, or wherever you— did you ever store them at home?"

"At home. Emm, sometimes. A few. If I needed access to them with some sort of immediacy. In the bedroom. You may remember. On the shelves beside the bed, there were some record albums. Just album covers, some of them, actually. Madonna. The Beatles' White Album."

"Where do you keep them now?"

"I've a storage place for them, with the equipment. For the moment. I'm sorry, I really can't be more specific." A car roared behind him.

"Do you ever get frightened, when you think about what might—"

"Perhaps sort of unnerved. Though it's hardly useful to think like that."

I had been frightened, was frightened for him. "Do you need somewhere to stay?"

"What?"

I had to gather my courage all over again. "Do you need somewhere to stay?"

"Why?"

"Because my flat's empty. And I thought, if you needed, if you wanted—"

"Seriously?"

"It would be fine. If it would be helpful." My heart kept speeding unevenly.

"Right." He gave a low chuckle. "Do you know how much longer you'll be away?"

"Not sure yet."

"Another week, d'you reckon? A month?"

"A week," I said. "Maybe two. Not a month. And you could look after the garden."

"Yeah?" he said. "You need someone to look after the garden, do you?" That note of amusement again. "Only if you're certain."

THAT LAST SPRING IN TORONTO, I would lie awake some-times in my basement apartment in my parents' house, looking up at Evan's painted moon and stars, and wonder how to recognize love. True love. How did you draw the line between love and selfishness, love and longing, love and tension, love and recklessness, love and violence, love and pain, love and self-sabotage, love and contagion, love and desperation? Did love make you a better person or worse? On good days, I felt that I had been twinned, or, no, that I could be two different people, live two different overlapping lives, that such a tricky balance was possible. On bad days I knew that I could not possibly go on like this, I'd have to choose. Yet I wanted to be true, figure out how to be true to myself. I was waiting to act only until it seemed absolutely clear what I should do.

"Love," Evan whispered in my ear one night as we lay in his third-floor room, "is like a braided silk cord that's tensile and tight, the one thing you can hold on to in the dark." Had he read that somewhere, made it up? That room was never truly dark. Orange ribs of light from two streetlamps spanned the floor, intersecting in the middle of the floorboards and across the double mattress and the two white pillows.

"If you truly love someone then you'll know what they're thinking when they're alone." Did he whisper these words on that night or some other night? I remember his hand stroking my hair as he spoke. I remember how breath spooled out of me, my body dissolving to pure ache in the face of this conundrum. If he knew about Neil, then we shared this knowledge, even if we didn't speak of it. And by this definition, he knew. Of course he did.

When I touched a finger to his scar—his cicatrix, he called it—his whole body quivered at my touch. I traced the *A* within its circle. *A* and *O*. He'd worked the edges of the wounds as they closed so that the scars did not heal smooth but in a bumpy raised ridge, the outline of the letters recognizable not only beneath my fingertips but against my skin as our bodies pressed together in the midst of making love.

And I—what did I know, thinking of him?

Alpha. Omega. From the beginning to the end. Without end. There had been an instant, that September afternoon in the ravine, when I was certain he would pass me the little blue-handled knife and insist that I cut myself as well. Mark me forever. But he hadn't.

"What goes on between us has nothing to do with anyone else."

Always when I knocked at Neil's door, there would be music playing. Anything from industrial-noise bands to Webern. Arriving, I'd time my knock for a moment when there was no one else in his hall, no longer in Frye College (where he'd had a bedroom off a shared suite) but in the graduate college, Ferguson, where he now had a single room.

I did not worry all that much about running into people. I could say I'd come to Ferguson to use the library. And these days Evan rarely came to campus unless for a class. Instead, he'd taken to working in the city reference library. He said he hated the university, hated his engineering program, which he'd switched into at the beginning of our third year. A decision that had stunned me. Why engineering, given all the things he could possibly do? Because it was practical, he said, which stunned me even more. Since when had Evan been driven by practicality rather than the romantic? I was only just beginning to see how nihilism might also be fueling him; how his acceptance of my father's work, for instance, which had relieved me when we first met, might equally derive from a kind of fatalism.

I should not have mentioned that my father had likewise majored in engineering (which Evan knew). When I did, Evan lashed out at me viciously. *This has nothing to do with your father.*

I knocked on Neil's door. Always I was nervous that he wouldn't be there, though we'd prearranged the time. That he'd forget or get waylaid or be on his own lax schedule. But the volume of music dropped suddenly, his solo voice bidding someone goodbye even as he opened the door, the brown phone on the floor behind him. We kissed. He locked the door. As I stamped the last snow from my boots, unlaced them, set them on a nearly melted square of newspaper beside his bulbous-toed, salt-stained black ones, he stalked toward the window, flapping his arms, and heaved up the frame, as if both gestures would instantly disperse the odor of smoke, the thin gray thread still curling up from the cigarette he'd just stubbed out in a saucer.

He didn't smoke in my presence, but ate pistachios instead, cracking the shells between his teeth and spitting them into his palm. He'd lie stretched out on his bed, ankles crossed, like some louche nineteenth-century opium dreamer, his head propped on two pillows, downing nuts by the handful.

The decor in his room was minimal. A row of empty beer bottles lined the base of the radiator. Milk crates full of albums, shoeboxes of cassettes. On the bookshelf above his desk, books were stacked haphazardly, some in long horizontal rows, some in tipsy vertical piles. A black-and-white postcard was propped against one stack—a Parisian street scene over which the sender (a girl, I'd checked) had smooched a pair of lipsticked lips. Beer was kept in a communal fridge at the end of the corridor. Tea, a tea bag purloined from the dining hall, came stashed in a mug that looked as if it, too, had been stolen from a dining hall. If I asked for water, he'd pour me the dregs of boiled water from his electric kettle.

We moved through half-light. Always when I visited he kept the blinds down, the window above the sizzling radiator propped open. The wind slurping the thick vinyl out through the gap at the bottom, then bashing it in, became, along with the low boom of bass notes, a constant background sound. Snow sifted onto the windowsill and melted.

The first few times I gave him hand jobs, burying my head against him, sucking out the scents of his body. He howled. I clasped a hand tightly over his mouth. One day, when I arrived, my pockets full of pistachio nuts, he drew off my coat and hung it over the doorknob. He unbuttoned the cuff of my shirt and, pushing the cotton toward my shoulder, began to move his tongue up my arm. "Don't worry," he said, though I felt very calm, quite buoyant, "I'm just going to eat you." He unfastened the buttons of my shirt, one by one.

From a Drum tobacco tin stored beneath the bed (his skinny single bed), he plucked a condom and ripped the packet open with his teeth. (*This has nothing to do with anyone else.*) *Was* it about secrecy or about privacy? Heat poured from the damp top of his head. When Neil came, he yelped, tiny high-pitched sounds, the muscles in his thighs and stomach deeply convulsing, long limbs all flailing gesture. Nothing like Evan. His cock nothing like Evan's. I cataloged (I could not help myself) all the ways in which his body was not like Evan's. Curious. Though I didn't come—too nervous, too guilty. Not then, not yet.

"What's important," Neil said, as we lay folded side by side in the bed, "is the nature of the encounter between two people—the attempt to truly *recognize* the other, which means that you approach any encounter in a spirit of openness in order to see what will happen, which includes being open to the possibility of risk or danger."

He'd return to these ideas, to words like these, to what lay at the heart of the I-Thou relationship, according to Martin Buber, whose books he'd begun to lend me.

"It's important not to fantasize," I said. "Not simply to idealize someone."

"Yeah." He nodded.

Or he'd rattle on about Wittgenstein, about the need for complex language to express complicated or paradoxical thought. "Of course, if something's impossible to say," he added, "then don't."

One afternoon, wrapping one long bare arm around my shoulder, he told me he'd had a three-year-old sister who died of leukemia the year he turned eight. (A tide of heat from the radiator washed across us, cold air gusting through the window, in waves, hot cold, hot cold, his fingers, his breath smelling of sex and smoke.) He buried his face against my breast. What he remembered from that day was his mother (who was Jewish) coming home from the hospital, pulling an oven mitt over one hand and methodically smashing her fist through the glass pane of the back door. Later that evening, his father (French Canadian, a doctor, a cancer specialist), got into the family car, which he'd left in gear and without the emergency brake on, turned the ignition key and drove right into the metal door of their garage. Neil laughed as he told me this, an uneven smile jigging over his face as if he expected me to find these things funny.

I looked at Neil and wondered what it meant to speak of recognition, not of love.

Neil was the one I told when, in late February, I was terrified that I was pregnant. My stomach roiled with acid. My tongue tasted punky. For ten days, I lurched around from campus bathroom to campus bathroom, islanded from friends by then. I sat for hours on toilets waiting for that telltale low ache, that familiar drip. Fear must have made me throw up (I did throw up), because I wasn't pregnant.

I told him that Evan wanted to marry me, the plain fact of this, while lying clothed on his bed, though what I saw and heard was Evan in bracing wind and freak March snow, under a tree in Christie Pits park. *Marry me, Arcadia, even though I've always thought I'd die young, and I don't want children, I want to be clear about that, I don't see the point of bringing any more children into this fucked-up world.*

Neil seated himself at the far end of the narrow mattress, bedsprings squeaking.

"What are you going to do?"

"I don't know." I frowned as I stared up at the cracks and watermarks on the stuccoed ceiling. "He told me if I broke up with him he was going to go up to his father's farm north of the city, bring back one of his father's guns, and shoot himself."

"His father has guns?" Neil sounded almost tranquil, languid—but not dismissive.

"A hunting rifle. Two German World War II pistols that belonged to *his* father. According to Evan."

"Would he really do that?"

"I don't know."

"Do you want to marry him?"

"I don't know."

"What did you say to him?"

"I told him I had to think about it."

Surely Evan must suspect something. I was convinced of this. It seemed impossible otherwise. Yet it baffled me that he'd done nothing, said nothing. Why didn't he at least *say* something?

What *was* the difference between love and longing, love and desire, love and blackmail?

Yet I didn't trust Neil, not in some essential way I needed to. I trusted him to keep secrets because there was a degree of self-interest for him in that. One afternoon, I told him I wanted to go to Paris. I wanted to sit in sunglasses drinking café au lait on the Rue de Rivoli and stroll through Les Jardins de Luxembourg. *Sounds like a good idea*, he said. He did not say, *Can I come with you?*

If I left Evan, Neil would bolt. This is what I told myself. Lightness would lift him away. He'd strand me. I'd be all right as long as I protected myself. My appeal lay in the fact that I couldn't make demands, I couldn't exact promises of commitment. Inaccessibility allowed me to outlast the others, the alluring comp-lit girls, the sulky philosophy grad students—the temporary glaze of hair across his clothes, now blonde, now red, now black; the lipstick-stained tissues in his trash basket; the bobby pins abandoned beneath the bed.

He wasn't dependable. On the other hand, perhaps I didn't have enough fecklessness. I longed for fecklessness while feeling addicted to risk. What did it mean that I could live like this, could go on like this? What did it reveal about me?

Yet, and this was another huge *yet*, to give up Evan would be to lose some crucial part of myself. Which I kept coming back to. The ability to love. To be loved.

Once I came by Neil's room as planned, knocked, knocked again (the room seemed oddly silent). A guy in a lumberjack shirt passed, sized me up and down, and said, "He went out about twenty minutes ago." Once I knocked (there was music), and when Neil opened the door, he looked stunned. "Oh fuck," he whispered, "what time is it?" He was stoned, his eyes swimming pink, the room thick with aromatic smoke. He waved his arms as if shooing me away, shaking his head.

I roamed the streets for hours after that, furious at him, furious at myself (*fuck, a good fuck*) and at the end of the afternoon, settled myself in the basement of the Davies College library, in a corner filled with books written in Cyrillic script, as quiet and out of the way as anywhere I could imagine. I yanked a book from the shelf and sat staring despairingly at upside-down Cyrillic. Neil found me there, which must have taken some searching, through the main stacks, through each of the college libraries. I caught his lope, the back of his tweed coat, bare legs between his hem and army boots, but refused to look up. The second time, he stopped, and when I looked (how could I not?), he yanked open his coat like any flasher—

FORGIVE
THE POOR
FOOL

—scrawled in black marker across his skin. All that skin. His face tipped at an angle, grinning wickedly but oddly scrunched up.

DO STATES NEED ENEMIES TO EXIST?

Does a state need an enemy in order to define itself?

Does one state need its opposite?

When I studied war theory, we would examine definitions of self-interest, as derived from the tenets of traditional game theory, in which, given two opponents in conflict, one could determine the position that most enhanced each party's self-interest, and thus what each would do.

In intervention studies, as in contemporary war studies, it's grown very hard to do this. The theories break down. Late-twentieth-century warfare rarely features a neat confrontation between two antagonists (or even two antagonists and their allies). There are too many other players: intervention forces, potential intervention forces, humanitarian (as opposed to military) interveners, the media (agents of intervention in their own right). An antagonist's response is no longer principally determined by the behavior of, or in relation to, a single opponent. Instead, a warring party may act, say, to gain the attention of an intervention force. Or the media. To manipulate and antagonize an intervention force. Bomb a hospital. Create a flood of refugees.

Capture soldiers—peacekeepers—to use as human shields, as happened in Bosnia. Kill them, as the Belgian peacekeepers were killed in Rwanda. So that wars (or non-wars) become at least a three-way conflict, if often a highly uneven one.

When people think of duels, they think of two figures—isolated, in black coats and top hats, say, pistols in hand, pacing away from each other across a stretch of grass. Yet most dueling histories are not like that. Formal duels were fought with a cluster of men surrounding the two central actors. Duelists were observed, their actions monitored. A doctor would be present to stanch wounds, to fight for the life of anyone who risked death. There were seconds, the duelists' representatives, who delivered the challenge, who mediated, attempting to work out terms that would avoid fighting, who, if diplomacy failed, made arrangements for the location. Who measured the ground, the distance that would separate the principals, who gave the orders to fire.

This is one set of rules. In other versions, the one who is challenged chooses the location.

I have no idea what rules they followed, or how closely they adhered to them.

In Ireland, so I've read, families once passed dueling pistols from one generation to the next and gave them intimate, besotted names like "The Darling" or "Sweet Lips." What does it mean to give your weapons names like these, to, in some sense, feminize them? Because women were perceived as agents of death? Because such men were half in love with the lethal risks the pistols bestowed on them?

In Paraguay it is still legal to fight a duel as long as you notify the authorities of your blood type.

There are days when dueling lore seems everywhere. Lounging with a newspaper on my parents' back deck, having riffled through the war news, I found an article about Fermat's Last Theorem on the science page, which included the story of the young nineteenth-century mathematician Evariste Gauloise. At age nineteen he was challenged to a duel by the fiancé of his lover in what may have been a true love triangle or, potentially, a political trap. What *is* known is that, the night before the fight, Gauloise feverishly scribbled out mathematical equations that would, over a hundred years later, help solve the intractable puzzle of Fermat's Last Theorem. If Gauloise had survived, would the history of mathematics have been different?

Downtown, amid the frantic crowds of early evening, I stood at the corner of Yonge and College, waiting, while passengers disgorged, to board a streetcar on the site where, in July 1817, a young student named John Ridout had fought a pistol duel in a field with a man named Samuel Jarvis. How many of the sleek-suited women, the brisk and bolting men, the voracious teen-agers, knew this history? These two hadn't fought for love but over money. Bad blood ran between their old Toronto families. Frightened and gun-shy, or quick-triggered and cocky, Ridout fired too soon and missed, then had to stand in place and wait to be shot. Those were the rules. Jarvis killed him (blood under our feet somewhere). Though tried for murder (those were also the rules), like many duelists he was acquitted.

From a phone booth on College Street West, before meeting Lux for dinner, I called Amir. He'd left a message at the house that morning asking me to ring him.

I'd begun to dream of him, fractured pieces of him. I'd dream the back of his neck, as I had pondered it, quietly revel-ing in this particular part of him, this private geography, mornings, waking in bed beside him. One night I'd dreamed a quality of movement, a magnetic field, an energetic blur, a rustle of shirt half glimpsed, and felt my own surge toward it, knowing it was his. I woke out of dreams of London: the corner of the Parkway and Camden High Street, no café I knew but one that I knew was London, desire like sparks of light in a mirror, the scent of sausages, baked beans, burning bread, the lurid lime green of the canals, my body pulled, tugged through the air like a swallow.

In London, in my flat in London, it would be nearly midnight. After four rings, I began to wonder whether or not he was there, surprised at my own anxiety, insisting to myself that as soon as the answerphone clicked on, I would hang up, as I was about to do when his voice broke in. An ordinary, if muted, hello.

Though not ordinary to imagine him in the London dark, padding barefoot down my hallway, white shirt untucked and flapping, one of my wineglasses in hand, making himself at home in my home.

"Hallo, you," he said. "You all right?"

Hearing only his voice, these days, I had to recreate a body out of it, limbs and gesture from its vivid rise and fall.

"I'm all right." And I was, I told myself, I was.

He just had a couple of domestic questions, really. The pilot light for the back burners wouldn't stay lit. Was that normal or was he doing something wrong?

Was there a reason I kept newspapers in the icebox?

And where (he'd been looking everywhere) did I keep the phone books?

"Actually, I noticed there are a lot of little green flies on the rose buds."

"Greenfly," I said.

"Greenfly," he repeated.

"There's a spray in the bottom cupboard by the back door, the one where all the gardening tools are. You could spray them with that, only don't do it in the middle of the day, not when the sun's out, anyway, it's better in the late afternoon or evening."

"Right," he said, "I'll do that."

I could tell him about searching for Basra. I could tell him that only half an hour before, as I'd stepped off the streetcar, I'd glanced across the street and thought, no, almost sworn I'd seen her alighting from a cab, the same lanky leanness, same tightly clipped back hair, white running shoes and denim skirt, her long, self-possessed face turned partway toward the young man heaving a guitar and amplifier out of the cab's trunk. I'd raised my hand, a frisson of recognition, of joy, of doubt—it *was* her, or was I imagining it?—leaping to the tips of my fingers, and had taken a step toward the curb, but made it no farther before she hefted the amplifier and the two of them disappeared behind the gunmetal-gray door of a three-story building.

I didn't tell him.

"My guest has left," he said. The last time we'd spoken, two days before, he'd asked if there was something I might consider, a small thing, though of course what I decided to do was entirely up to me. There was a woman, a woman in transit, who needed a place to stay for a night or so; she was Sudanese, a Dinka woman from the civil-war-torn south, who'd been smuggled into England and was en route to Canada, by which I presumed he meant he was helping her. In tricky circumstances like these, he sometimes did put people up, briefly, in his flat or at his office, when there wasn't anywhere else, only at the moment, as I knew, he'd left his flat and was looking for an office (he'd found somewhere that looked possible, likely even). And the canal boat was otherwise occupied. If this did not feel right to me, he understood, he understood completely, but he needed simply to ask.

I thought about saying no. The thin edge of the wedge. That sort of thing. I thought about the brutalities of the civil war in southern Sudan (which I had written about but where I'd never been). About the latest bodies dug from mass graves in Srebrenica (where I had also never been). About women in Bosnian refugee camps who'd been raped by Serbian soldiers, a defilement worse than death in their culture. About the massacred bodies left to rot on the grounds of the church at Nyarabuye in Rwanda, left where they'd been felled, as testimony to the genocide, where (so I had read and people had told me) the grass had grown back lush and fertile. About all the ways in which information and theory can masquerade as knowledge but are not knowledge. I did not know what it was like to walk across that bone-strewn grass. I could imagine but I did not know what it was like to flee across a desert or in a little boat along the coast of the Horn of Africa, toward Mombassa, Kenya, a boat crammed with survivors frantic for food and water.

There was a cot stored at the back of the hall closet, I told him, clean sheets in a drawer in the bedroom. I did not ask him, now, where the woman, this stranger, had slept. It seemed obscene to feel a stab of jealousy, though I did. I merely asked if she had gotten off all right and he said, yeah, she had, and arrived safely, and I told him I was glad.

"Have you decided yet when you're coming back?" he asked.

"Soon, I expect." Because, in a sense, I'd given up. Perhaps I'd found all that I could hope to find. I'd made the return. I'd seen my parents; even if we hadn't talked much, surely this counted as some gesture toward reconciliation.

"You'll tell me when, will you?"

"I won't just show up on the doorstep and kick you out."

"Arcadia—Arcadia, come on. It isn't that. I miss you."

Something stirred on the tip of my tongue, beyond sparring. "In the next few days," I said. "Next week at the latest. Soon, I do miss—I have to book a seat. As soon as I know, I'll tell you."

"I'll clear out. "

"No," I said, "don't be silly, I'm not asking you to, not—" I listened, with curiosity, to the lurching in my chest, something stumbling to its feet like a strange and shaggy animal. "It's all right," I said. I closed my eyes. "I'm not judging you. I don't want you to think that after everything I said— I don't condemn what you do. I do concede difficulties. And I suppose

I do reserve the right to judge, if only one act at a time, taking into account all the particular circumstances."

"Come back," he said.

"I'm coming back."

"I was frightened you might not. That you might not want to have anything more to do with me."

"No," I said. "Yes. I mean, I do."

"Have you found what you're looking for? Here?" Lux asked as we sat at an outdoor café table, lancing antipasti with our forks.

"No," I said, "not really."

"How much longer are you staying?"

"Another week. I *have* got a job to get back to." Although traveling in my line of work was not so unusual, Ray didn't mind, as long as I kept in touch, and I *was* doing some writing.

Lux nodded, and I stumbled against the sense, some vague skittishness in her, that made me think she might be hiding something.

The only person that Neil and I had ever run into together was Lux. (At least that we knew of.) In a convenience store on a no-man's-land-ish stretch of King Street, far west, among gas stations and decommissioned warehouses, across from the dilapidated building where Neil was house-sitting a fellow graduate student's apartment during March break. We'd spent the night together. Two nights. While Evan visited his mother in Montreal. For the second morning in a row, Neil and I woke, surprised and groggy, beside each other. Showered and ravenous, we stumbled out the door. Safe, or heedless, cushioned by a bubble of skin, by all those uninterrupted hours, by how far west we were, I basked in some lovely pheromonal glow, impervious to consequence, until I turned from the convenience-store counter where Neil was paying for doughnuts and eggs, and there was Lux. A long pink knitted scarf wrapped about her neck, the laces of her black boots coiled around and around her ankles. Beneath a wool coat, she wore a pair of skin-tight green pants that I had never seen before. Her face blanched. I had no idea what she was doing there. Was there someone (one of her radio-and-television-arts friends) outside waiting for her? Was she alone? Had she been out all night? Did she smoke, was she buying cigarettes? Manic questions sluiced through me. I had no sense at all of her private life. Was she making a bid to escape the family home, out looking for an apartment?

When I introduced them, Neil nodded and held out his hand, as unperturbed as ever, but Lux did not reciprocate, or speak, just turned on her heel and bolted.

We had never spoken of that moment.

"Lux," I said (she was my *sister*, Neil had insisted at the time, what was she going to do, and in any case what was the point in worrying about it?), "are you still doing deliveries? You know. Running errands? Whatever you want to call it. When you travel?"

A fleck of rhinestone, not ruby this time, glittered in her nostril. "No," she said, "not at the moment."

"Why's that?"

When she looked up, her eyes shone oddly—not fearless. "I got stopped."

She would not tell me what had happened until later, until after we had finished dinner and split the bill and set out down the quiet, house-lined streets, the shadows of leaves jittering over our arms and legs, the shrieks of invisible swifts rending the night air.

"It was in the spring," she said. "On that trip I took to South Africa. To Johannesburg. Well, when we finished shooting in Johannesburg, we had these plans to take a trip to Kruger National Park, and also this little expedition across the border into Mozambique, to Maputo. To meet up with these musicians and do a little shoot with them. But also take them some stuff. Money. Equipment. They're these great guitarists, but after the civil war they had nothing. So we were taking them a couple of amplifiers and some guitar strings. And some money. We weren't trying to get them out of the country or anything.

"I knew it was supposed to be sort of dangerous. The drive to Maputo. But I was with Paul, my videographer, and Sipho, the producer we'd worked with in Johannesburg. And he said he knew someone who'd driven it recently. And it was okay. As long as you didn't drive after dark. And stayed on the road. Because of the mines. And I thought, it's only a couple of hours across the border to Maputo, anyway. And we'd been fine in Jo'burg—we'd been hassled on the street a bit, but basically everything had gone okay, and I'd said I would do this, and after Kruger, after seeing all those animals, we were feeling pretty relaxed and I thought, okay.

"So we crossed the border. That was fine. And then, like maybe twenty minutes later—we're driving on tarmac, pot-holed but still kind-of tarmac, and every so often there are these abandoned hulks of cars and trucks left over from the war—when we came to this vehicle pulled up and kind of blocking the road, and these men in camouflage suits with guns, waving us to stop."

Trees fanned above the street in front of us. They began rustling.

"So we stopped," she said. "We didn't really have much choice. They said, it's an inspection. They didn't say what for or who by, but we didn't really feel we could argue. They wanted to know where we were going and what we were doing. They took our passports. They were very interested in the video equipment and the amplifiers. Then they made us get out of the car and took us away one at a time and questioned us. They were mostly pretty young and they all had guns and seemed a little jumpy. And there wasn't a lot of traffic on the road. Maybe a couple of trucks, but they waved those by.

"Then Sipho got kind of angry, which was probably a mistake. Because they got angry back. They took us away from the road. They tied us up. One of them tried to scare us, not shooting at us but like shooting on either side of us. And they pistol-whipped Sipho. By this point it was nearly the end of the afternoon and I was getting really worried about what was going to happen when night fell. They'd hold their guns to our heads and demand to know what we were filming and nothing about the musicians seemed to make any sense to them. It had been about four hours by then and they hadn't given us any water and I kept freaking out, thinking they could not only shoot us, but garrote us with the guitar strings. Or do other things. If they felt like it.

"Anyway." She shrugged. "They let us go. They took almost everything. All the equipment, money, our passports, even our shoes. But they left us the car and told us to go back."

"And?"

"So we went back, but when we reached the border, we decided that we were going to report what had happened. So we pulled up outside the Mozambiquan border station. Maybe we were hopelessly naïve, but we went inside and the same man was there who was there earlier, and Paul and I began to tell our story, and when I looked up, there (I absolutely swear this), standing in the doorway to the back room, was the man who'd pulled us over.

"He said, it is bandits or ex-guerillas from the civil war. They are impossible to track down. This road is dangerous. People like you should not be on this road. Do you wish to report what has happened? And we said, no, no, we were just passing on the information. And we got out of there as fast as we could."

"Why haven't you mentioned anything about this?"

"I have," she said. Her pale collarbone shone. "I've talked about it a lot with some people. I guess I just didn't tell you." She waved her hands in front of her. "Anyway, anyway, I'm telling you now. So I was completely freaked out. Always before, I'd known there was a chance something could happen but it didn't. I was lucky, but what I *felt* was that I was good at this, I had some kind of knack. I was inviolable. Inviolate? And then I lost that, I lost it completely."

Our footsteps shushed along the pavement, through the pools of light and dark.

"The first night afterward, we stayed in this convent, not far from the border, a place where a lot of aid workers stay, or used to stay on their way into Mozambique, when there were more refugee camps, during the war. And I kept telling myself, we're okay, we're okay, but at night I was in this little room by myself and I couldn't sleep and when I finally fell asleep I kept having these dreams in which things were exploding or glowing, weird things, like cars, or, like, parts of my body. And then, in the middle of the night, I woke up and totally freaked, because there *was* something, there really was something glowing in front of me. Something green. Floating in the dark. You'll never guess what it was."

"I've no idea."

She gave a shaky half-grin. "A glow-in-the-dark crucifix."

We dashed across treeless Dundas and came to a stop on the south side, close to a streetcar stop, a block from Lux's apartment, where Haydee was waiting for her. In a Portuguese men's club with turquoise walls, middle-aged men in short sleeves tossed back tiny shots of coffee and exhaled clouds of smoke. I was on the verge of saying to her, *I have dreams like that, too, dreams in which things start to glow,* when, stuffing her hands into the pockets of her shorts, Lux furrowed her face again, crabbed and quizzical as a small child's.

"How does Dad seem to you?"

"Dad?" The question appeared out of the blue.

"Does he seem okay to you?"

"Yeah," I said. "I guess so." Perhaps a little distracted, a little reclusive, though I'd put some of that down to residual awkwardness at my return. And in any case, not having shared a house with him in ten years, I had no clear idea what counted as normal behavior on his part, what was within the range of acceptable moodiness for a nuclear safety engineer in his late fifties, especially given a recent spate of reactor shutdowns. "Why?"

A streetcar rumbled toward us, shooting sparks, slowing as it approached. I threw my arms around Lux, hugging her close, as perhaps I should have done moments, if not hours before. To comfort her.

"It's okay." She shrugged, loosening my grip, though her gaze stayed leery as we kissed good night. "Just wondered."

It wasn't until later, as I stood on the front porch, rooting in my bag for the keys my mother had loaned me, that my fingers slid along an oblong of paper that had not been there before. An envelope. I pulled it out and examined it under the porch light. It was sealed, no name written on it. I turned it over a couple of times in bemusement, eyeing its smooth white surface, before I tucked it under one arm and, key in hand, unlocked the front door.

SHE MUST HAVE SLIPPED IT into my bag back at the restaurant, between dinner and coffee, when I'd gone to the ladies' room and left my leather knapsack on the seat beside her, asking her to watch it. More likely this than that she'd tried some tricky maneuver in the dark as we walked down the street or embraced good night. And I presumed Lux was responsible, because who else?

I switched on the kitchen light and dropped my keys on the table, cleared by my mother for the night. No voices from upstairs. The dog, who'd risen to greet me, nuzzled my shins, licking away the salt of old sweat until I shoved her away. First, I rang my airline, hoping I might actually reach a human at this hour, and when I was told a seat was available on a night flight in five days, I booked it. Then I sat down and, with one finger, tore open the envelope's sealed back. From inside, I pulled a folded square of newspaper, which I unfurled to find a photograph of Haydee. Which seemed peculiar. Midair, midflight, hair windmilling, she hurtled like a horizontal rocket toward the open arms of the male dancer waiting to catch her, though, in the instant the photograph captured, she was still inches, no, feet away.

At first I simply studied the picture, as if it were a clue, as if there were something I had to puzzle out—perhaps Lux had sent it as some coded message about trust. Love. And/or unconditional trust. Presumably the photo had once accompanied a review, but the text had been cut off. I turned the paper over.

On the back was a page of obituaries, center row intact, others sliced through. To the back, Lux had stuck a tab of yellow paper, on which she'd drawn an arrow and, beside it, a question mark, the arrow pointing to the name on one of the dismembered obituaries, one at the bottom.

All this I registered simultaneously—the obituaries, the tab of yellow paper, the arrow, the name, the name hurling itself at me like a fist to the solar plexus.

Neil Charles Laurier, suddenly—

Everything convulsed. For how could this be possible? How could a photograph of Haydee, Haydee dancing, Haydee as she was now, appear on the back of an announcement of Neil's death?

There were dates in other obituaries, some at the end of May, others the beginning of June—but June of two years ago. Along the perimeter, Lux had squeezed in tiny block letters: FROM THE VANCOUVER PROVINCE. A paper, the *Province*. (A geography which other obituaries corroborated—death in a Burnaby nursing home, funeral service in West Vancouver.)

Not in Toronto at all.

There was nothing to say that this was the same Neil Laurier. Other than that his name, even his surname, was not that common, as I knew from my phone-book searches. And Neil Laurier, that particular combination of French surname and Scottish first name, was rarer still—and what were the odds of finding someone else who shared his middle name?

It wasn't proof.

Yet how many others would be *survived by parents Rachel and C— of Montreal and by brother Dani—*?

My hand shook.

Neil's father's name was Charles. He'd had a younger brother named Daniel. He'd once shown me a photograph of the three of them, playing croquet on the hummocky, tufted grass outside their cabin in the Laurentians, a photograph whose sheer absurdity must have appealed to him. Neil skinny and adolescent, fair and pudgy Daniel, Charles with a pipe drooping from his mouth, all wearing baseball caps at rakish angles, gripping their mallets with antic ferocity as if ready to whack each other in the balls.

Not dead in a duel. This drummed in my head like a mantra. I clung to it like a handhold. Not dead in a duel. But dead, *suddenly*, eight years later.

Now I was starved for facts, desperate, ready to gorge, because without more facts, I could only conjecture.

I dashed upstairs to retrieve my computer from the guest room. Descending, I did not stop in the kitchen, other than to grab the newspaper clipping, but opened the door that led down to the basement. At the bottom of the stairs, there was a lock on the door, which had been installed when I moved into that suite of rooms, and which I'd kept locked while living there, although my father left the door open. Now, from the inside, I locked it, for the last thing I wanted was to be disturbed.

I cleared some space on my father's desk and set up my laptop, stomach growling. I replaced the phone line that led from the wall jack to his modem with my own line and adapter. Seating myself in his desk chair, I cracked my knuckles and waited for the computer to go through its interminable start-up.

Through the window in front of me, which had been left partly open, curtains undrawn, came the shushing of wind, swift and insistent, through the trees in the ravine. And, like an echo, blood slushed through my veins, surged through my arteries, speeded by anxiety and adrenaline. I listened to the contraction and expansion of my heart's ventricles, swayed to the ceaseless slurping of blood.

I lay down on the floor. I lay down on the floor and stared up at the white ceiling, thinking about blood, lay where I'd lain without moving for the better part of three days, a little over ten years before.

I *had* tried to visit him, right at the beginning, as soon as I found out which hospital they had taken him to. I had no intention of calling any of them to discover where they'd taken him but, phone book thrown across my lap, was determined to try every hospital I could think of until I found him. It proved easier than that—right on the first try—the closest hospital, of course this was where they would have gone, given how much blood he was losing. One of them must have had a car, at least one of them, amid the general panic, must have been thinking straight.

Neil Laurier was in intensive care, I was told. Critical condition. Still receiving transfusions. Absolutely no visitors. That was all the information the woman at the information desk would give me, although she offered to put me through to the nursing station.

I went anyway. I went because I was desperate for absolution. Because even if I couldn't talk to him, even if I could simply see him through some glass partition, that would still be proof that he was alive—the relief, the release of knowing this already sent parts of my body singing.

I showered. I showered, as if it were an ordinary morning, as if I could wash away what clung to me. I bought flowers at a florist's on Yonge Street, a stem of scented white lilies, though no sooner had I paid for them and had them wrapped than I thought, white lilies are an emblem of death. Of funerals. Not death, I told myself. Easter. Resurrection. I remember telling myself this. I couldn't bring myself to trash them, but clutched the paper wrapping as, wreathed in their perfume, nearly sick to my stomach, I rode the subway south.

Somehow I must have believed that I could bolt past the nursing station, swing through some double set of doors, that the urgency of my mission would help me find him, my need, without delay, because there was no more time to lose.

But the nursing station was like a barricade, they wouldn't let me through; one of the nurses reached for the flowers, one of them said how lucky he was to be alive, another that they were trying to save his leg. One of them, huge eyed, leered toward me and asked, *What exactly happened to him?*

At that, I fled.

At home, I locked the basement door. I closed all the curtains. I lay down on the floor, wracked with dry sobs, because even though he was alive, nothing was in any way all right. Even when he called on the second afternoon, at the sound of his voice speaking into the answering machine, his wrecked and mumbling, half incoherent, horribly transformed voice, there was no solace, and at his words I did not, could not move.

Now I moved. I sat up, stumbled back to the desk, and logged on, listening to the dweedling sounds of the modem waiting for its connection, then the rush of static as the lines fused. I had searched for people in this fashion before, using on-line search engines and directories. I had even looked for Evan and Neil in this way, now and again, in recent years, when certain moods struck me—but always as if they were alive. Never had I tried to search for a dead person.

Could I access a two-year-old obituary from the *Vancouver Province*?

Perhaps there'd be an article, depending how grisly and

spectacular "suddenly" had been. A murder, a train wreck, a car crash, a *motorcycle* crash, a heli-skiing accident, a suicide.

Though by now, whatever it had been, it would be old news, buried by newer, more spectacular acts of violence.

I could have called Lux to see if she knew more than this, though I suspected she did not, otherwise why wouldn't she have told me? On the other hand, why had she slipped the envelope to me in such mysterious fashion? Why not simply hand it to me across the restaurant table and tell me how she'd found it? I wondered if she'd held onto the obituary for two years and only now decided to pass it on (and if so, *why now?*) or if, by some crazy fluke, some stroke of luck, she'd just recently stumbled across it.

I could have called her—it was late, but I suspected she'd be up—only at that moment I did not want to talk to her.

I set my fingers to the keyboard. All I knew was that someone named Neil Laurier had met a sudden death in Vancouver twenty-seven months before. This was what I told myself. I did not yet feel grief, not true grief, just franticness.

Often enough, in the course of research, I had sought out information on atrocities, I'd logged through reports of casualties, of brutal deaths, I'd scanned photographs, and occasionally I had encountered reports of the deaths of people whom I'd met or knew of professionally, but I had never set out on a private search for one particular body.

And though I was certain that what I wanted was out there somewhere, I could not find it. Too much information. Too many Neils. Wouldn't another one do instead? Why not a biography of the Canadian prime minister named Laurier? I was drowning in a sea of information whose levels, at every instant, kept rising.

Later, far later, when my face in the window in front of me shone lurid and spectral, I sought out accident Web sites, which a friend in London had told me about, because (late at night, in certain moods) she haunted them. Some featured bodies, some just mangled wrecks in which you could perhaps make out the trace of a body or were left to imagine the particular wreckage of the body. Some sites were devoted to car crashes, others to different sorts of accidents. All featured photographs, some video clips. Some victims were named, others were not.

Through the open slit between window and screen, birds grew audible, singing to the soft blue light: robins, sparrows, red-winged blackbirds, a mourning dove.

I disconnected the computer. I went to the bathroom, threw up, flushed the toilet. I tossed cold water against my aching eyes and ran it over my burning arms. I leaned my forehead against the cool of the mirror, as if against a palm, a human palm, as if it could comfort me.

If Neil's parents were still in Montreal, which was likely, it should not be hard to find their phone number. As I could have done all along, but had never dared to. Nor did I know how, without being needlessly cruel, I was going to ask them what I wanted to know, or how, in order to win their confidence, I was going to identify myself.

There were other ways to search through the land of the living. There was Daniel.

Through a haze of half sleep, I heard my parents' voices on the floor below and tried, in some bleary way, to distill content from tonality: was this idle morning chatter or something more emphatic? The front door clacked shut and my mother's shoes tamped their way down the driveway. For a long time, though perhaps I slept, there was silence, then I breathed the odor of coffee: my father brewing a fresh pot. I opened my eyes. My computer lay in its case beside my bed. He spoke into the kitchen telephone. A little while later, he left. (We were like foreigners passing each other.) He did not take the car, either. By then, it was almost eleven-thirty.

I rose and showered, hoping a flood of water would help wake me. I dumped my father's grounds and made myself a pot of coffee, as thick and black as I had ever tried to drink it. I only glanced at the Monday morning paper, had no appetite for world affairs, for global bellicosity, the deaths of dictators, no fluency for anything other than the search at hand.

At 12:29, 9:29 Pacific time, sitting at the kitchen table, I tried a phone number in Venice, California.

After two rings, a male voice, brusque and husky, picked up.

I said, as I had done at the other numbers I'd called, that I wished to speak to Daniel Laurier.

"Speaking."

"I'm looking for a Daniel Laurier from Montreal who had a brother named Neil."

"Yeah," the voice said bluntly, while I listened for any vestigial trace of a Canadian accent, any hook for hope. "Why? Who's this?"

"Am I speaking to the right person?" His curtness alone almost made me hang up.

"Who *are* you?"

"I used to be a friend of Neil's." I tried to keep my voice calm, not to waver, tried to sound reasonable. "I used to be quite close to him. A long time ago."

"Listen," the voice said, its terseness uneasily softening, "Neil's deceased. He died two years ago."

"I know." (Had there been other girls who'd called, others whom he had talked to or roughly comforted, since with Neil there had always been other girls?) "I'm sorry, I'm so, so sorry. I heard he died. That's about all I know."

There was silence on the other end of the line.

"I'm sorry," I said. "Did I wake you?"

"No." He gave a sharp exhalation. "You didn't wake me."

"Would it be possible to talk—"

"About?"

"Neil. A little. About what happened to him."

"When, *now*?"

"Whenever, whenever might be good for you. I could call back. It's just, in a way, to know so little is almost worse than not knowing anything at all."

Was he going to swear at me or drop the phone in outrage? Whenever would be *good* for him. He gave another sharp exhalation as I began to sweat. "Okay. Now. Whatever. Just give me a sec." Then he did drop the phone, which clunked against something, a table or a chair leg. His footsteps retreated across a hard floor and I wondered if he would in fact return. Yet, after a low thunk, as of a door closing, his footsteps clumped back. "Sorry," he said.

"Are you sure now's all right? It's not too early?"

"You called now."

"I just hoped to catch you. Before you left for work. Or leave a message."

"I work at home." Perhaps his bluntness was nothing personal. Perhaps this was simply his manner—nothing like Neil's. Sometimes, in families, the links between siblings, visual or auditory, are so obvious, while in others there are no clear clues at all. "So," he said, "what do you want to know?"

"Someone sent me an obituary. Recently. Only part of it had been torn away. He was in Vancouver when he—"

"Yeah."

"He lived in Vancouver."

"Yeah."

"How long had he lived there?"

"Since law school."

"Where did he go to law school?" *Law school*. Each fact more startling than the last.

"I mean he went there to go to law school." He swallowed a sip of liquid—coffee? "There's a lot you don't know."

"I knew him at university," I said. "Grad school. In Toronto. Then we fell out of touch." I touched a finger to my moist temple, to my damp hair. "Did he go right there, from Toronto, right to law school?"

"No," Daniel Laurier said, "he was in China for two years. Well, first Hong Kong, then Shanghai, then back briefly in Hong Kong."

"Doing what?"

"Teaching English. You know, what most people do." Never once in the time I'd known him had I heard Neil express any interest in China, in Asia, other than to debate the comparative merits of fried dumplings at Chinatown restaurants on Spadina Avenue. No feverish yearning to travel to the other side of the world. No mention of law school.

"He was a lawyer?"

"Yeah."

"What kind of law did he—"

"Criminal law."

"Did he work for a firm?"

"For a crown prosecutor. He was part of kind of a star team. He was going to be a great lawyer. He played kind of a crucial role in a murder trial, this guy everyone thought was going to get off, they weren't sure there was enough evidence, and then the main prosecutor fell sick, and Neil basically had to take over the case. And he got the guy."

"When was this?" Blood beat against my scalp, against the backs of my eyes. Everything hurt. What hurt was the effort of cracking open the picture I'd held of him, all the futures I'd imagined, including early death, which were not this one. Not

only Neil who'd almost died from a gunshot wound, but Neil
Laurier the hot young lawyer, beloved and stranger (Neil in a
suit, Neil in a courtroom pursuing murderers), had been snuffed
out.

"This was about eight months before he died."

"Were there newspaper articles?"

"I don't know, I guess so." I should have found them.

"How did he die?"

"In a car crash."

"Did someone hit him?" I stared at the pale-green wall in
front of me, the tops of the kitchen chairs, the still and unre-
markable table.

"No." There was a new tightness in Daniel Laurier's voice.
"The official word is that he lost control."

"He was on a street, a highway?" Every word hurt. I, too,
was cracking open.

"On an overpass. Out near the airport. How well do you
know Vancouver?"

"I don't," I said.

"Where are you calling from, anyway?"

"From Toronto."

"You don't sound like you come from Toronto."

"I'm *from* Toronto but I live in London. England."

"Only right now you're in Toronto. And you want all the
gory details."

"No," I said. "Just some of them. Just enough to make sense
of what happened."

"Okay." That exhalation again, almost a snort. But perhaps
terseness was a response to grief. Pain speaking. Or perhaps a
form of self-protection. In the beginning, there'd been three of
them: Neil, then Daniel, then Emilie, the sister who had died at
three of leukemia; now there was only Daniel, and Daniel had
to live with that. "He was driving a white Honda hatchback.

That's what he drove. He wasn't driving into the sun. Not exactly. He was driving south. Though it was sunny, which, as I assume you know, is highly unusual for Vancouver."

His voice maintained the same unemotional inflection. "It was early afternoon, around about two. Traffic was pretty light, it wasn't crawling, things were moving along. Maybe something blew in his eye. A wasp. Coroners look for things like that afterward. They didn't find anything, which means if there was something it didn't bite him. I've thought about all these things. Maybe someone cut in front of him. One witness said there was another white car that was speeding, but no one else remembers it. And no one remembers him speeding, but he swerved and went through the railing. He fell fifteen meters. He almost hit a busload of schoolchildren on the road below, but he didn't. I'm not joking. He landed right way up. If he'd landed upside down, he'd probably have been killed instantly, but he wasn't. He was trapped. He was paralyzed and hemorrhaging and perhaps had suffered some brain damage. His skull was fractured. It took the emergency crew forty-five minutes to free him. He died on the way to the hospital."

"I'm sorry," I whispered. "I'm sorry to have made you do this."

"No, you're not," he said. "Not really. This is what you wanted to know, isn't it? At first they thought maybe there was a chance of foul play. Because he'd also been doing some work in the Asian community—been involved in prosecuting some members of Asian gangs. But the police said there was no evidence of any kind of tampering. Or of any kind of mechanical failure. It took them almost a year to release the report. The official word is that he lost control."

"Was he married?"

"What?"

"Was he involved with anyone when he died?"

"No. I mean, he had been involved with people, *women*, but he wasn't seeing anyone right then."

"Were you close to him?"

"I don't know. Yeah. Kind of. Intermittently. We're brothers."

"What do you do?"

"What do *I* do?" Almost a whistle of breath. "I'm a screenwriter. Like 99.9 percent of the world down here." He offered up the name of a television program, asked me if I'd heard of it. I hadn't. "Maybe because you're from England. I wrote an episode of it." He'd been in film school in New York when he'd sold the script, his lucky break, the kind of crazy thing that was never supposed to happen. He'd moved to L.A. Now he was working on a feature, had been working on it for a while.

"About?"

"Two brothers. A comedy. A tragicomedy."

When he asked me what I did, and I told him, he didn't respond in any obvious way, other than to ask me my name.

"Unusual name," was all he said.

"Why did Neil go to China?"

"*Why?* Because he wanted to."

"When I knew him," I said carefully, "before I left for London, he was a graduate student in philosophy. He was planning to write a Ph.D. on Kant." Even at the time, I wasn't convinced he had the discipline or the will to see this through, that he wouldn't find some other outlet for his debating skills, his charm, his restless smarts. And it wasn't that I believed, afterward, after the duel, that he'd just go back to doing what he'd done before—that there wouldn't, for all of us, be some kind of rupture.

"People change," Daniel Laurier said curtly.

He didn't ask me how I knew Neil or how well I knew Neil.

What I wanted to know was what Daniel knew. What explanation had Neil ever offered for his gunshot wound? To the hospital staff. To the police officer sent to question him in his hospital bed, who would have been called, no matter what Neil said, given evidence of an incident involving a gun. To his fierce mother, who flew in from Montreal, to sit beside him. To protect him. To guard him. To his father, his brother, to anyone, then or later. For I couldn't believe that for all those years you could keep the fact of fighting a duel a complete secret, that Neil wouldn't have admitted something, let something slip, at some point.

"Did he limp?" I asked Daniel.

"What?"

Blood and grief pressed against my collarbone, against the tight muscles in my throat. *Had* my name set off any alarm bells in him? "Wasn't there an accident of some kind around the time he left Toronto?"

Perhaps he ought to know. Perhaps he had a right to know what Neil had done, because there had to be some connection between the duel and the criminal lawyer that Neil had become. I had to believe that.

"No," Daniel said after a pause. "He didn't limp."

"There's no reason to think he—in the accident, the car accident—that he might have meant—"

"No!" Daniel Laurier cried. "Why would he? There was no reason for him to—"

"I'm sorry," I said. "I'm sorry to disturb you. I loved him. I know it was a long time ago. And we messed things up completely. We played a dangerous game together. We wrecked things. I'm not saying things would ever have worked out. But I've never forgotten him. Ever. I've never stopped thinking about him. I remember, I'll always remember even the smallest things, like the shape of his hands, the way his sweat smelled like burning bread—"

"A lot of people loved him," Daniel Laurier said.

ONE AFTERNOON, at the end of April, Evan asked me to meet him at the Alborough Avenue house.

I let myself in the front door with the key he'd given me. The house seemed empty, its rooms silent and weightless, although at all times the place had the stranded, melancholy air of somewhere people didn't inhabit but merely camped. Peter had never properly redecorated. True, he'd bought new leather sofas to replace the old maroon chesterfield that Delia had repossessed, but there were still ghost outlines on the walls where prints and photographs had once hung; he'd never removed the red dots from books and records that she had claimed but never taken.

There was no sign of Evan in his third-floor room, only a lingering trace of the yeasty smell that I associated with him. The cat, Eddypuss, lay curled like a life buoy on one of the pillows. On an orange crate beside the mattress stood Evan's two brass candlesticks. His desk was tidied, not as if he'd broken off in the midst of studying—his engineering texts piled neatly and the computer, which he'd bought just after Christmas, turned off.

Downstairs, I checked the front hall: his wool army jacket, his laced leather boots were there. No sign of his running shoes, which meant he could be out training for the marathon he planned to run. Or else he'd slipped out, coatless, down to the corner for a carton of milk.

On the kitchen counter, I set the bag of food I'd brought to make dinner—fresh linguine, cream, oyster and portobello mushrooms. I opened the back door and peered out across the garden, which Evan had reclaimed from rampant weediness, since Peter never touched it. As soon as I closed the door again, I heard something. A faint thwack. Uneven pause. Another thwack. Like an arrhythmic heartbeat. I switched on the light at the top of the basement steps and stood for a minute, listening. Then I began to make my way down, dampening the silvery tang that rose at the back of my mouth.

Light shone around the door of the room at the front of the basement, beyond metal shelves stacked with old skates and skis, dusty jars of homemade jam, a red suitcase. *Thwack.* When I knocked, the door swung open. Evan stood there, red faced, clad only in sweatpants and sneakers, gripping a hockey stick. The room itself had been gutted of belongings since I'd last seen it. Once it had been a children's playroom, then a teenagers' lair with shag carpet stapled to the walls, now stripped to scuffed Sheetrock. A lime-green tennis ball rolled across the cement floor. He looked as if he'd been there for hours: glossy with sweat, sinewed, taut as a flagellant.

"You came."

"You asked me to."

Turning away, he snared the ball with his stick and dribbled it, using tiny flicks of his wrist, back into place.

"Evan, stop for a moment."

He glanced up, eyes bitter and hooded. "Am I a fuck-up?"

"No," I said.

"I'm going to quit."

"Quit what?"

"Quit engineering."

"Ev," I said. We'd been through this before. "You have one week of classes left. Then exams. That's it."

"There's no point anymore."

"No point? Then switch majors. Take another year." As I was doing, to get a four-year honors degree in history. "Go back to chemistry. Or English. Or German."

"I'm not going to fucking major in German."

The week before, he'd called me up in the middle of the night, past two by the clock beside my bed, his voice ratchety and slurred. He said he'd been out with Fergus. He'd drunk most of a bottle of cognac. *I know what you're up to. You're sleeping with Fergus. Aren't you? You bitch you whore you cock tease you cunt.*

Then he'd hung up.

"Or philosophy," I said. "Or history. Or something interdisciplinary. On the Enlightenment. Or William Blake." Whose cosmology, whose revolutionary theories on the union of mind and body, on the link between the divine and the sexual, Evan loved.

"I just want to read Blake, I don't want to fucking analyze him." His eyes kept darting, his cheeks blisteringly red. "You see. I'm a fuck-up."

"Evan, stop."

"Do you love me?"

"Yes," I said. "I do."

He whipped the ball—not toward me, though each ricochet off the wall careened it madly in a new direction, so that I jumped to avoid it. "Stop!" He did not look at me as he reached out to hook the ball with his stick and tamped it to the ground.

"Then why won't you marry me?"

"Evan, we're too young, I *feel* too young, I can't—"

Only then did he drop the hockey stick and, slicing his arms across his chest, stare in pain and fear and self-protection and defiance. "Arcadia, what are you so frightened of?"

The next night, the Sunday of the first week of May, we went out for dinner. I'd just finished my last paper, on the French and Indian Wars. Because it was raining, Evan came to pick me up in one of his father's cars, the Saab. He knocked on the glass doors at the back of the basement, as he had a habit of doing, and I let him in.

We went to a restaurant where they made their own ravioli, and talked about what we would do during the summer, how much time we'd be able to spend up at the farm and whether we had the money to travel and if so, where. I told him, shifting my ravioli carefully around my plate, that I was thinking of moving out of my parents' house. That one of the university librarians had told me about a room in a house on Palmerston Avenue that a friend of hers was renting. With a flat glare, he said, "You can't do that."

Afterward, we walked back to the car to find the windshield coated with the pale-green dust of tree pollen that the rain had washed down, so that when we settled ourselves inside, into the plush leather seats, the absinthe haze of it closed us in. And as I buckled my seat belt, I thought, I no longer feel any kind of safety around him—nor a thrill of danger or excitement or passion or an unsettled jaggedness that could pass for passion, but simply exhaustion. And I was frightened of him. I reached out for the latch of the glove compartment, twisted it back and forth, and heard myself say, "Evan, I can't do this anymore."

"Can't do what?"

"Any of this. All of it."

He didn't say anything at first. Then he said, in a perfectly reasonable voice, "I'll count to twenty and you can change your mind."

"Ev, listen."

He pulled back the left cuff of his shirt. "I'll give you thirty seconds to change your mind."

"Please—we could talk—"

He held up his right hand. "Are you changing your mind?" As if calling time out or warding me off, his voice rising a little now, as if it were futile to acknowledge the outrageousness of what he was doing.

He dropped his gaze back to the watch on his wrist. After a pause, he released both arms and shook his cuff back. Gripping the steering wheel, he stared into the green haze in front of him. "That's it." He turned to me with a look of arctic bleakness. "You've got what you wanted. Now get out."

I was stunned, I suppose, startled at my own behavior as much as anything. When I leaned over to kiss him goodbye, he jerked away. "Get out."

This was it? After three years, it was going to end like this— no pleading, no drama, no argument, no tumult? *Was* this what I wanted? Surely there had to be more than this. Yet what was the point in my being just as unhappy as he was? I unbuckled my seat belt. The skin around Evan's eyes had grown puffy, as if he were about to cry but would not do so in front of me. What shocked me most was that I could no longer touch him—the swiftness of this loss was like falling off a cliff. "Goodbye," I said. I climbed out of the car. I shut the door behind me.

All night I lay in bed by myself wondering if Evan would kill himself. If I should have stayed with him so that he wouldn't. Panic seized me. I buried my face in the pillow to escape his painted moon and stars. Should I have taken his threat seriously? Only I wasn't responsible for him. And what kind of relationship was it if he used blackmail, not love, to keep me with him?

The next day, in the library, I dropped books. I tore pages by accident. Helplessly. Things kept breaking on me. Staplers. Microfiche readers. The jamming of the photocopy machine made me weep. In Bloor Station, every limb in my body stiffened when the escalator I was riding stalled inexplicably. The day after, I biked to work instead. I kept waiting for a phone call. From someone. Speaking in a grave and mournful voice. About Evan. I tried to call him but got only the machine. When I tried his father's line, a woman answered (no one I'd met, though I'd last been in the house only a week before), and said, *Pete's out of town.*

Five nights later, on the Friday, as I biked up Bedford and was crossing at the lights on Davenport, a figure, two figures—one in a black tux jacket, the other a thin girl whose hair was cinched in a bleached-blonde ponytail—burst through the door of a café. The neon lights above the door blinked JUST DESSERTS. Swollen cakes and puffy pies gleamed in its windows.

"Cay Hearne." I clamped my brakes so hard that I almost fell off my bike, as Fergus dropped the girl's hand and began a strolling approach.

I searched his face for grief, for haggardness, for any sign that Evan might be dead or ill or wounded. But did not find it. On the other hand, he did not look friendly.

"Is Evan all right?"

"No." He kept his hands in his pockets. "He's not all right."

"But he hasn't—he hasn't done anything to himself?"

"He's upset, Cay. Very upset." Already I was mourning Fergus, too, the loss of Fergus. And although I had known there would be a whole sequence of losses, not just of Evan, it had been impossible to predict exactly what they would be or how deeply they would cut.

Fergus scuffed the sole of one shoe against the pavement, the flick of his gaze turned suddenly canny and sharp. "Have you talked to Neil Laurier lately?"

One of those nights during March break, when Evan was out of town, Neil had convinced me to go with him to hear a band. I'd hesitated. *Come on,* he'd jibed. *Live a little.* It would be late, the hall on Queen Street East would be loud and dark and crowded, and it was all these things; we could simply arrange to run into each other, which we did, downstairs, by the washrooms. We were standing upstairs in a corner, holding plastic cups of beer, Neil's leather arm squashed against my suede one as he shouted in my ear about the history of industrial music, how it had really begun early in the century with the Futurists, when I happened to glance up toward the balcony, and through the fog of smoke, the maze of bodies, there was Fergus—or someone who looked like Fergus—staring down at me.

"What?" I said now. "No."

A volley of expressions curved across Fergus's face: disbelief, possessiveness, disgust. He stepped closer.

Why did he do it? Because he'd been drinking? (I could smell alcohol on his breath.) I've no idea what difference that made. Desire? The desire to hold the balance of power for a moment and shift it, spill a secret, intercede and see what would happen? Fury? Because he could not help himself? Because he felt he ought to? "Evan's challenged Neil Laurier to a duel over you."

Sounds contracted to a curious, tinny drone. The traffic pouring around the bend in the road looked flattened, almost toylike.

Fergus stepped closer. Shaping the fingers of one hand into a pistol (long first finger for the muzzle, thumb for the trigger), he pointed it at me, right at my chest, tapped me with his extended finger, popped the make-believe gun. "A duel, Cay."

I flinched back. "You're joking." Wiping sweat from my upper lip. Sweat ran down my back.

Behind Fergus but visible to me, the girl wriggled her hand in the air and a cab veered toward the curb at her side. At the sound of its back door scraping open, Fergus glanced behind him. "No, I'm not."

"When did he tell you this? Where are they going to fight it? When?"

"I can't tell you, Cay. I'm afraid I'm not at liberty to tell you." Plucking his hands from his pockets, he glanced nervously at the girl as she slid into the cab. "Look, I'm not supposed to be talking about this, but I thought you should *know*."

"Fergus, you can't just—"

But he shook his head and retreated quickly. Gripping the door of the cab in one hand, he lowered himself inside. The girl's pale face floated in the cab's rear window, though Fergus did not look back as the taxi pulled away.

What was the first shock? The duel, that whatever they were going to do they were calling it a duel, or that Fergus knew Neil's name? Perhaps it was nothing but a trap, a sick joke, Fergus's concoction, Fergus's protectiveness and belligerence in defense of Evan. (Even if he'd seen us at that concert, this in itself that didn't *prove* anything, there was no rule to say I couldn't *go out* with people. Fergus might know who Neil was — though I didn't *know* this.) Maybe all he had to go on was hazard and suspicion, and what I should have said to save myself, oh fool that I was, was simply *Neil Laurier? Who's he?*

When I called Evan's number, I got the message that had been on his machine for the last two months, which began, *You've reached the headquarters of the Pterodactyl Society.* I hung up and leaned my forehead against the metal frame of the pay phone.

I'd seen Neil twice since leaving Evan. The night after Evan and I had split up, I'd called and asked him to meet me for dinner in a Vietnamese *pho* restaurant on Spadina. When I told him I'd left Evan, he set his china spoon beside his bowl of soup and said, *I'm sorry,* and the calm compassion in his voice stunned me, and then his first question stunned me even more somehow; he asked, *Is Evan okay?*

He said he would call me and we'd make plans to get together two nights later but I didn't hear from him. By now he had moved out of his residence room into a house on Grace Street with three other graduate students. Another guy and two girls. He had a room on the ground floor, just off the kitchen, which was in some ways the least private, but, as Neil pointed out, there was no one right on the other side of the wall at night. Three days a week he tended bar in a pub restaurant on Bloor.

Home from work, I called him. Someone else, male, answered. There was music in the background, a woman laughing. "Hey," Neil said, when he picked up, and I couldn't tell if what I heard was pleasure or surprise.

"I thought we were supposed to get together."

"Yeah?" Real surprise, or faked? "I wasn't sure. I didn't hear from you." The woman's voice larked—giddy, pleased with herself. "You can come over if you want."

"I'm already at home," I said. "I don't feel like coming all the way back downtown."

I didn't want to rush things, I told myself. To exert pressure. Better to give things time.

He called me later that night, so late that I was convinced it would be Evan, although I wasn't asleep, just lying, staring into the dark. "Wanna go to a movie?"

What strange impetuousness was he suggesting? "When? *Now?*" What would be on at this hour other than porn movies?

"I had in mind a little later maybe. What if I met you somewhere near the library after work?"

We went to a movie—it didn't matter what movie—the second, and last, we ever saw together. I was aware, above all, of Neil slouching beside me, his fingers tracing the outline of my fingers back and forth. I laid my hand across his thigh. And afterward he drove me home on the motorcycle that he was always talking about selling, but hadn't.

Nothing felt normal. To walk down the street beside him didn't feel normal. To be so visible. To have so much open space clanging around us.

At the end of my parents' driveway, I slid off the bike while Neil switched off the engine. "Do you want to come in?" I'd lost the sense of comfort that I used to feel around him—to nervousness, to the humiliation, more acute than ever, of still living at my parents' house. Yet he'd never before seen where I lived.

"Not tonight." His gaze skimmed the shrubs lining the driveway, the chestnut tree, the bushes on the far side of the front lawn. "Too exhausted. But I'll see you soon, okay?" Easy lies that anyone could toss off. He gave me one kiss on the lips good night.

When had Evan issued a challenge? How had he? Had he accosted Neil in person, phoned him, written the details up in a letter? If he'd done any of these things. And how did he know who Neil Laurier was? Fergus might have told him— Evan himself might be casually acquainted with Neil. Perhaps he had spotted us together, spied on us, followed us. Perhaps someone else had told him. Perhaps he'd seen us together months before. Had the idea been stewing in Evan for long, or had he hit on it only now, mad impulse springing from whatever despair he'd pitched into when I left him? Had he made his move right after or waited and plotted for the better part of a week? (*When* had he found out about Neil?)

And what exactly did he hope to prove by it? The idea was crazy. So crazy that nothing would happen. I wasn't sure exactly how Neil would respond, only that he would know this was Evan's overreactiveness, his penchant for drama, for grandiose self-dramatization talking. He would find a way to be diplomatic or ignore him, assuming that Evan would calm down eventually.

But the knowledge might make him cautious. Make him retreat a little. Because I was touched with Evan's craziness. Made dangerous. Not worth the trouble. He'd known—Neil must have known the night he drove me home. Perhaps this was all Evan wanted, anyway. His manic strategy. To drive a wedge, to fuck things up between Neil and me.

I didn't call Neil. I simply turned my bike around and headed south. Down St. George. Past the library. West along Harbord. I saw Evan everywhere. In phone booths. In school yards. Outside old brick houses. In parked cars, bus shelters, laneways. Pointing a pistol, aiming a gun.

When I pulled up, shaky and breathless, outside the Grace Street house, there were no lights visible: the porch darkened, no signs of life inside. I wheeled my bike along the alley at the side of the house, leaned the bike against the wall beneath the unlit windows of Neil's room. In the dark back yard, I could make out the hump of tarpaulin under which Neil stored his motorbike. Straining for voices, I heard nothing but the wind through the fingerlike leaves of the ailanthus that grew in the middle of the yard.

Someone was sitting in a chair on the cement patio tiles. In the dark. The red tip of a cigarette smoldered, moved as the head behind it turned. "Hey," Neil said, his perpetual greeting, always that unquantifiable mixture of pleasure and surprise.

There was a beer can on the ground at his feet, and, in front of him, at the base of the tree, as if he had been contemplating it, a painted bust of Elvis, which one of the roommates had planted. Someone had strung outdoor lights shaped like chili peppers around one of the tree's lower branches. In the dark, they were reduced to little blobs like worms or termites.

I was the one who asked him what he was doing.

"Cogito ergo sum," he said. A mouthful of teeth flashed white. He reached out with a finger to poke me in the thigh. *"Et in Arcadia ego."*

"No, you're not," I said.

"But I want to be."

Goose bumps riddled my arms and legs. Inside, in the stuffy kitchen, I opened the fridge, seeking something to drink, and pulled out an open bottle of wine. After a minute, Neil followed me in. I made my way toward his room, and, once we'd both entered, closed the door. I rolled down the blinds but did not switch on the light. Holding my wineglass, I stepped out of my dress, which was wet and sweaty anyway, and wove a passage between the still-unopened boxes, past a chess set spread out on the floor, to his mattress, where I seated myself. I drank in the scent, the tang of him, lime and toast and smoke, and watched him flex his fingers in the dark. Someone had given him the mattress. And the desk and desk chair and a set of bookshelves. People, women especially, he'd told me offhandedly, liked to give him things.

At every moment I meant to say something. I kept waiting for him to say something like, *I got this wild note from Evan.* Treating it lightly. Which of course he'd do.

He grunted as he rolled onto the bed, huffing as I unbuttoned his shirt.

And afterward he lay with his cheek mushed up against his pillow, scratching one arm.

"Happy?" Arm slung around me, he began to rock us both, pulling me hard against him, our foreheads furrowed as we stared at each other.

Did he think everything was fine just as it was, despite all its unsettledness? Would he one day twist his head to the side and, with a coy and slippery grin, say, *Cay, I'm not sure about all this.* Did I love him? How could I know if he loved me?

I told him I had to leave early because I had a morning shift at the library, though it was a Saturday. I did not bike to the library, however, or home, but to Evan's house.

With the key that was still on my key chain, I unlocked Evan's front door. I prayed for silence. I prayed that Evan had gone out running, as he had done every morning between eight and nine, no matter the weather, for the last eight months. I prayed that Peter was elsewhere—out of town or up at the farm—and if he did keep guns, an old set of pistols, that they were not easily accessible. Not here.

On my way upstairs, as I passed the second-floor bathroom, I heard voices—a woman giggling, making soft bleats. The gush of a shower. The lower rolls of a male voice that chuckled, then rose in a reedy cry. I swallowed, my tongue thick in my throat; kept swallowing.

On the third floor, all was quiet. Evan's room looked as it had always looked—the duvet pulled up meticulously over the mattress, the cat curled in the center of one pillow, the surface of his desk cleared apart from the computer and a black metal file stacked with papers. At the back of the desk stood his pair of brass candlesticks. A bottle of cognac. The two fragile, bulging snifters. The only sign of wayward life, the stiffened and spattered clothes he wore for painting houses, lay tossed on top of a wicker hamper in a corner.

It was as if I had never been there—no residual clue that my presence had ever permeated this place. No sign of any interior despair or disarray. I listened for sounds from the hallway, the stairs, moving as fast as I could as I tossed aside the pillows, flipped over the goatskin rug, scanned under the mattress, among the files of papers on his desk, between the pages of his Greek dictionary, his chemical engineering texts (two exams still ahead of him), his volumes of William Blake—and as I searched, a strange fury built in me. I longed to sprawl the impress of my body across the bed, kill the cat, rip the pages, anything to offer some mark, some evidence . . .

Sitting at his desk, I tugged open the top left-hand drawer of his desk and found an envelope, laid facedown over a box of staples and his checkbook, not where he usually kept envelopes—and not one of his, not the thick, white bond paper he usually used. Cheaper paper. Only the back and the jagged slit where the envelope had been opened were visible. Not hidden exactly. Carefully placed. Anyone looking with any thoroughness would have found it. And anyone who discovered it would have to pick it up and turn it over in order to read the address, to identify the handwriting of whoever had written it.

I could have stopped there, not turned the envelope over, not slid the folded piece of paper from it, the hook under my ribs driving farther and farther up.

But I didn't stop there.

ONE WAY OR ANOTHER we'd killed him—not directly, no, but indirectly. The link may not have been causal, but it was consequential. One thing led to another: if there had been no duel, if any of us had acted differently, had intervened, then Neil would not have been on this particular trajectory, which led to Vancouver, to law school, to car crash, whether accidental or— We were not guilty in any conventional sense, but we were guilty.

The clock above the kitchen sink read just after one-thirty. Only one brief hour had passed since I had picked up the phone to call Daniel Laurier. The house, with its drawn blinds, the windows shut tight by my mother to keep out the heat, felt more oppressive than ever, its green stillness suffocating, offering only the creepy illusion of calm, beneath which clamored a host of imagined voices in whose presence I could not bear to be a moment longer.

Yet no matter how fast I hurried down the tree-lined sidewalk or how I hid under sun hat and dark glasses, there was Neil, slouched and loping, light and springy on his feet, hovering now and forever out of reach.

Each step was lament, each clack of my shoes a wail going up, for now there was grief.

He'd survived. Until now I'd never known for certain that he'd survived the duel. He'd been shot in the groin and walked away, golden and lucky. Though how being shot had maimed him—if the shot had left any noticeable scar—I did not know. That the shot had changed him seemed certain—how could it not have done so?

And yet what good had being saved done him? *No*, no, only the time given, the second chance had been so freakishly brief. His hands—I had loved the strange, hyper-flexible double-jointedness of his hands—even now I could see them, feel them. I nearly walked into a telephone pole.

There was still so much I didn't know—to catch sight only to have him torn away. Why China? Had he gone there simply because it was the farthest point that he could travel to? Had he *fled* there, as an escape? Running from the duel, some repercussions of the duel, or, just possibly, in response to my own flight from Toronto? On the other hand, perhaps his motives had not been as desperate as all that: he'd simply decided it would be better to shuck off the turbulent, tainted past and start over.

He would have made a good lawyer. As hard as it was to picture him in a suit in a courtroom. (As hard as to imagine him speaking Cantonese.) Philosophy, he would have argued, and he liked to argue, was ideal training. Yet what I wondered above all was if he'd been passionate about the work, truly committed to it (why criminal law, why prosecution?) and where that passion had come from.

Had he fallen in love—later? Had he whispered in a woman's ear that he loved her? Surely he had. And yet he had not married. He had not, at the time of his death, been living with anyone.

In Lawrence Station, I fumbled my token into the subway

turnstile. In the bag slung over my shoulder, I carried a pad of scribbled notes, notes for a chapter on international war-crimes tribunals, which was not precisely a form of intervention but of due process that went hand in hand with current philosophies of intervention, linked by the belief that human injustices were more important than the sanctity of borders. I would go to a library. Downtown, I would find a library, for libraries had always offered refuge. I would try to work. Work had always consoled me: concentration would rinse me clean of everything other than the particular intensity of my work. Its paradoxical safety. That was some solace. Only not the city reference library where Evan used to steam over his engineering texts. *Not* the university library.

Perhaps what I needed instead was to talk to someone. A live person. Not just a voice over the telephone. There was the peace-and-conflict specialist. A woman in the political science department whom I'd been meaning to meet. Someone, anyone, lucid in the language of U.N. missions, current on the stalemate in Cyprus, fluent in the possibilities for post-Dayton mediation in Bosnia (who would not be aghast were I to burst into tears).

A woman staring at her reflection in the darkened subway window crossed her fingers, as if for luck. The metal wheels of the train shrieked as we rounded the curve at Union.

When I stepped aboveground on the corner of College and University, the mirrored wall of the Ontario Power building blinded me, its reflected rays and mottled squares of sky a burning scrim of light. A hot-dog vendor's grill choked the air with smoke. Everything seemed cacophonous and strident. Signs pointed the way to an underground copy center. Huge, dim-windowed tour buses lumbered down the avenue.

Perhaps what I needed was something altogether different. Non-war-related. Perhaps I should lose myself in the quiet halls of the art gallery.

South on University, hospitals rose on either side of the wide street like the sides of a ravine. A mile of hospitals. To my left, the Hospital for Sick Children, whose name Basra had memorized. None the one to which Neil had been taken.

On my right, a man stepped through the gray front portal of the Princess Margaret—the cancer institute. He stopped on the front steps, blinking in the sun. He wore a gray suit and held nothing and appeared (though perhaps it was simply the light) a little disoriented.

He had not noticed me as he set off down the steps until I waved and called out.

"Arcadia!" My father's face had the exploded look of someone deeply jolted. From which he quickly recovered. "What a surprise—you caught me—" He shook his head and gave a bemused smile, light silvering his hair and racing along his cheekbones. "Where're you off to?"

"The art gallery."

"Particular show?"

"No, no, just thought I'd wander."

"Had a meeting." He indicated the stone edifice of the hospital behind him. And there was nothing inherently suspicious in his exiting through its doors, for as part of his consultancy he regularly performed safety evaluations of medical radiation equipment. Though he did not say what sort of meeting. And his manner seemed a little strained. If anything was mysterious, there were a number of possible explanations. He could have been to visit someone. Although this opened up another set of questions. Who exactly?

Awkwardness clung to us, which could simply have been the residue of the awkwardness that had hovered between us since my arrival. Nor had we much experience at bumping into each other unexpectedly. And anything I felt at that moment, I felt through the distortions of my own already jangled state.

"Have you had lunch yet?" I asked, because it seemed odd to part so quickly.

"No, I haven't actually." He glanced at his watch, frowning, though, again, it could just have been the light. "I probably have time for a quick bite."

With the familiarity of someone who knew this stretch of blocks well, he guided me around the corner to a coffee shop that he said he used to frequent when he kept regular hours at Ontario Power. One of the waitresses appeared to recognize him, smiled as he slid us into a corner booth. He ordered for both of us: my tuna salad and coffee, his chicken salad and coffee, no, cancel the coffee, he'd have a lemonade instead. He asked me, with studious politeness, how it felt to return to Toronto after all these years. Did the city seem different? Was I managing to get any work done on the book, as I'd said I'd wanted to do? What did I think of the future cohabitation of Hutu and Tutsi populations in Rwanda, *génocidaires* and victims, now that the Hutus had been forced to return? The intensity of his questions seemed genuine, although he also seemed to be deflecting the conversation away from the personal, from himself, from potentially awkward territory. Covertly, I tried to size him up: did he look more tired than usual? What was usual? More evasive? Didn't his work, especially these days, give reasons for both of these?

What kind of meeting did you go to without a briefcase? Not usually a business meeting. *Meeting* might be a euphemism then, slur or fudge. Every so often, at the sight of his long fingers encircling his plastic water glass, or my hand, or the salt shaker, I'd think: *Neil's dead.* A keening cry rose up inside me. I wanted to lay my head on the table and weep. Because there was no longer any possibility of reconciliation, no matter what I wanted.

Only afterward did the deeper oddness of the encounter settle upon me. "I'll see you later," my father said amiably enough. "Around dinnertime, presumably."

"Where are you off to?" I asked.

"Oh, home, probably." He gave a light shrug.

Only once it seemed unlikely that he would look back did I turn to watch him as he made his way through the afternoon crowds toward the subway. There was, possibly, a hesitancy to the way he moved, a fragility, a lack of assertion. But I couldn't see clearly. I could simply have been overreacting.

I went to the art gallery, but stopped outside and instead of going in, turned and made my way back to University Avenue.

As I headed south, the buildings—office towers, bank towers—rose higher and higher. When I began to look up, window washers were everywhere: they inched along on their risky-looking suspended platforms, hung from delicate swing-like harnesses, one man lifted like a homunculus in a wooden compartment clasped in the jaws of a crane. Reckless and fragile. Did men have a greater propensity toward reckless behavior, I wondered. I thought of Neil in his car, my father and the lure of tritium.

Clouds came scudding in now, speckling the visible patches of real afternoon sky and the virtual blue of windows, clouds that had the stock white puffiness of painted clouds, as the window washers, sweeping their arms like wings, tried to smear them away.

Down below, office workers spilled onto cement plazas from boxy entrance vestibules. Blue DANGER MEN AT WORK scaffolds barricaded sections of sidewalk, droplets of water scattering across the pavement.

Across an intersection, at the edge of one plaza, two window washers, who had shed their harnesses at the end of their workday, sauntered, buckets in hand, toward a red truck pulled up to the curb. SKY HIGH WINDOW CLEANING was scrolled across its cab. A third man sat in the driver's seat. The two window washers wore shorts and T-shirts, one young and slim and dark, the other a little older, his hair straw blond and beginning to recede. He dropped his bucket, peeled off his gloves, and shook his birdlike hands. The same stubborn purposefulness—recognition was instant, indelible—though he was perhaps a little stockier now. To find him here—here, doing this. I remained invisible, rooted to the spot. What I felt, as bizarre and improbable as it seemed, was the utter inevitability of this trajectory.

WHY DID WE DO NOTHING, knowing what we knew?

I was not the only one who could have stopped them. Fergus knew. And Carl, Neil's second. And the medical student who agreed to accompany them, to administer to wounds.

It was, after all, the seconds' responsibility to find a diplomatic solution, to do everything they could to avoid the risk of fighting.

Perhaps they had tried. And Evan had refused to listen.

Any of them could have told someone. Told Peter, Evan's father (though that was hard to imagine). Or Evan's mother in Montreal. Or called the police, as I could have done, once I, too, knew the date and the time they planned to meet, and the location.

And if I had, would the police have believed me? And then what? *Arrested both of them?*

Even Neil could, at any point, have halted things. This was not the nineteenth century, we were rattling toward the end of the twentieth. His honor was not at stake. There was no need for him to let Evan under his skin.

But he didn't.

In the guest bedroom of my parents' house, at a doll-sized desk more ornamental than functional, I sat and tried to decide what I should do—not what I should have done in the past (though that, too, obsessed me) but what I should do now, in the present. When I arrived home, my father, there before me, had left a message on the kitchen table. *Someone called—a woman? Will call back.* When I asked him about it, he said whoever it was wouldn't leave a name. Another mystery.

But mostly I was thinking about Evan. I had watched him climb into the cab of the red truck. I had not approached him— not then, but I did not want to approach him then, like that.

In a sense, I was no more surprised to find out what Evan was doing than what Neil had done—and perhaps, after the first shock, even less so. For Evan had always had a temperament capable of willful rejection—the flip side of idealism, the reverse of passionate embrace. Rejection itself a kind of passion. A nihilist's gesture. To throw away everything, all the promise in him that the duel itself had already skewed and contorted.

Perhaps the gesture was more penitence than nihilism. An atonement. A retreat from the world, a cleansing, a stripping away.

Perhaps, in his sharp and nasal voice, he'd insist that all he'd ever wanted was to do something practical. Useful. Which this was. As long as he had time in the evening to read Rilke or William Blake. Life reduced to the elemental—including the embrace of physical risk.

Was I, after all this time, still angry with him? Or did I long simply to meet him?

And so, what to do? I wanted to speak to him, but I did not want to accost him without warning in the street.

What I had in mind was something a little different.

———

In the morning, I called Sky High Window Cleaning, whose number, needless to say, *was* in the phone book. Each ring of the phone frazzled me, although I told myself there was little chance that Evan would pick up. He'd be out on a job. Before calling, I'd checked weather reports, even stuck my head out the front door and peered upward, where the milky clouds were innocuous and dry.

"Sky High," lifted the man who answered.

"Does someone named Evan Biederman work for you?" I wanted to be sure. To make no mistakes at this point. How strange to say his name in a context where his live presence was palpable.

"Yeah. What's up?" He did. He *was*.

"I wondered if I could leave something for him."

"You wanna leave me a message or do you wanna page him?"

"No," I said, oddly serene, "no, I wondered if you'd give me the address. I wanted to drop something off."

The door at the bottom of the basement stairs was shut, my father behind it. Or so I presumed. I had not heard him go out. There was no sound as I descended the basement stairs, past a pair of canoe paddles leaning by the side door, and knocked.

"Be with you in a minute," he called.

He opened the door, shirt sleeves rolled to the elbow, in stockinged feet, the dog rising to its haunches behind him like a co-conspirator. He appeared to have been reading. Files of papers lay piled around his leather armchair, the desk chair pulled into use as a footrest. A glass of water and the telephone were on the floor within reach. Nothing seemed obviously suspicious. "You all right?" I asked him.

"I'm fine."

I wasn't sure if I should press him. "I'll be back later in the afternoon, if anyone calls," I said. "If you could get a name. Or a number. If possible."

"Yes," he said. "Have a good time then."

As instructed, I rode the Queen streetcar east to Broadview, where I got off and began walking south. At the bottom of the street was a wrecking yard, where smashed cars, now flattened, Volvos, a white Honda, lay sandwiched in thick accordion layers, within a chain-link fence. Along the verge, the grass had been left to grow long and go to seed, interspersed with Queen Anne's lace and milkweed.

I followed the sidewalk east, under a railway bridge where pigeons hooted and the walls reverberated with the throb of speeding tires. On the far side, I stepped out once again into a dazzle of early-afternoon light, in the midst of which a sign appeared, SKY HIGH WINDOW CLEANING. I crossed a small parking lot scattered with Chevrolets—American cars. At the far end, a red touring bicycle was locked against another stretch of chain-link fence. Feet crunching on gravel, I made my way toward a squat, aluminum-sided building.

When I pushed open the door, a bell trilled. I stepped into a chilled world of wood veneer—veneer counter, veneer paneling on all four walls.

"Can I help you?"

I tipped up my sunglasses in order to pull the figure into focus: a middle-aged man in a short-sleeved, shiny shirt, whose skin had the flaccid pallor of someone who never went outdoors. His looping voice the voice of the man I'd spoken to by telephone.

"I'd like to leave something for Evan Biederman." I drew an envelope out of my bag.

"For Evan?"

"Stan!" a voice yelled from an interior room. "Is it Vivian? Evan said she was dropping off the car so he could pick up Tristan."

Vivian. Tristan. The ordinary seepage of information.

I laid the envelope on the counter. "I'm not Vivian," I said.

SHE CALLED AND THIS TIME I was at home and as soon as I heard her low and slightly halting voice asking for my name, I knew exactly who it was. Yes, she was all right, she said, she was well, she was wondering if I could meet her. There was a place called the Transit Lounge, on Parliament Street south of Dundas, would this place be possible? I said I didn't know it but I was familiar with the east-end streets and I was sure it would be easy enough to find. How, I asked her curiously, had she got my number? Someone had given it to her, Basra said. *You have been looking for me.*

On first sighting, she looked much the same—young and slim, the clipped back hair, white running shoes—as she had when we first met in London and that time I thought I'd glimpsed her on College Street. From her seat at a rickety café table, she rose, blue skirt falling over her hips, and held out both hands and we kissed. On second glance, I thought, no, no, not the same at all. What had struck me, on first meeting, as simple willowiness now seemed, in retrospect, to have been a kind of bony strain, which was missing. She did not look relaxed, exactly, but some taut core of fear had migrated.

On the table beside her was a palm-sized tape deck (some clone of a Walkman), a bowl of popcorn, a cup of black coffee. The menu on the wall was Ethiopian. Plus spaghetti. A man in a white apron approached and waited near my elbow. "Please?" he asked. I ordered a black coffee, which he brought with another bowl of popcorn.

"Are you singing?" I asked Basra.

"Oh yes," she said. "I am singing." As I'd walked down Parliament Street, past the prostitutes and loud cars and apartment towers, to meet her, I thought I'd heard a woman's voice, though it could have been my imagination. Basra ducked her head to look at her hands, long fingers clasped at the edge of the table. "I wish to ask you something."

I guessed it would be something to do with music, a message, a request to pass on to Lux, presuming Basra remembered who my sister was and what she did.

"When we were in London, you gave me two phone numbers. One day I called to thank you. This one. The place you work. The Centre for Contemporary War Studies." She pronounced each word carefully, as if months before, she'd memorized the name.

I nodded.

"It is your job. War Studies."

"Yeah." I nodded again.

"So then it is your job to travel to wars."

Was this a question? "Well, yes," I said.

"Sometimes you must travel to Africa?"

"Mmm," I said. "Possibly."

Her forehead wrinkled. "Maybe you travel through Nairobi."

"It's possible," I said. My mouth was sticky. "Why?"

"You have asked, is there a way to help me. And now I think maybe there is, yes. If you go to Nairobi. In the camp where I was. In the northeast. It is one day, maybe two, by road. My sister is still there. If it is possible, you can take something to her."

"You'd like me to deliver it."

"Yes, if it is possible."

"First," I said slowly, "you'd have to tell me what it is."

She glanced around the restaurant, which was empty, apart from a woman ordering takeout food at the counter. Basra ran one long, steady finger up and down the red checks of the tablecloth. "A passport."

"Is it from the same man who got you here?" My heart began to race.

"Maybe," she said. "I think—it is from his—people here, he works with them."

"Does he know you're speaking to me?"

"No. I say to them only, I think maybe I know someone who can take it. Because for my sister, now, it is dangerous. There and at home. There is no one to protect her."

"What about your brothers?"

"We do not know where my brothers are."

"Where did you get the money for the—"

"I give a little now. His prices are not so terrible. And more later."

"Listen," I said. I could have told her it was folly, the request outlandish, though I genuinely wanted to help her. "I'm supposed to leave for London in three days. It's possible. But I'll need to think about it, at least overnight."

"This is okay," she said.

From there, I walked across town to the Argonauts Sporting Goods Store, which I remembered from outings with Evan: it had been the source of the fingerless gloves he used to wear at his desk in the winter. When I stepped inside, a bell jingled and a young man feeding a roll of paper tape into the cash register looked up. I nodded as I walked past him, through the racks of camouflage gear and hunting caps toward a door glimpsed at the back. GUN ROOM, read the sign above it. But the door was locked. "I'd like to see your firearms, please," I said, as I approached the front once more. Outside, a fleet of children tottered past, in pairs, sun hats on their tiny heads, clad in orange vests, clutching a knotted rope as if descending from an ark.

The young man nodded. "Just a sec."

He wore a neat, white T-shirt. His hair was cut short over the ears and at the back, left a little longer on top, like Amir's. His boots, visible when he stepped from behind the counter, were black lace-ups in shiny patent leather.

I followed him calmly back through the camouflage gear, the rain ponchos and fleece vests, past oil lanterns and flashlights and flares and tin camping utensils.

So this was how it was done. This was how you did it. It was this easy.

"Might I ask if you have a permit?" He spoke in this particular, elaborate way.

"No," I told him.

I thought about Vivian. I wondered who Vivian was, if she was Evan's lover, or his wife, and how long they had known each other. If Tristan was her son, or theirs. Tristan was a name I could imagine Evan choosing, for all that he had insisted that he never wanted children. What did it mean, though, to name a child after a hero of medieval romance who succumbed for life to a love potion, who loved a woman who was another man's wife, who married a woman who shared the first one's name, for whom love was as much peril and pain as pleasure?

And what of the scar that Evan had carved into his chest? I

wondered if it was still there, and, if it was, how he explained its presence. He could have had it surgically removed. *I'll love you forever*, he'd sworn, and I, through all these years, had been crazy enough to believe him.

"I trust," the man said, "you know that you will be restricted from buying any firearm other than a starter pistol." This, after all, was Canada.

The door to the gun room divided in two, so that top and bottom opened separately. He extracted a fistful of keys from his pocket, fishing through them until he found the one he wanted, then slipped it into the lock. He shut the bottom half of the door behind us but let the top half swing open. A safety device, I suddenly realized, and, turning, noted that now there was another, older man at the front of the store, who kept us unobtrusively within his line of vision.

"However," the young man went on, "be forewarned that you can still do significant damage with a starter pistol. Training, I reiterate, is essential in the handling of any firearm." He told me about an American preacher who, while warning his congregation about the dangers of high-stakes gambling and the particular perils of Russian roulette, had pointed a starter pistol at his temple and shot the blank toward himself. He'd died from the impact of its compacted cardboard shrapnel.

Sorting through his keys once again, the young man unlocked the glass doors of a wall-mounted glass cabinet, in which were displayed the starter pistols—replicas of actual firearms. A Colt .45. A Ruger. A Walther PPK, like the real one I'd once, in a London hotel room, pulled from Patrick O'Daire's jacket pocket. I wondered how the young man sized up his customers and if he had particular categories he slotted us into, and if, to him, selling guns was truly different from selling camp gear or camouflage jackets.

Every day people bought guns. Some (though not others) would know exactly what they wanted to do with them. Few would be thinking about honor. Or about the origins of war. Some might (just possibly) be thinking about how to smuggle passports between countries.

"What sort of thing are you looking for?" he asked.

"Self-defense," I said. About lovely, terrible testosterone.

Behind him, on the far wall of the small room, hung a rack of hunting rifles and what a sign called Decorator Swords. Replicas of various historical armaments for those who wished to indulge in a little military fantasy. A fierce two-headed ax. The swirl of an antique scimitar.

"Alternately," he said, "we have something a little different." He led me to the glass-topped counter and, unlocking one of the display cases beneath, withdrew a small gold tube. "The lipstick knife." He pulled open the cylinder to reveal the blade within. And it was true, it did look exactly like a lipstick tube. He handed it to me. "Very, very nice," he said. "Very discreet. Very elegant." I swiveled the lid back on, then removed it again, turning the blade this way and that, watching it wink in the light. "Or, in a somewhat similar line, the defense stick." A longer metal blade housed in a metal tube still small enough to dangle from a key chain. "Or—for a starter pistol is not precisely or terribly practical as a defensive weapon"—he swept one arm along the glass cabinet to the next display case— "any one of our selection of switchblades."

I WOKE BEFORE MY ALARM, slipped out of fitful sleep, as I had done on a late-May morning just over ten years before. Outside, when I peered through the curtains, the ink-colored sky was nearly cloudless. Only this time I was thinking not just of the woods, and what might await me in them, but of flying back to London and what I would tell Basra Alale.

In the end, I thought jaggedly, as I tugged on jeans and a green sweater, used clothes I'd bought (lacking anything suitable) at a Goodwill store, in the end the questions are the same. Everything converges. Are we to intervene or not? Who are we to let slip within our borders? Who's a stranger? Whom do we allow ourselves to love?

Knapsack riding my shoulders, I closed the bedroom door behind me, just as, some moments later, I closed and locked the front door to the house, soundlessly, I hoped. From the next block came the *thunk, thunk* of newspapers landing, the purr of a car's motor, as a pair of headlights crept forward.

I have to believe, I told myself, that some kind of reconciliation is possible. And that there is something to be gained in the attempt at explanation, by offering some sort of testimony, for private acts as well as public ones, despite the gaps and distortions—and that this is different from simply accruing information, and, in the end, this is the knowledge I've come to believe in. And that the duelists' story is not complete without the girl's story.

Was I frightened as I set off in my secondhand running shoes down the still-dark street? No, not exactly frightened.

I've wondered sometimes why they chose the site they did, why a ravine, if one that was nearly downtown, closer to Evan's home than the Grace Street house where Neil was living. Evan was the one who knew the ravines, not Neil (or not that I knew of), though by most rules of dueling, either the seconds or Neil, as the one challenged, would have chosen the location.

There were parks close to Neil's place, studded with trees, block-long parks where there were stretches of flat and open ground. Perhaps too open. Or why not Philosopher's Walk, the green dip of land behind the museum and music conservatory, near the university, where once, at the sound of a whistle, I'd started as I walked and there, behind a bank of shrubs, was Neil in his leather coat, beckoning.

Perhaps they had conferred, or conferred through their seconds, before Neil had committed to paper the note and the map that I had found and that were, convincingly, in his handwriting. Perhaps Evan had persuaded him to consider the ravines, as most private of all—where there was the least risk of gunshots being heard. Although it would be more complicated to get an injured party to a hospital—this was what struck me.

And I—for I, too, was there, I was present, I saw it all—at what point did I decide to go? Right until that final morning, I insisted to myself that someone (presumably Fergus) would phone and announce the whole thing had been called off, it had been a joke, a provocation. Or Neil, in his lighthearted way, would call and say, *Guess what?* The act of deciding would be taken out of my hands. Only no one called. Each new moment began to tick through me in a kind of frenzy—to go, not to go? I hovered on a precipice of motion. If I didn't go, I could claim to know nothing (though Fergus could rebut this). Whatever happened. What did I *want* to happen? If I went, I gave myself every opportunity, right until the last instant, to stop them.

A chain blocked the path that led down into the ravine, a chain strung between two metal poles. I knew the path well, because it was one that Evan and I had often taken, especially in the first year we were together. In those days, it was a dirt path, studded with loose stones, scarred with tree roots, cutting in a long diagonal down the side of a slope. In the years since—so I could hear from the crunch of pebbles underfoot and sense by the pale line that descended between the trees—it had been covered with gravel.

Both times I took a taxi downtown. Now, I'd called one from a pay phone. The first time, reaching Yonge Street, I'd simply waved my arm madly as one came speeding, roof lamp shining. I remember that its shocks were bad and that I spilled change all over the backseat and that I could barely bring myself to look out the windows. Then, as now, I asked the driver to let me off a block south, so that I approached on foot: first, the wrought-iron gates that led into the gardens where Evan and I would sit sometimes and watch the coddled dogs; then, just to the north, the point where the path into the ravine opened up. I was jittery above all because I did not want to be seen. My plan, both times, was to be the first arrival.

I climbed over the chain. There was just enough light for me to be able to see my way along the path, to distinguish the black of the trees from the iris patches of sky between the branches. As the air in the woods grew cool and damp, the skin at the back of my neck began to prickle—at the thought of what might lurk invisibly behind the trees, at each bang and rattle of my footsteps, the explosions of stones and twigs under my shoes. I strained to run back but did not.

The first time, even before deciding for certain that I would come, I'd plotted how I would proceed. Where the path began to descend more steeply toward the ravine floor, I would cut away, between the trees, and make my way across the hillside until I was peering from above into the clearing. It did not matter how much noise I made as I crashed through the undergrowth. No, because they were not there—there was no one there to hear me.

It had grown a little brighter, slate distilling itself toward lavender, lavender touched with lime, the air still breezeless. Birds had begun to sing, cries I identified without thinking: robins, red-winged blackbirds, a goldfinch, a whitethroat. The world grew greener—leaves the pale and delicate shades of early summer. I picked out a maple, its trunk thick enough to shield me should anyone turn and glance in my direction, and settled behind it. The calm of the woods lulled me, relaxed me enough to give in to wonder, at the paradisiacal beauty of such a place at such an hour and the strangeness of finding myself in it, so that I could almost have fallen asleep and, whatever happened, failed to wake up.

Hugging my arms hard around my knees, I waited. My feet grew cramped. I wanted to pee. Then I heard something.

Voices were carried on the still air, hushed, barely louder than breath. Footsteps crackled. When I turned around, I could not see clearly back to the path through the haze of foliage and slats of trunks—just enough to make out figures in motion, the brightness of clothing. Black and white. Lurid in the wan light, my stomach jumping. Was that a tuft of blond hair? A chuckle I recognized?

They disappeared below me. I knew the path: they would come to a rickety wooden bridge over a tiny creek, after which the path branched; they would take the right fork until they came to a smaller trail that led through poplars to the clearing, invisible from the main path.

Forty-four beats of my heart until Neil and Carl Landauer stepped into the clearing.

They stepped, they stopped, they looked at each other, they glanced around them.

Tall Carl wore the tan trench coat in which I'd always seen him and beneath it a white formal shirt, as if he, like Neil, were dressed for a special occasion. From the pocket of his shiny black jacket, Neil pulled a cigarette pack, extracted one, handed the packet to Carl. He'd slicked back his hair, which gave him an unlikely lounge-lizardly appearance. But he did not light his cigarette when Carl offered him a match, he shook his head, flicking the cigarette between his fingers; then he dropped it into his pocket and rubbed his fist back and forth across his mouth.

I longed to run to him, to touch him. And it was not too late (and as long as I thought like this, I warded off incipient panic, though even to think this *was* panic). If I told him I loved him, pulled him away, convinced him to run off with me—no matter what happened afterward, or what I truly felt, at least I would have saved him.

Yet I also hated him for being there. You could not—could you?—fight a duel as a lark. Perhaps he'd embraced the duel as a philosophical proposition. Here, in some perverse fashion, was an opportunity for action that he could not refuse, no matter what the risks were: through it, he would define himself. He was serenely not thinking about consequences, beyond the lure of risk, some ludicrous theory of risk—*not* of what it truly meant to pick up a gun and chance killing someone or being killed himself. Over and over, I saw his mouth in the dark of his room in the Grace Street house, the way his lips kept parting, and was entranced, repulsed.

And part of me, some compulsive part of me, wanted to test him, to wait and see exactly what he was going to do.

Was he—*was he*—acting out of love?

Then I'd lost my chance to intercept him, for there were more voices, more footsteps approaching along the path.

In August, the leaves are a thicker, tougher green. I did not cut away from the path this time, but continued to the bottom of the slope, crossed the new metal bridge that had been built over the creek, and took, without faltering, the fork that led toward the clearing. I waded out into the wet, tall grass. Once Evan and I had brought a blanket and picnicked here; we'd lounged, spitting watermelon pips toward our feet.

There were fewer trees. Or they were taller. Here was where Neil had stood when they appeared—Evan in a white tuxedo jacket, Fergus, the medical student with the black bag—before he stepped forward to shake Evan's hand.

Once, in a London minicab, I'd found myself in conversation with the driver, a Bosnian man. We were talking, naturally enough, about the Bosnian war. All of a sudden he twisted to face me with such forcefulness that the whole car swerved toward the curb. *People always say, oh, no, no, this cannot happen to them. Where they live, they do not behave like this.* With dexterity, the harnessing of passion, barely glancing round, he brought the car back into its lane. I'd told him I was Canadian. He told me he'd recently met a woman from Quebec. *I speak to her, here.*

She says to me, her people, they are not violent. And I say, you may not be violent but you can become violent. This was, to him, the crucial distinction, the message he was forwarding to anyone who would listen.

That day, I was also thinking about Rwanda. A winter day, a thick rain streaming down. I'd spent the afternoon at the office poring over documents that by then were coming out of Rwanda, among them the story of a Hutu priest who had given refuge to hundreds who'd begged for protection, then facilitated their slaughter, then denied it.

It doesn't absolve you from responsibility, though, does it? I said, as I rested my arms along the vinyl top of the cab's front seat. *To argue that at root, violence is circumstantial.*

No, no, the driver said quietly, *because not everyone becomes violent.*

Evan lowered his knapsack from his shoulders to the grass. From it, he pulled a bundle wrapped in a blue towel, which I lost sight of as the others gathered close around him. Carl stubbed out his cigarette. The sun was rising, long rays gliding between the frail green leaves, gilding their bodies, their backs, their hair, so that as they huddled they appeared touched with radiance, nearly glowing.

I was too far away to read their expressions, could only attempt to decipher them, Evan's from the fever of purpose that seemed to burn from him, stubbornness and doggedness above all, as if the most important thing was his determination not to be deterred from what he intended. The unease in my stomach grew toward nausea.

I assumed, though I could not see, that he was loading the pistols. His father must have shown him how. (Recently? Years before?) I could not imagine that Neil knew anything about loading guns. When Evan stood up, it was Neil's turn to crouch. They could have been invisibly intent on snakes or card tricks. But they weren't. When Neil rose, the others parted around him, as if he'd grown charmed or dangerous.

Because Evan had brought and loaded the pistols, Neil had first choice of a weapon: though I observed them, it wasn't until later that I made sense of what they did.

From the edge of the clearing, Fergus and Carl dragged a dead branch to the middle of the grass. They began to march out paces, first in one direction, then the other, marking each end point with smaller branches. Fergus strode while Carl counted, both of them stamping down the grass as they walked. From behind my tree, I counted with them. Fourteen, fifteen paces. The medical student stood stiffly near the line of trees, arms folded, black bag at his feet, and watched—as did Evan and Neil. Evan still, Neil pacing.

My tongue clogged my mouth. It was as if I'd loosened some hold on my body, aware of it only as a source of sensation—the damp ground beneath me, the chilled air, the rigidity of tendons, the swill of adrenaline and nerves, the scent of torn leaves and wet earth. Maybe I am simply making excuses for myself. They both held guns. I was frightened that if I moved, I'd be shot—a genuine if not a realistic fear, given the distance that separated us. But there was also the theatricality of the scene below that made it seem impenetrable. Unreal. A hushed, extraordinary aura clung to them and made their actions both terrifying and beautiful, impossible to intrude upon, as if a scrim separated me from them.

They conferred again. I could hear only the murmur of voices, not what they were saying. Fergus took a coin from his pocket, the tiny disk dazzling as he tossed it in the air. To see who would be the first shot? No, to choose position. For Neil stepped forward, peering toward one end of the clearing, then the other, while Evan stared at the ground. Then, when Neil headed toward the southeast side of the tamped-down path, Evan trudged toward the northwest.

From here, Neil was closest to me, half in profile, close enough that I could make out the way he pushed his lips together and released them, close enough that I might have called out to him. I had never seen him look more serious; under the slicked-back hair his face seemed longer and more sallow.

Each had the rising sun to one side, Neil to his right, Evan to his left, each a horizon of poplar saplings, though Evan would fire into greater shadow, Neil into brighter light. Everything seemed so green: the grass, the leaves, their skin.

Neil moved with less certainty as he took his position, shifting a bit, as if covertly, vulnerably, eyeing Evan to figure out how he should stand—turned, so that less of the body was exposed—and what he should do with his arms. Dew shone on Evan's boots. Dew must have made the grass slippery. Both held their pistols lowered to the ground until Fergus, standing parallel to the field's midpoint, raised a square of white cloth and, with a curt shout, lowered it.

Shots rang out—not simultaneously, one an echo of the other. *Was one the echo of the other?* Neil fell. Did he begin to turn before falling? Did he turn toward Evan while taking his shot, or from the gun's recoil being stronger than he'd anticipated, or in the instant of being shot? Only because he turned did Evan's shot hit him in the groin—whatever Evan had been aiming for.

Someone yelled. Someone else hissed for quiet. Evan was still standing. Arm lowered, he stood, staring doggedly, cheeks flushed.

I don't remember crossing the creek. I remember scrabbling up the far bank, dirt coming loose in my hands. They were all running. Except Neil. "Cay," he said with languid surprise as I stumbled toward him.

"Get away from him," Evan shrieked. He was pointing his pistol at me.

Already there was so much blood: blood on Neil's jeans, above the damp calves of his jeans, blood in the wet grass.

I don't remember picking up Neil's pistol. I remember holding it, the hard awkwardness of it, and pointing it at Evan, in the same instant I was convulsed by the knowledge that Neil could really be dying, that Evan, that we, might really have killed him.

"Can you treat him here?" That was Carl. "Can you get it out? Can you walk?"

"Put down the guns," Fergus said—clever Fergus, gingerly holding out the blue towel so that none of his fingerprints ended up on the metal.

Evan dropped to his knees. He was weeping. "You left me nothing to believe in."

"Oh, fuck." Neil's voice rose and gasped. He bleated, he giggled. "You bastard," he said. His face was jumpy and pale, his whole body twitching. "You tried to shoot me in the balls."

"Get out of here, Cay," Fergus said, "just get out of here." While the medical student leaned back, speaking over his shoulder to Carl as if, this way, Neil wouldn't hear him. Something about *the iliac artery*. Even he looked frightened.

"Unload the pistols," I said.

"Cay," Fergus said, "there's only one bullet in them."

Blood on the grass, blood soaking Neil's jeans, blood on his T-shirt. *He's alive*—but any relief this thought offered was extinguished by the next, more virulent thought that he could be dying. The medical student was wrapping gauze and cotton padding around Neil's thigh, which seemed hopelessly inadequate, tightening another strip of cotton so fiercely it looked to be a vise. Carl had stripped off his coat and was swaddling Neil into it, stuffing his arms, like a child's, into the sleeves. By now the seriousness of what they were in the midst of had seized them, panicked them. Fergus stuffed the pistols, wrapped in the towel, back into the knapsack, which, after hesitating, he handed to Evan. Yoking Neil's arms over their shoulders, Carl and the medical student stumbled to their feet and set off at as much of a run as they could manage, half dragging Neil between them, Fergus and Evan clustered close. If any early-morning walker encountered them on the path, dueling would not be the first thing the onlooker would think of.

The grass in the clearing was mangled and smashed. I began to jog after them. "Go home, Cay," Fergus rasped from the edge of the trees. More ferociously than ever. As if I were the source of horror. "Now." He was the only one to look back. I kept going until I tripped on the path and stumbled, the five of them disappearing ahead of me—a posse, a blazing wall. And it was easy enough to convince myself then that none of it, none of it, had anything to do with love.

Is violence inevitable? Once Amir had asked me this, as we lay in my garden, although he had been talking specifically about war. Still, this is one of the questions I have come back to again and again, as I sit at my desk or wander the streets or when I wake out of sleep in some wan hour of the night. Is it? Do I believe it is?

And if it is, doesn't this doom any attempt at intervention to failure? Make it no more than a stopgap, or even part of the cycle of violence? No, because even if violence is inevitable, this doesn't mean it's inevitable in all cases, under all circumstances.

When I've asked myself why they did it, why they fought— no, specifically why Evan fought—I've wondered if these were the only circumstances that ever aroused him to violence. If I had been the only person to do so. No one else.

Grief is one thing, pain another, yet violence isn't inherent in either. He wasn't threatened with violence. He did not simply respond in self-defense.

If he had really wanted to kill Neil, however, a duel (in which he risked being shot himself) was hardly the best way to go about it.

Which came first—fear or aggression? This is another one of those questions with which war theorists, like anthropologists, like to puzzle themselves. Were our brains shaped, as our shaggy ancestors stepped down from the trees into plains of grass, by being predators or prey? Waking in the dark or prowling the streets, I worry this question, too. Though determining which came first doesn't mean you can separate fear from aggression.

Should I have followed them? Perhaps. Though by doing so, I might have distracted them and made them lose crucial time on their way to the hospital. If Neil had indeed been hit in an artery, or close to an artery, every moment counted, and any moments lost might well have killed him.

I'd held a pistol and pointed it at Evan. Would I have shot him? If there'd been a bullet in it—had there, by some chance, still been a bullet in it? I assumed, as Fergus had told me, that the pistols were loaded with a single bullet, but did not know this, just as I return again and again to those moments in the woods, trying to clarify, if I can only concentrate hard enough, whether what I'd heard was clearly two shots or one shot and its echo.

Was I capable of shooting him? But I did not. This I repeat to myself. I did not.

Now I waited for Evan. I paced back and forth through the grass, the burrs, the Queen Anne's lace, the goldenrod. At dawn, I'd written. I'd explained where, though there was no question he'd remember. I'd mentioned forgiveness, reckoning that even after all these years, or because of the passage of years, such a gesture might carry weight with him, too. That we owed each other this. I still had some claim on him. Though I'd written what I'd written before I knew of the existence of Vivian and Tristan.

Perhaps he'd never received the letter: the man had forgotten to give it to him. My plan wasn't foolproof: there were any number of points at which it could have broken down.

Pink clouds were blooming on, were bloodying the eastern sky, above the heads of the trees. The ricochet of speeding cars on the Don Valley Parkway traveled through the still air. A breeze began to tremble the poplars, as I listened, as I craned for any sound, scanned for any particle of human movement.

I waited. At the edge of the trees, I stood as still as possible, breathing deeply, concentrating on calm. A stick cracked— what was that? I removed the starter pistol from my knapsack and slipped it within the waistband of my jeans.

Ordinary morning sounds began: a screen door slammed; someone whistled; the jingle of dog tags accompanied the crunch of footsteps on the path; children shouted.

And with the advent of ordinary morning, as such sounds grew, rage boiled up. He hadn't come. He wasn't coming. I would chase him down, wherever he was, I could find out where he lived, I had enough clues; pistol in hand, I would pound on his door, disrupt his reconstructed life, force him to confront me, confront the fact that, one way or another, we had all been twisted and reshaped by the duel. *Neil's dead*, I would shout at him. And, *He should have charged you.*

What kind of reconciliation is possible when there's only one of you? What good does it do to know that duels have been fought in dark rooms, fought naked, fought between women, that Aaron Burr killed the U.S. Vice President, Alexander Hamilton, in a pistol duel on a ledge above the Hudson in June 1804, when I can never, never know if Neil meant to aim wide and miss Evan, or whether he shot to hit, and chance and inexperience and the nature of the pistol misdirected his shot, or whether, making himself into some crazy sacrifice, he did not shoot at all.

All I heard was his voice that morning on the telephone from the hospital, slowed and brutally slurred. *Nearly out of the woods, I think—hey, Cay, my mother's here—don't say anything, if anyone—it's better if we don't—listen, I want you to know I'm not going to charge him.*

I strode back to the place in the clearing where Neil had fallen, not far from where Evan had spread out our blanket in the heat of that other summer day. A palimpsest of loss. I stared up toward the place on the slope where I had crouched, which was almost completely hidden by now, lost to the depths of green foliage, so that anyone concealed there would be virtually impossible to see. Squirrels chirred in warning. A blue jay gargled deep in its throat.

I could not go on like this. I could not. I would walk out of the woods, though part of me would never completely be out of the woods. None of us ever is, really.

I turned and made my way back the way I'd come. I would walk back up into the city. Amid people on their way to work, I would hail a taxi. I would call Basra. I would ring Amir and tell him I was coming. Hope rose. And out of sadness, as I was released from a kind of fear, a strange joy, like a slim green stalk grew.

I used to long for love as a clear and steady state, though perhaps there is no love that does not hold the seed of something else—just as there is no steady state of the body, and no state at all without some inconsistency, some internal contradiction, some trace of weather patterns, the possibility of migration or other turbulence. Perhaps the question is simply whether love enfolds an ambivalence you can live with, or one you can't.

THE TAXI PULLED INTO THE DRIVEWAY of my parents' house. Once I'd stepped out, folding change into my wallet and closing the door of the idling car behind me, I glanced up, along the side of the house, down the paved path that led, beyond the driveway, from the side door into the garden, and caught sight of something—a flare of brightness, cloth, a coat, the corner of a coat—disappearing around the corner of the house. It was after nine. By now my mother should have been at work. Perhaps my father had let the dog out, though what I'd seen was human, or at least not dog. Perhaps my father, wearing a coat, had stepped out with the dog, though a coat made little sense on a dry, mild morning in August. A bathrobe?

Behind me, the taxi sped down the driveway in reverse.

Could it be Evan? And I'd miscalculated. We were still playing some game of brinkmanship and he was determined to catch me unawares, meet me once again on his terms, not mine.

Or—far-fetched but not impossible—a simpler intruder, the stealthy, gun- or metal-pipe-wielding, break-and-enter kind?

I edged forward, past the side door, past the wild snapdragons

that my mother had planted, toward the path, sliding my knapsack off my shoulders—

And when I turned the corner, my father, wearing an overcoat, clutching an overnight bag, was locking the French doors
behind him. I gasped. Because in that first instant my mind
rejected what I saw as unrecognizable—the coat, the confusion
of his face. He blanched (like Lux in a convenience store once),
in greater disarray than the afternoon I'd surprised him on the
steps of the hospital.

"What are you doing?" I demanded.

"I thought you were in bed." His voice cracked, no guile or
strategy in it; he simply sounded sabotaged.

His face kept contorting, as it had done the evening before I
ran away to London, the evening I had refused to open the
basement door to him and in a fury he'd unlocked the door
himself—the day after Neil had called from the hospital,
the day my mother had appeared outside the French doors
and rapped upon them, peering in consternation through the
chiffon-curtained glass. I'd roused myself from the floor and
let her in. She said the library had called her, wondering where
I was, bewilderment growing as she took in the stale air, the
Kleenex box, the nest I'd made of my duvet on the floor. I let
her coax me onto the sofa, place a damp cloth over my forehead. *Hush now,* she whispered. I could sense, from her reading of the state I was in, that she thought I was pregnant, or
simply that Evan had left me. *Arcadia, what is it? Please tell me.*
I told her because I wanted to crack her belief that she could
protect us, keep us safe forever within some imagined haven.
Because violence took peculiar forms. Because I wanted her to
comfort me. And once I'd told her, I begged her, made her
promise to tell no one, least of all my father, and she cupped
her hand against my forehead and, in a fierce and steady voice,
promised me.

Later I heard their voices overhead. I heard my father shouting before his steps drummed down the basement stairs.

He grabbed me by the shoulders, not a violent gesture in the larger scheme of things, but hard enough to leave small bruises, still turning yellow by the time I moved into the flat in Turnham Green. His anger shocked me more, its explosiveness something I'd never seen let loose in him. Anger or fear? He began to shake me, lifting me into the air. *Two men fought over you? Two men fought over you with guns? You should have told someone. Why—why didn't you do everything you could to stop them?*

"You ordered a taxi, didn't you?" I asked now, and, indeed, a new set of wheels scrabbled their way up the driveway.

My father nodded. Even in his coat and summer suit, he looked worn, as if the optimism that had buoyed him up for years was ebbing away. A new map of pain and trepidation lay upon his skin.

"What is it?" I held out my hand for his bag, which he surrendered. I reached out with my free hand to touch his arm hesitantly, then, when I took hold of it, felt his weight heave a little in my direction. "Look," I said. There were tears in my eyes. "I could say 'Don't go,' and mean it, but, please, before you go anywhere, at least tell me—tell us—where you're going."

"GO," LUX SAID. "You have to go. Just come back soon, that's all."

My father has cancer. He is not imminently dying, but is in hospital for four days of radiation treatment, not to cure him, for what he has is incurable, but to treat his symptoms and relieve his pain. He was off to catch a flight to New York when I ran into him that morning, to visit someone he knew, someone he'd worked with once, a doctor who specializes in the type of bone cancer he has, which is exceedingly rare, like leukemia but not leukemia, and who had arranged to offer him a second opinion. At least this was the explanation he gave—the one he insisted upon.

Just as he insists that his cancer is completely unrelated to his line of work. There is absolutely no evidence that this particular cancer is caused by radiation exposure. Absolutely none. We can read studies if we want. He has some in the basement. *If* he's suffered any work-related radiation exposure, and there is scant evidence of that, either.

"What causes it then?" We were sitting, that morning, bags at our feet, at the kitchen table.

"Bad luck, bad genes—some genetic malfunction. It's rare, but more prevalent among men." He gave a rueful wink, aiming for cheerfulness. "Just one of the risks you run."

He had known for two years and told my mother six months ago. He was going to tell Lux and me—"soon, but I didn't want to alarm you. Especially when there's nothing to be done."

He didn't want to alarm us. And what, now, was the point in being angry with him?

"So what happens?"

Or in ruing the past when what lay ahead was what we had to contend with? Which did not mean ignoring the past, or denying it.

"The prognosis? Three to five years." He spoke as coolly as if he were talking about the state of an aging nuclear-power plant. "I'm hoping for five, needless to say. Gradually my bones will start to shrink and fracture easily and I'll be in greater and greater pain. They'll try to treat the pain."

"Are you in pain?"

"Now?" Tiny bubbles of sweat had gathered along his upper lip. "Yes, rather a lot of pain."

I changed my flight; I stayed.

By the third day in hospital, he was sitting up in bed, and had shaved, his skin softer, his cheeks slightly flaccid. My mother had shaved him. I'd watched her delicately clasping his chin, although it seemed to me there was some strain in her, a kind of pain, as if there were lapses and secrets that lay between them for which she might not be able to forgive him. Yet, wreathed in a trace of male cologne, he seemed remarkably calm: being ill wasn't necessarily going to transform him.

"Lux," I said. She was driving me home, back to Glenmaple Street. Two children carrying orange balloons raced through drizzle along a downtown Toronto sidewalk. How strange to feel the silvery touch of other people's happiness—or, if not happiness, at least to watch them shine in the blurred, gray air. "There's one more thing I want to know."

I'd told her about my conversation with Daniel Laurier, that the obituary had been for the right Neil Laurier; I'd told her briefly how he'd died. I had not mentioned Evan, or that I'd buried a starter pistol in a small pit at the bottom of the garden. To tell her would be to implicate her: there were things she perhaps did not need to know.

"Afterward—do you know if Neil ever called the house? After I left?" I'd settled on this one question. There were others I'd decided I would not ask.

"You mean, call us, upstairs, to see if we could tell him where you were?"

"Yeah."

She nodded. She was gazing straight out through the windshield, into the arc the wipers had cleared. "Yeah, he called."

"Did you speak to him?"

She nodded again, fingers steady on the wheel.

"You knew who it was. You remembered? He mentioned his name?"

Once more she nodded.

"What did you say to him?"

She was quiet for a moment. "All I knew was that there'd been some kind of a fight. Mum and Dad were barely talking. No one would tell me anything else." She paused. "I said you'd gone to China and you'd told me you weren't ever, ever coming home."

When I arrive, when I arrive in London, I will take the Piccadilly Line from Heathrow to Holloway Road, and, from there, a minicab to the Centre for Contemporary War Studies. With luck, Ray Farr will be in, even though it is early, because he often squirrels himself away to work before the phones start ringing. And because we've been in touch, I know he's in town, not off in some war zone.

Inside, I'll drop my bags and greet Ray; then I'll switch on Moira's kettle.

"How's your father?" Ray will ask.

"Better. Thanks. Going home tomorrow."

In the back room, bleary and jet-lagged as I am, I'll pull up a chair beside Ray's desk.

"Ray," I'll say. "I'm planning a trip to Kenya. To the northeast. Up to where some of the Somali refugee camps are." This is unlikely to surprise him. To him, it was never more than a matter of time: I was bound to undertake a trip like this one day.

"Right you are," he'll say, "and while you're out there, perhaps you'd feel up to a trip into southern Sudan as well. I've been wanting to send someone in as an observer. You could go in overland with one of the aid groups. From Kenya. Out of Logichokkio. I'd like to get some independent information about the behavior of government troops—if any are actually involved in the slave trade. Or simply complicit. If there's any sort of active policy, you know? As part of the GoS war-waging policy. It may be a bit dangerous. But you'll be careful, careful where you go, of course." And as far as Ray is concerned, it's decided. "This will, in fact, be extraordinarily useful." Only the practical arrangements will remain to be taken care of. I'll need a flak jacket. Among other things. Nor is it inconceivable to Ray that I could arrive groggy in London and, visas and transport willing, be ready to leave again in another few days.

But first, from Moira's phone, I will call my flat and, with luck, Amir will answer.

"Where are you?" His astonishment as bright as pleasure.

"In Highbury."

"Whatever are you doing in Highbury?"

"A meeting. I'll be there in minutes. Promise. Just hold on."

Or if he's not at the flat, I'll try him on his mobile. I'll be patient. I'm ready to be patient. He's out there somewhere.

He does not need to know what's sewn into my pocket. Not yet.

Outside the airplane window, the moon shines down upon the tiny waves, lighting them like pebbles. The plane shudders, but it is not unusual for jet aircraft to do such things. On the screen at the front of the dimmed cabin, a man points his gun. At every instant, the world realigns itself, it continually realigns itself in its compulsive dance of sadness and joy and grief. This, too, is normal. These risks are normal. There are earphones in my ears, an open cassette case in my lap, a package in my pocket, and as we roar through the darkness, the air fills with the sound of a woman singing.

Acknowledgments

Numerous books and articles were consulted during the writing of this book. Among the most useful: *Blood and Belonging* and *The Warrior's Honour*, by Michael Ignatieff; *Blood Rites*, by Barbara Ehrenreich; *Civil War*, by Hans Magnus Enzensberger; and *The Transformation of War*, by Martin van Creveld. Thanks to Mary Flanagan for passing on an invaluable source, *The Duel*, by Robert Baldick. Thanks to David Sheps for putting me on the trail of two wonderful nineteenth-century texts, *The Art of Duelling*, by 'A Traveller,' and *The British Code of the Duel*.

For their generous financial assistance, thanks to the Canada Council, the Ontario Arts Council, the Toronto Arts Council, and Concordia University. Also to the MacDowell Colony and Yaddo for offering me havens in which to write significant portions of the manuscript.

Enormous thanks to those who offered their support along the way: to Rob Nixon, for his perceptive eye through numerous drafts; to my agent, Denise Bukowski, for her unstinting energy and enthusiasm; to Dawn Nichol, for giving me back the use of my muscles; to Nigel Hunt, for his generous encouragement; to David Lea, for his hospitality in London; to my editors, Iris Tupholme at HarperCollins Canada and Elisabeth

Kallick Dyssegaard at Farrar, Straus and Giroux, for their vision and wisdom.

I'm also hugely grateful to the many who answered my questions and gave crucial information, including Stephen Anderson, Jennifer Bush, Joan Hoey, Mark Kingwell, Ed Lee, Katherine Moshonas, Soheil Parsa, and Art Weinreb. And to the friends who offered advice, read the manuscript, and stuck with me, especially André Alexis, Eliza Clark, Douglas Cooper, Jean Hanff Korelitz, and Kate Pullinger.